Beyond Your Dreams

A Novel

Amy Martin

Beyond Your Dreams
Copyright © 2014
Amy Martin

This book is a work of fiction and any resemblance to any person, living or dead, or any events or occurrences, is purely coincidental. The characters and story lines are created from the author's imagination or are used fictitiously.

Cover design by ninjaMel Designs

CHAPTER 1

This morning, the morning of the first day of school after winter break, the only thing on my mind should be the fact that I'm about to begin my last semester of high school. But instead, all I can think about right now is my boyfriend—my boyfriend who doesn't remember I'm his girlfriend.

I peek out the front window at our empty gravel driveway carving a gray path through the winter-deadened grass down to the blacktop of the county road. Not only is the driveway gray, but the sky is also gray, and even the usually white walls of my living room appear to be a dingy gray in the dim light of an early January morning. Everything in my life right now feels like it's been drained of color, but as I hear my mom coming up behind me, I stand up straight and try to replace the scowl I sense I'm wearing with a more neutral expression.

"I put some coffee on," she says, hunching down into her flannel bathrobe. "Want to take some in a travel mug? I know you've got a big day ahead of you."

I give her a sad smile.

"It's just school, Mom. No big deal."

But we both know today's not just another day. Not only is today the first day back after Christmas break, but it's also the first day back at school for my boyfriend Kieran Lanier, which wouldn't be a big deal if not for the fact that he doesn't really know who he is right now—or who his sister is, or his parents…

Or me.

Kieran, as of a few days ago, has amnesia, which is merely the latest in a bizarre collection of afflictions he's had to deal with in his life. And while the amnesia is supposed to be temporary, unless a miracle occurred sometime after I left the Lanier house two nights ago, his sister Kayla and I will spend today helping him adjust to a life he doesn't recall.

Mom puts a hand on the back of my head as I rub some lingering sleep out of my eyes.

"You know, you don't have to ride to school with Kieran and Kayla this morning if you don't want," she says, stroking my hair. "You can always drop me off at the store and drive yourself."

In the days before the Laniers moved to town, I used to drive my mom to her arts and crafts store, Doodles, every morning before heading to school in our only car. And our routine continued uninterrupted for the first few months the Laniers lived here until Kieran and I finally moved out of the "friend zone" and took our relationship to the next level. Since we've been a couple, Kieran has picked me up every morning and I've ridden to school with him. Or, rather, Kayla and Kieran pick me up and Kayla drives the three of us to school. Thanks to the narcolepsy-like disorder Kieran's suffered with since birth, he doesn't drive, although now that his sleep disorder has been successfully treated, I guess he would be able to get a license.

On the other hand, the treatment for his sleeping disorder is what left him with the amnesia in the first place, so at the moment, he wouldn't remember anywhere he'd want to go even if he did have a license.

"Thanks," I say to Mom, and I mean it because I realize she's trying to save me from what's probably going to be a pretty awkward drive to school. "But I can't pretend this whole thing isn't happening. And the more time I spend with Kieran, the sooner he might get his memory back. He needs to be exposed to as many familiar places and people as possible right now, and like it or not, I'm about as familiar as it gets. And, I mean, I can't just ignore him. I promised—"

4

I stop myself and Mom narrows her eyes.

"Who did you promise? What?" she demands.

"Jilly," I say, heaving a sigh. "I promised Jilly when she was here in August I wouldn't turn my back on Kieran and his family if things got all weird with the treatment."

"Jilly" is Jillian Lanier, the ultimate cool, crazy aunt, who told me as far as she was concerned, I was as much a Lanier as her blood relatives and that once Kieran came through the other side of the treatment, the family would need my support more than ever. I wasn't completely sure at the time if she understood what the treatment's possible side effects could be, but I gladly agreed to stand by the Laniers no matter what happened, no matter how bad.

And then Kieran underwent the treatment, and the amnesia happened. And judging by the weird, distant conversation Kieran and I had two nights ago on New Year's Eve, things are going to be bad. Really, really bad.

"Jilly had no right to expect promises from you," Mom tells me. "I know you love the Laniers, but you shouldn't be burdened with helping them through everything. You're only seventeen and in a few months, you'll be out of high school. Life should be non-stop fun for you right now, and instead…"

Mom shrugs and her voice fades out.

"It's not like Jilly made me swear a blood oath or anything," I explain. "And, I mean, I told Kieran before the treatment we'd always be in each other's lives, no matter what."

"Not like you should be held to *that* promise right now, either, given your conversation the other night," Mom says dryly, and I shoot her a look.

"Mom, come on. Yes, the other night was tough to take. But whether I ride to school with him here in a few minutes or wait and run into him at school, being around Kieran while he's like this will be hard. And, I mean, we're supposed to be going over to the Laniers' for dinner tonight, remember? Or are we backing out of the invitation?"

I've got Mom in a bind. The Laniers had invited my mom and me, plus my grandparents and Kieran's birth father Morgan Levert, over for dinner tonight in the hope that being around familiar people might jump-start his memory recovery process.

"No, we're not backing out," Mom says through a sigh.

"So, then I'm going to see him tonight, no matter what. I might as well be with him on the way to school, too."

"Sorry." She stops stroking my hair. "I don't mean to be so crabby about this whole thing this morning, but I ache for you right now, you know? I've always admired how determined you are to face things, but I wanted to tell you that if you needed to put off facing this head-on first thing in the morning, I'm totally willing to help."

I give her a crooked smile.

"Are you also willing to homeschool me until May?"

"Don't push your luck," she huffs as a horn sounds in the driveway. I peek through the curtains to find Kayla's black Jeep idling outside our carport—my conversation with Mom had distracted me just enough I didn't hear the car rumbling up the gravel path.

"Gotta go, Mom," I say, giving her a kiss on the cheek and bending down to grab my backpack. "Love you."

"Love you, too, kiddo."

I'm out the door and to the back passenger-side door in seconds, and already, everything's wrong. Kieran's sitting up front with Kayla. Kieran never sits up front with Kayla. He always sits in back with me while Kayla spends the entire ride—which is, thankfully, less than two miles—complaining about how she's not our chauffeur and doesn't appreciate being treated like one.

6

"Hey," Kayla says to me over her shoulder as I throw my backpack into the backseat and crawl in after it.

"Hey," I reply, before saying "Hey, Kieran," to the back of Kieran's head.

"Hey. How are you?" he mumbles, turning his head a little but not enough for his eyes to meet mine.

"Good. Thanks."

We sound like business colleagues getting ready to start a meeting. I glance up at the rear view mirror and catch Kayla shooting me a pained look as she backs into the grass so she can drive forward down the driveway.

The drive to school lasts a few long, quiet minutes of Kieran staring out the passenger window while I do the same, sitting right behind him, the silence louder than any conversation we've ever had. Soon enough, Kayla pulls into a parking space a few spots from the side door to the school—one of the perks of being a senior—and shuts off the engine, turning to the two of us before she's even had time to drop her keys into her backpack.

"When we get out of the car, the two of you need to hold hands," she orders us. "You can keep holding hands down the hallway until we get past the gym, but then we might run into teachers, so make sure you let go after that."

Titusville High School has, first among its list of ridiculous rules, a "no PDA in the halls" rule, so even holding hands would put us at risk of detention. Kieran, of course, wouldn't remember, but judging by the vacant expression on his face as he listens to Kayla's instructions, he also doesn't remember that holding my hand is— *was*—one of the most natural things in the world to him.

"And try to smile sometimes," Kayla says to Kieran. "Just like we talked about last night. People are pretty much going to ignore you anyway because they think you're the weird narcolepsy kid, but you don't want to be standing around looking at things like some kind of a moron because you don't remember. That's just going to tip people off that something's wrong."

"But I *don't* remember," Kieran insists. "I don't know how to act..."

"We'll help you," I tell him, shooting Kayla a harsh look as I lean forward and put my hand on the corner of his seat. "Whatever questions you need to ask, just ask us. If you're confused, tell us. We're all going to get through this together, right?"

I glance back at Kayla, who nods her head but is mashing her lips together as if she doesn't buy into a word I've said. Kieran, meanwhile, says, "Thanks," and gives me a version of the grin that's turned me inside out since we first met. The grin isn't entirely the same—this one's not quite as broad or familiar somehow—but it's still The Grin. It gives me hope that the Kieran I love is here with me, even if he's not aware of it.

"We should go," Kayla says, watching the steady stream of people hunkering down into their coats as they head for the door. Kieran slides out of the passenger side as I hiss, low enough so he can't listen, "Way to be positive, Kay."

"He needs to be prepared," she points out, her voice at its normal volume. Kieran, now outside, turns and stands stock straight as if he's afraid to make a move until we're next to him. Kayla watches him for a second and then glances back at me. "And it's not like the two of us can follow him around all day. He's not in most of our classes."

I heave a sigh and get out of the vehicle, offering my hand to Kieran.

"Ready for this?" I ask, nodding toward the school as we lock gloved hands.

"No," he mumbles. "But I'm glad you and Kayla are here with me."

His face is frozen in a frown as if he's not really too glad at all, but he realizes he doesn't have much of a choice.

"Whatever you need, we're here for you." I say, looking past him to Kayla, who is now on his other side. He and Kayla exchange polite nods as I quickly add "But don't text us. You can't use phones at school, not even at lunch. You're pretty much forced to sneak a peek at your messages while you're in the bathroom or something. I don't know if Kayla told you or not."

"She mentioned it, but it sounds like there wouldn't be anyone who would be texting me anyway, so..."

The bell signaling that we have ten minutes to get inside and to our first period class goes off, and we trudge to the entrance, saying polite hellos to the other members of Titusville's teenage population we pass along the way. Luckily, there isn't time to make much meaningful conversation with anybody since we need to hurry to our lockers, grab our books, and head to class, and—as Kayla so eloquently put it—since Kieran's "the weird narcolepsy kid," people other than our close friends aren't going to invest much time in talking to him anyway. Once we pass the gym, Kieran and I drop hands as directed and head through the lobby to the senior hallway, where I stop at my locker halfway down while Kayla crosses to her locker across the hall. Kieran, meanwhile, stops about a foot away from me and watches as I hang up my coat and grab books from the bottom locker shelf for my history class. When I stand upright again, I find Kieran's standing so close to me his mouth is mere inches from my ear, and I can't say I mind.

"I'm not really sure where my locker is," he whispers, embarrassed. "Is it down there?" He points in the direction of the school lobby. "Kayla drew me a map of stuff and wrote down my combination, but I'm kind of disoriented and..."

"It's over there, across the hall," I whisper back, nodding in the opposite direction and as I do, he leans in even further and we bump heads, his dark hair grazing the side of my head.

"Sorry," we both mumble at each other, and as he pulls back from me, his face breaks into a version of his grin that seems a little more familiar. I lift my left hand to smooth my dirt-blonde bangs out of my face after our collision.

"This is really pretty," Kieran says, catching sight of the bracelet around my left wrist. Of course he wouldn't recognize the silver charm bracelet he gave me on our mutual birthday last year, and he definitely wouldn't remember the significance of each of the charms. And with time ticking away before our first period classes, now isn't the time to remind him and pray for those memories to come back, although I'm assuming he would have read about giving me the bracelet in the mini-autobiography I helped him write before he underwent the treatment. If reading about giving me the charm bracelet and all the different times he's given me charms on special occasions hasn't jogged his memory, then I'm not sure seeing the actual bracelet will make much of a difference.

"Thanks," I mumble, pointing down the hall. "Anyway, like I said, your locker's over there, right across from boys' bathroom."

"That's convenient, I guess."

I match his smile with one of my own. Maybe we're going to get through this day after all.

"Did Kayla write down your locker number?" I ask, getting serious once again.

"Yeah."

"And you've got trigonometry first period." I turn and nod toward the other end of the hall. "Room Two."

"And I won't see you again until English this afternoon, right?" His voice has a note of hope to it I latch onto like a life preserver.

"We have the same lunch period. So does Kayla."

He shakes his head, closing his eyes.

"That's right," he mumbles. "Kayla wrote that down, too. I'm never going to be able to keep all of this straight."

"You'll be fine." I unconsciously reach out to touch his arm and immediately realize what I'm doing, jerking my hand back before I make contact. "I'll meet you at your locker and we'll go to lunch together. It's what we always do."

I can't keep the sadness out of my voice, and he looks away. Luckily, the warning bell sounds, saving us both.

"I have to go upstairs," I tell him. "You'll be okay?"

He shrugs. "I guess I'll just go to trig. I don't think there's time to go to my locker now." His eyes flash with mild panic. "I *think* my book's in my backpack."

"I'll walk you," I offer. "The stairs are that way anyway."

We start to walk off but stop when we see Kayla elbowing people out of the way to get across the hall to us.

"It's go time, big brother," she says, falling in step next to him. "Ready to get your trig on?"

"Did I even like trigonometry…you know…before?" Kieran asks as we continue down the hall.

"No," Kayla and I both say in unison, prompting Kieran to heave a deep sigh as he heads off to the classroom. Kayla and I keep pushing down the hall toward the lobby and the stairs, not saying anything until we're safely in our seats in the back of our history classroom, having narrowly avoided being late on the first day back.

"Is he going to be okay?" I ask as the bell goes off. Coach Denton—*Mrs.* Denton when we're in the classroom and not on the basketball court—welcomes us all back from winter break and we get a few more minutes to whisper while she writes notes on the board.

"I hope so," Kayla says, leaning across her desk so I can hear her. "I drew him a map of the school, wrote out his schedule, and told him not to talk to anyone unless he had to. I spent all day yesterday quizzing him about our life here, who people are, stuff like that. I hope it's enough to get him—"

"Ms. Lanier, I'm ready to start class whenever you are." Mrs. Denton has her arms crossed over her broad torso, glaring at Kayla.

"Sorry," Kayla mumbles, and Mrs. Denton orders us to open our textbooks to the page she's written on the board. From the corner of my eye, I catch Kayla scooting her notebook toward the edge of her desk, and I lean over slightly to read that she's finished our conversation in the right margin of the page—"I hope I've prepared him well enough to get through the next few weeks."

Just a few weeks—we're hoping with repeated exposure to familiar people and places, Kieran will come out of the amnesia in a few weeks. Cooper Halloran, adopted son of the nation's tenth richest man and the only other known person who suffered from the same sleeping disorder that produced flashes of the future, only had amnesia for about three weeks before his memory started coming back. Three weeks seems like an eternity right now, but that time will be worth it if Kieran comes out the other end of this able to live the normal life he's never had.

I give Kayla a weak smile as Mrs. Denton notices my attention isn't on the front of the room.

"Zara," she says, hand on her hip while using my given name, as most teachers do during the school day, "if I have to tell either you or Kayla to pay attention one more time…"

She lets her threat hang in the air unfinished as I apologize and make sure I don't so much as blink at Kayla for the rest of the period. But my mind isn't on history class or Kayla or anything else other than Kieran, and how he—and how all of us who love him—are going to get through these next few weeks.

CHAPTER 2

Cassie Newbaum and I have been friends since birth—longer, if you count the fact our mothers knew each other when they were pregnant—and we've played basketball together nearly as long. So when something isn't quite right with me, Cass can sniff the problem out like a coonhound on the hunt. And right now, as we're changing in the locker room after practice, she's apparently getting a big whiff of something being off with me.

"So, what's up with you and Kieran?" she says, sliding her head through a red knit sweater and gathering her long brunette locks in both hands to pull the ends out from the collar.

"What do you mean?" I struggle to make my voice sound as innocent and unknowing as possible as I fasten my charm bracelet around my wrist.

"I'm not exactly sure. Things seemed kind of weird with you two at lunch."

"You think Kieran's weird all the time anyway," I point out, not doing a very good job at deflecting her concerns. Reaching behind me, I grab a hairbrush from my locker and start sweeping my hair into a loose knot at the base of my neck, holding the strands secure as I toss the brush into my gym bag and fumble around for a ponytail holder.

"Well, yeah. I'll be the first person to admit the guy's a total cutie, but personality-wise? Not my type," Cass agrees. "I'm not only talking about him, though. I mean, you seemed kind of weird, too. It was like there was...I don't know...this *distance* between the two of you. I can't put my finger on it."

I can put my finger all over it, of course, but I'm obviously not going to say anything to Cassie. Kieran usually spends his lunch periods with me at the "Jock Table" reading and ignoring the school sports talk and general gossip going on around him, only looking up to say something on the rare occasion he has something to contribute to the conversation. But I often lean in close to him to whisper comments about whatever's going on around us, whether Cassie and her eternal on-again, off-again boyfriend Cody Hull are bickering about whatever or Jake Tomlinson is trying for the millionth time to eat five hamburgers in one lunch period—he always fails—or Ashley Keep is arguing with Rick Matthews over when they're going to stop randomly hooking up and become a real couple, and then the two of us giggle together until everyone gives us annoyed looks for being off in our own world.

Now, Kieran and I are in two separate worlds, and naturally, Cassie would be the first person to notice.

"Does any of the weirdness have to do with him not having narcolepsy anymore?" Cassie asks.

I stop reaching around inside my bag and let my hair fall loose around my shoulders. Sitting up straight on the bench and hoping I'm masking my shock well enough Cassie won't notice, I mumble, "Um, what?"

"He doesn't have narcolepsy anymore. Or, I mean, he's on medication for it now or something."

My mind races, attempting to figure out a way to get the information I want out of Cassie without revealing that I, Kieran's beloved girlfriend, doesn't have the information to begin with.

"How did you find that out?"

"I guess he went to the office after lunch with some note from his parents saying he's taking medication every morning now to control his narcolepsy thing, so he doesn't have to go to the nurse's office for a nap during his study hall period," Cassie explains. "So Principal Rosner called Mrs. Lanier to make sure the note wasn't a fake or whatever, and then signed off on him having study hall instead. Mrs. Gillette texted Marcy about the whole thing, and then Marcy texted Ashley to ask if she'd heard any other details. Ashley was checking her phone in the bathroom before fifth period and she told me the whole story."

I sigh at the fact that the Titusville gossip circle now stretches beyond state lines. Marcy Gillette, our former teammate who's now a freshman at some school in northern Wisconsin, was always the first to find out everything going on at school thanks to her mother's position working in the school's front office. Her college life must be extremely boring if she's still getting Titusville gossip as soon as it happens and had the time to share her mother's news with Ashley.

But what disturbs me more than Mrs. Gillette and Marcy being unable to keep quiet about anything is the fact that the Laniers have concocted another story to hide something strange about Kieran and they—or, more specifically, Kayla—have neglected to share that information with me.

"Narcolepsy or no narcolepsy, Kieran and I are fine," I tell Cassie, brushing off my hurt feelings. "In fact, I'm going over to his house for dinner tonight. My mom, too—I'll bet she's outside waiting for me right now."

"Just checking," Cassie assures me. "And I hope Kieran understands if he hurts you in any way, he'll have to answer to me."

I lean over and bump elbows with her.

"Thanks, Cass," I say, smiling, and I hear my phone buzz in my gym bag. "That's probably my mom. See you tomorrow."

"Yeah. See you."

I sling my backpack on my shoulder and grab my gym bag off the floor, saying goodbye to the rest of my teammates as I make my way out of the locker room and down the hall to the outside entrance.

As I expected, my mom is idling in a parking space a few feet away, and I hurry through the cold and snowflakes to the warmth of her car.

"Hey, kiddo," Mom greets me, leaning over to kiss the top of my head as I get settled in. "How was school?"

"Educational."

"Because you learned the Young Mr. Lanier's memory has returned and now this dinner isn't going to be the most awkward social event ever?" she says, pulling out onto Main Street and almost immediately making the left turn onto the county road that runs in front of our house and the Laniers'.

"Because the Young Mr. Lanier's 'narcolepsy' is apparently under control thanks to medication, and I'm the last person at school to hear the news."

Mom's brow furrows in confusion, but she doesn't take her eyes off the road. Before she can ask, I jump in with an explanation.

"I used to be the first person to know all about the Laniers' lies and cover-ups and strange explanations for things. I guess now that's changed along with Kieran."

"First of all, Kieran hasn't really changed," Mom points out, although I'm not sure I agree. "He's just temporarily…"

As she thinks of the right words to describe Kieran's current state, Mom slows the car for the turn into the Laniers' driveway.

"Temporarily taken leave of himself?" I suggest.

"Very poetic, daughter-of mine." She smiles. "And I'm sure there's a good reason why no one told you about the latest Lanier cover story. Maybe there wasn't time."

"Maybe," I muse, but I can't help but feel left out. The Lanier family intrigues have been such a big part of my life over the last year that not being among the first to know about one—or even helping to dream one up—seems pretty strange.

We park in the driveway next to my grandparents' truck and make our way to the front porch of the Laniers' two-story farmhouse, a house that was owned by the family of my mom's high school boyfriend until the Laniers moved here from North Carolina, seeking to escape the imagined threat of Kieran's ex-con birth father, who meets us at the front door.

"You guys are right on time," Morgan tells us, standing aside so we can come in out of the cold. "Carlie's putting the food out."

He takes our coats from us, and I notice his hand lingers on the back of my mom's neck for a second before he moves to hang our coats on two empty pegs inside the front door. Mom and Morgan are currently engaging in some sort of undefined relationship neither wants to talk about in much detail, which doesn't seem to consist of anything more than hanging out and sharing secret smiles. The two of them exchange glances and walk off toward the dining room as Gram toddles out from the kitchen to intercept me.

"How was practice?" she asks, enveloping me in a hug. She smells like apple pie, and I breathe in the comforting scent.

"Good," I say against her sweater before lowering my voice a little. "Although I guess that's not really the most important thing right now, is it?"

Gram pulls back enough to plant a kiss on my forehead. "Just trying to put you at ease a little," she whispers. "Is it working?"

I don't have the heart to tell her no, so I only nod at her.

"Is he…?" I tilt my chin toward the dining room.

"With Kayla and Brad," Gram says, keeping her voice low. "Gramps and Jim are in there, too—I've been helping Carlie get the food out from the kitchen." Gram pauses for a moment, glancing back over her shoulder before looking at me once again. "Kieran…he seems a little…lost. I'm not sure what I expected, but…"

I shrug at Gram as Carlie's voice booms—as much as her whispery voice *can* boom—from the dining room.

"Everyone ready to eat?"

Gram drapes an arm around me and we enter the Laniers' dining room, the table set for ten almost too big for the space. I slide into the empty seat at the end of the table next to Kieran, my usual place at these combined family dinners. Kieran greets me with a warm smile and a "Hey," which I return, restraining myself from what would be my normal behaviors of searching for his hand under the table or brushing my knee against his. Instead, I concentrate on not touching his hand when he passes me bowls and serving trays of food and on listening to the various snippets of conversations swirling around me, most of the talk revolving around Sumner College. Gramps is retired from the Department of Art and Design, while Jim Lanier is the head of the Sumner College Counseling Center and Morgan works on the grounds crew, and right now, the three of them are detailing the highlights of the latest exhibit at the Sumner College Art Gallery. Kayla and Brad, sitting on Kieran's other side, are murmuring amongst themselves about something I can't hear, while Mom and Gram appear to be listening attentively to the art conversation.

Carlie, on the other hand, is freaking me out a little.

I'm pretending to be invested in the discussions taking place across from me and at the other end of the table, but when I take a few moments to cut into my pot roast, I shift my eyes to Carlie sitting to my left at the head of the table. She's not eating, she's not talking, she's not doing anything but glancing at Kieran every few seconds, as if she doesn't want to miss his reaction to anything, as if she's expecting that any second now, Kieran's going to drop his fork to his plate, take a look around, and announce, "Oh, hey—I remember you people." And I understand her anxiety, because we all know Kieran's

19

memory returning could be as sudden—all it took for Cooper Halloran's memory to return was hearing a crappy song by his pop star ex detailing a breakup conversation they'd had. So, I'm sure Carlie's too on the edge of her seat to eat anything, just waiting for someone to utter whatever magic word or phrase that will bring Kieran back.

"This is all really good, Carlie," I say, pointing to my plate with my fork, hoping a compliment will distract her from the torture I imagine she's putting herself through inside her head right now. She breathes a "thank you" as Kieran piggybacks on my sentiment.

"Yeah, Carlie. This is delicious."

Everyone at the table cringes to the point the expression almost makes a sound. Kieran picks up on his mistake and corrects himself, saying, "*Mom*—I meant *Mom*."

"Thank you," Carlie says, her voice barely audible.

A lull in the conversation, filled only by the sounds of silverware clanking against plates, hangs over us for about a minute before Brad leans forward so he can look at me at the other end of the table.

"How was practice today?" he asks.

"Good. Really good. Given the way the season's going so far, I like our chances to go undefeated this year."

"Basketball, right?" Kieran asks me.

"Yeah."

"When's your next game?" Kayla asks as if she doesn't already know. But Kieran had developed an interest in basketball over the last year, which was mainly due to his relationship with me, so keeping this particular conversation going has as much of a chance of sparking his memories as anything else.

"Friday night," I say, pushing some vegetables around my plate with my fork. "At home. We play at five and the guys play at seven."

"I like basketball, right?" Kieran asks, and the almost audible cringing from everyone at the table happens once again.

"Let's just say you were developing an interest," Kayla offers, and Kieran nods before turning back to me.

"Do people go to the games? I mean, is that a popular thing to do around here?"

I'm almost relieved to be talking to Kieran about basketball—I can pretend I'm having a normal conversation with someone who's just some guy and not the guy I'm in love with.

"More people go to the guys' games than ours," I tell him. "But it's weird because we're doing so much better than they are this year. I mean, they have a losing record and we're undefeated, and they still get more people at their games. It's like…tradition or something for people to watch men's basketball instead of women's."

Kieran listens attentively to my mini-diatribe and shifts his attention to Brad and Kayla.

"Well, we should go—to both games. You want to?"

Kayla mumbles a "yeah," and Brad says "Sure. I don't have to go back to Evanston until Sunday, so going to the game sounds like a plan."

Kieran smiles at me, and once again, I assure myself I'm going to get through the next few weeks until whatever brings him back brings him back.

We all make more meaningless conversation throughout the rest of dinner and dessert, the highlight of the evening being Carlie and Jim sharing the story of how they told Kayla and Kieran they were moving the family to Titusville from North Carolina, another obvious ploy at shaking Kieran's memories loose. But rather than announcing he's remembered something, when Kieran finishes the last morsel of his apple pie, he instead says to me "Do you want to come up to my room and hang out for a while?"

Everyone in the room stops eating, talking…*breathing*…and waits for my reply. I'd burst out laughing right now if the situation were anything other than what it is.

"Yeah. Sure," I tell him, glancing around at the adults in the room bobbing their heads in almost desperate approval. They all look so ridiculous, I almost want to yell "I can't wait until we're alone so we can *totally* make out," except everyone at this table knows making out is probably the last thing that's going to happen when we get upstairs.

And even weirder is the fact that everyone at this table probably wishes Kieran and I *were* going up to his room to be all over each other just so we could go back to being normal boyfriendy-girlfriendy again.

Kieran and I head upstairs as the adults adjourn to the living room and Kayla and Brad clear the table and start cleaning up. I enter the room ahead of him and sit down on the edge of his bed while he sits cross-legged on the window seat a few feet away and shoves his hands into the front pocket of his black hoodie.

"So, do we do that a lot? The dinner thing?" he asks.

"Not a lot." I shrug. "Mostly when there's something significant going on."

"Like?"

I decide to charge right into the metaphorical thousand-pound gorilla in the room.

"Like when everyone's hoping that if we all get together, we'll do or say something to bring your memory back."

Kieran exhales and smiles, and I think I've lifted a weight off his shoulders.

"It did kind of seem like everyone was kind of trying too hard, didn't it?"

"Yeah," I agree. "Funny thing is, we were all trying so hard to act normal we couldn't really act normal at all."

He takes his hands from his pocket and runs them through his hair, saying, "Um…yeah. So, acting normal is kind of what I wanted to talk to you about."

"Okay."

Kieran stands up and looks around before sitting back down again, his nerves obvious. I fight the urge to go over and put my arms around him to calm him down.

"First of all," he begins, "I want to thank you for helping me out at school today. I don't think I could have made it through the day without you."

"Don't mention it. I didn't really do much."

"You told me how to behave at lunch and got me to the right English classroom and…" He shakes his head. "Just…thanks. You made a day that was going to suck no matter what suck a lot less."

"You're welcome." My voice sounds quiet and formal, mostly because I'm not sure what his point is yet in asking me up here.

"It's just that, I know part of why you helped me today was because you're my girlfriend and you're, like, supposed to or whatever, but I can also tell, just from being around you and from reading stuff in my old journals, that you're a nice person, and you would have helped me out anyway, even if we weren't together."

I bob my head slowly, still clueless as to where this conversation is headed.

"You're so *nice*," he says, standing up from the window seat. He paces back and forth in front of his desk for a few seconds, stopping to lean against the edge near his computer. "But everything's totally weird right now, you know? It's like…it's like I'm

23

supposed to be playing the lead role in a movie, but no one's given me the script. Nothing's *natural*. I mean, I'm reading those journals and I'm listening to everything Kayla and my parents are telling me about my life, but nothing's real to me. And this Cooper kid keeps sending me messages every five minutes, wondering how I'm doing and asking if anything's come back to me. This life I'm living right now…it's someone else's—not mine. I'm not sure what my life even is."

Once again, I have to stuff down the urge to go to him. I want so badly to feel his hair on my cheek, to breathe in his scent, to measure his heartbeat against mine, even as I know those sensations mean nothing to him now.

"Just…I can't do this to you. I barely know who you are, but I'm sure you don't deserve this."

"This?" I mumble, starting to get a clearer picture of how our conversation is going to end.

"I can't pretend to be the perfect boyfriend—assuming I was the perfect boyfriend to begin with."

"You were," I tell him and, realizing my mistake, I quickly backtrack—"You *are*."

"See? There." he says, holding his hands out in front of him. "This whole thing is too weird—for both of us. And you seem like a good person, and I don't want to hurt you. In fact, I want more than anything to be your friend."

Here we go—I'm about to be sent to the "friend zone" by the love of my life. I take a deep breath and start to move this discussion along to its inevitable conclusion.

"So, what are you suggesting?"

"I'm suggesting we tell people we aren't together anymore," but he quickly adds "but we're still friends."

24

When I was in seventh grade, the Titusville Junior High girls' basketball team was playing Sumner Township and when I went up for a shot on one possession, Brynne Lostrand slid under me. As I came down, my belly crashed right into her shoulder. I spent a few minutes lying on the court—and a few minutes on the bench after that—trying desperately to catch my breath.

This moment with Kieran feels *a lot* like that moment in seventh grade.

Chapter 3

I take a minute to focus on breathing like a normal human being before I ask him "And what happens if you wake up two days from now or two weeks from now and you remember everything?"

He shrugs and says "I guess we'll tell people we got back together. I mean, that's believable, right? I'm guessing people break up and get back together all the time, right?"

"Yeah. Okay," I mumble, willing myself to mimic Kieran and make like this is happening to somebody else. This is somebody else's life—not mine.

"And I'll go along with whatever you want to tell people," he says, staring down at the floor. "This must be hard on you and I feel like an ass because you're so nice—"

I *so* wish he'd stop calling me *nice*. *Nice* is one of those words people use when talking about a person they don't know very well. Acquaintances are *nice*—the love of your life had better be a little more than *nice*.

"I'm trying hard to do the right thing here," he continues. "I don't want to hurt you even worse than I probably already have because I can't be the person I've always been for you."

Unfortunately for me, what he's doing right now almost makes me love him more, especially because when I was trying to talk him into undergoing the treatment, I convinced him I'd be fine without him if he didn't remember me. Guess now's the time for me to put my money where my mouth was back before Thanksgiving.

"No, I understand," I tell him, proud of myself that my voice sounds normal and not shaky or upset. "We can tell people we started fighting a lot over Christmas break or something and decided to be just friends for a while. Nobody at school saw us for almost two weeks, so they'll buy our story. Most couples around here can't go two minutes without fighting, much less two weeks, so a breakup is totally believable."

Kieran nods and says, "Okay." He pauses briefly and shoves his hands back into his hoodie pocket. "And I really do want to be your friend, Zip. From what I understand, you're an amazing person. How could I not want someone like you in my life?"

"Thanks," I mumble. "You wouldn't remember this now, but I promised to be in your life no matter what. I'm not one to go back on my promises." He gives me a grateful smile, and I continue, "And you don't realize it, but you're a pretty amazing person, too. Keep clinging to those thoughts, okay?"

"Thanks."

An awkward silence settles over the room, and I search my brain for a quick method of escape.

"I think I'll go help Kayla and Brad with the dishes. My mom will probably want to leave soon, and I don't want them to get stuck with all the work," I tell him.

"Yeah—I have homework and stuff I should probably get to," he says, shifting his eyes to his backpack on the floor next to his bed, obviously searching for an out like I am. I give him a little wave and a "Bye" before darting for the door and heading downstairs to the kitchen, swallowing down the sob working its way up my throat.

This is for the best—I'm sure of it, and I believe deep in my heart our separation is only for a little while, only until Kieran gets his memory back. But my heart doesn't understand what's going on as well as my head does at the moment.

I rush downstairs and don't stop in the foyer long enough to see whether or not the adults have noticed I've come back to the first floor alone. Instead, I walk at warp speed to the kitchen, stopping next to Brad at the kitchen sink.

"Here—let me put that away for you," I motion to the platter he's drying and he hands it to me. "Kay, where does this go?" I ask as if everything's normal.

Kayla takes her hands from the dishwater and dries her hands on a towel.

"It goes right between 'Who cares?' and 'Tell me what you and my brother talked about upstairs,'" she huffs, sitting down at the kitchen table. I set the platter on the counter behind me and suck in a breath—might as well cut right to the important stuff.

"Well, he broke up with me, basically."

Kayla's eyes widen in disbelief, and she darts up from the table as if she's realized she's sitting on a bed of needles.

"Okay—no. Not happening. Unacceptable." She turns on her heel and seems to be headed for the hallway, but Brad rushes over in front of her and places his hands on her shoulders.

"Kayla, no."

"Brad Wallace, if you don't get out of my way right now…"

Brad blows his overgrown bangs out of his face and looks past Kayla to me.

"Zip?" he says, and I understand he's prompting me to continue relating what happened upstairs which will, hopefully, calm Kayla down a bit.

"I'm fine, really," I insist, which I immediately realize isn't the thing to say when you're trying to convince someone you're fine, really. "Kayla, this had to happen. Going upstairs to yell at him or talk him out of breaking up with me or whatever you're planning to do isn't going to change anything."

"Still not convinced," she says, sweeping both Brad and me up in her scowl as she slides back into one of the kitchen table chairs.

"Look," I begin, sighing. "Today was awful. The other night was awful. He's not Kieran right now—he's not himself. I can't expect him to fake a relationship with me when he basically has no idea who I am. We can't pretend everything's okay and think people aren't eventually going to pick up on the fact things are the total opposite of okay. Cassie's already wondering if something's wrong with Kieran and me. It's only a matter of time before everyone else starts noticing things aren't right between us."

"And what happens when he gets his memory back and realizes you two are the most disgustingly happy couple on the face of the planet?" Kayla asks and Brad raises his eyebrows at her. "Besides us, I mean," she assures him.

"Then we get back together, I guess."

"And people are going to buy that? You two just breaking up for no reason and getting back together for no reason?"

I can't avoid rolling my eyes at her question.

"I know you've only lived here a year, but Cassie and Cody Hull have broken up over nothing and gotten back together over nothing so many times they've practically turned breaking up into an Olympic event," I remind her. "Kieran and I getting back together won't be a big deal. Or it'll be a big deal for, like, a day and then everyone will move on to something else."

Kayla looks to Brad for confirmation, and he says, "She's right, Kay. People at school have short attention spans. If you're lucky, Cassie and Cody will go through another blowout around the same time Kieran gets his memory back and no one will even notice Kieran and Zip got back together out of the blue."

"Or maybe they'll be too preoccupied with Kieran being on medication now to control his narcolepsy," I say to Kayla with a little bite to my voice. And, as usual, she isn't caught off guard at all.

"I was going to tell you about that," she says, barely missing a beat. "There just wasn't time."

"Were you going to tell *me* about it?" Brad asks. "I have no idea what Zip's talking about."

Uh oh. Kayla hiding things from Brad almost broke them up once before, so I don't know how he's going to react to her hiding things again.

"We had to come up with a cover story for why he wasn't falling asleep all the time anymore," Kayla explains, more to Brad than to me. "Nobody here knows that Mom and Dad had Kieran on every narcolepsy drug in existence when he was a kid and nothing worked, so telling the school he's on something now was a pretty easy explanation. And since part of the story was that he takes the medication at home every morning, we didn't need to deal with filling out forms or providing doctor's information so Kieran could take the medication at school—all we needed was the note from Mom and Dad that he was on something that worked."

"Another lie about his condition," Brad says through a breath. Brad, who's hoping to be a doctor someday, always gets a little twitchy when he finds out the Laniers have bent some rules on anything involving medicine. I think he's made peace with Jim and with Carlie, a physician herself who hasn't practiced in years in favor of hovering over Kieran, and how they've lied to the school about Kieran having narcolepsy. But he really struggled with Carlie working in secret with the Halloran researchers—all of whom had everyday, legit jobs as researchers with Halloran subsidiary companies—to devise a corrective for Morgan Levert's homemade drug that induced the sleeping and dreaming symptoms in Cooper Halloran and Kieran in utero. So, I'm not surprised Brad would be struggling with the Laniers devising another lie about Kieran's true medical condition and that Kayla had conveniently forgotten to mention anything about it to him until she had to.

"We didn't have a choice," Kayla points out. "We couldn't send Kieran back to school without an explanation or people would wonder."

"And not sending him back to school wasn't an option?" Brad challenges. "Mr. Halloran kept Cooper out of school until his memory came back. Your mom couldn't homeschool him again for a while?"

"Okay—you've *met* my brother, right?" Kayla huffs. "He may not seem like the same person right now, but deep down, he's still the same stupid, stubborn-as-hell Kieran he's always been. Mom suggested keeping him home for a few *days* to help get him used to things and he nearly lost it. He may not remember anything, but he understands the basic facts—he's almost nineteen, he's already behind in school, and he's supposed to graduate in a few months. There's no way we were keeping him home."

"And you couldn't have explained any of this to us before now?" Brad nods over at me as he questions Kayla.

The cover story basically came together late last night," Kayla breathes. "There wasn't time to tell either of you."

"But you have time to send me dirty text messages at two in the morning." Brad points out, and I pile on with "Yeah, Kay—modern technology sort of eliminates the whole 'There was no time' argument.'

Kayla fixes her gaze on Brad, her blue eyes almost shooting sparks.

"I thought you *liked* getting dirty text messages from me at two in the morning," she says.

Brad shakes his head at her. "Kind of not the point right now, and you know it," he fires back

"And a little more information than I needed about either of you, to be honest," I chime in. "I mean, ewww."

Kayla ignores me and keeps her attention focused on Brad.

"Look, I also didn't tell you guys right away because I know you're both sick of it," she begins. "You know—sick of the lying. And I know you both think lying about my family stuff is as natural to me as breathing—" she gazes at Brad rather than me as she says this last bit—"and maybe after all these years, it kind of is. But I don't like lying, especially to people I care about. But this is the last time—it *has* to be. If we can get Kieran through the rest of the school year and off to college without any problems, he'll get to live a whole new life…we both will." She takes a long pause. "He has two college interviews with portfolio reviews in Chicago over Presidents' Day weekend—we just found out this afternoon. He's so close to getting everything he wants…*wanted*."

Kayla closes her eyes and shakes her head. Apparently, none of us knows whether to refer to the facts of Kieran's life in present or past tense, his college applications included.

"Does he have any idea he'd applied to colleges?" I ask, recalling with some sadness that the prospect of being able to go away to school was what finally convinced him to undergo the treatment.

"He does now," Kayla mumbles. "Dad and I sat him down before everyone came over tonight and told him where he'd applied and that he'd already been accepted to Sumner. Dad said that if he thought he didn't want to major in art anymore—or even if he did—we could look into him applying to some other schools. And Kieran *did* say he felt more at home during art class today at school than he did anywhere else, so I don't see him changing his mind about his art school applications."

"But timing's an issue, though, right?" Brad asks. "I mean, what happens if he decides to apply and go somewhere else, but then he remembers where he really wanted to go? Or what if he's in the middle of his interview in Chicago and his memory comes back all at once?"

Kayla's shoulders hunch forward. "I have no idea," she breathes, her voice full of defeat. "I guess we'll figure all of that out if any of it happens."

Brad leans over and gathers her into a hug. "I'm sorry," he murmurs in her ear. "I hate that this is all so hard on you. I wish I could do something to make things easier."

"I wish you could, too," she breathes. "But just having you here makes things easier. I wish you didn't have to go back to school on Sunday."

He kisses her forehead and barely pulls away as he says "You're welcome in Evanston anytime, you know. Caleb told me he doesn't have a problem with you visiting because he can always stay across campus with his girlfriend."

I've gathered over several conversations that "Caleb" is Brad's roommate at Northwestern, a fellow future doctor from a small town in Pennsylvania who probably found an on-campus girlfriend to crash with once he realized he'd be sharing his room most of the time not only with Brad, but also with Brad's off-campus girlfriend.

"Speaking of Northwestern," Kayla starts, looking over Brad's shoulder at me, "any news from them yet?"

I shake my head. In between worrying about Kieran and playing in the Sumner Township Holiday Tournament, I barely had time to pull my application together before the due date. Kayla, meanwhile, had heard about her early decision acceptance right before Christmas.

"It's way too soon," I tell her. "I don't think I'm supposed to hear anything until April. I just hope I wasn't so distracted by stuff that I screwed up the essay."

"Oh, come on." Brad dismisses my concerns with a wave of his hand. "I'm sure your essay is fine, and I bet you'll have no problem getting in. I had straight A's and I got in, and you and Kayla both have straight A's and *she's* in. It makes sense for them to accept you, too."

"Well, put in a good word for me with the right people anyway, okay, Wallace?" I tease.

"Sure thing," he teases back. "I'm in with all the important people on campus. The president, all of the deans, everyone in admissions...I've got your back."

I shake my head at him as Kayla says, "Just wait, Zip. Everything's going to work out. Kieran will get his memory back, and we're all going to end up in Chicago—you, me, Brad, *and* Kieran.

The slight tremble in Kayla's voice betrays that she's not any more certain everything's going to work out than I am. As much as I want to go to Northwestern, if another school somewhere offers me more scholarship money—especially if they offer me scholarship money to play basketball—then I'd be crazy not to consider. And who knows what's going to happen with Kieran's college plans or anything else about his life, for that matter.

"And at least you still have basketball season to worry about, right?" Kayla points out, as if I need a reminder. "At least you've got something else to focus on while you're waiting on Northwestern and..." She pauses, nodding down the hall as if Kieran's standing outside the kitchen. "...other stuff."

I don't answer her, but I shrug my shoulders and think *Yup— at least I still have basketball.*

CHAPTER 4

I set the inevitable in motion by texting Cassie as soon as I get home, telling her in a series of sentence fragments and abbreviations how she was right about everything—Kieran and I really *were* having trouble and hadn't been getting along since Christmas, and we'd decided to take a break and be friends for a while. She asks if I need to talk, but I put her off until school the next day when I'm sure she'll want to do more talking about the whole thing than I could ever possibly imagine.

Sure enough, she's practically on top of me the second I enter the school through the side entrance the next morning. In order to ease any awkwardness between Kieran and myself, I'd texted Kayla I was going to return to my old routine of dropping my mom off at her store in the mornings and driving myself to school, at least for now. So when Cassie ambushes me, I'm alone without Kayla to run interference. But I'm also without Kieran, which, given Cassie's attitude, is definitely a good thing for him.

"Oh, my God," she starts, falling in next to me as I shuffle up the hall. "I am so totally kicking Kieran's ass for this. I mean, he gets that, right?"

"This is a mutual breakup and we're still friends," I remind her. "No ass-kicking necessary."

I glance over at her as we make our way through the overcrowded hallway to my locker. She's giving me this kind of pouty, sad-eyed expression like I just lost my best friend—which I guess I kind of did.

"But thanks for offering to kick ass for me," I tell her. "Knowing you have my back means a lot. But like I said, Kieran and I are still friends, so I'm good."

"Really?" She's obviously skeptical, and I don't blame her. At the moment, I'm too numb to be sure if I'm okay or if I'm only faking being okay.

"Really. I mean it."

Cassie pats me on the back before heading off to her locker, her gesture being the first of many back-pats I receive from various girls in my first few classes. Kieran was my first boyfriend, and now I'm learning how to go through my first breakup—apparently, when one ends a relationship, one is the recipient of lots of mournful expressions, lots of comforting pats on the shoulders and back, and lots of "Hey, I was really sorry to hear about you and Kieran. Relationships totally suck"-types of comments. The whole situation is weird and foreign to me, and by lunchtime, I'm baffled as to how I'm supposed to get through the rest of the day and not be miserable. Here I am, trying so hard not to be depressed, but everyone else is insisting on throwing me a giant pity party and bringing me down.

I make my way through the lunch line—where I am on the receiving end of more sad stares—and pay for my something-or-other resembling shredded beef and French fries before heading back to my usual seat at the "Jock Table," where Kayla's already picking at the mystery main dish with her fork.

"If you value your life at all, don't eat that," she warns, casting a glance at my tray before giving up and pushing her own meal away. I sit down and she asks me, "So, how'd your morning go?"

"Well, everyone's acting like my dog just died and I've never owned a dog. So, there's that."

Kayla laughs a little before assuring me "I think people are trying to be nice. Remember what you and Brad both told me—in a few days this will all blow over and everyone will move on to something else."

"Yeah. You're right," I say as Ashley sets her tray on the table and flops down in the chair next to me so hard her body careens sideways and she bumps me in the shoulder.

"Oh, wow, Zip. I'm sorry. I'm really, really sorry."

"Ash, it's fine. You bumped me a little. I'm okay."

"I know. But you're having a rough day and I feel so bad for you and…"

Her voice trails off, and she gives me a soft pat on the shoulder she'd bumped a second ago. I sigh and look around the table at the usual suspects who are now all assembled and staring mournfully at me—Ashley, Kayla, Lauren, Cassie, Cody Hull, Rick Matthews, and Jake Tomlinson—and I kind of lose my mind.

"Look, guys. I'm okay," I insist, my voice rising. "I'm serious—I'm okay, Kieran's okay, everybody is totally *freaking* okay."

"Well, Kieran sure seems okay, anyway," Cody points out, and I follow his gaze across the cafeteria to where Kieran's sitting at a table populated by most of the Junior and Senior Class representatives to the Student Council, along with several members of the dance and cheerleading squads. In other words, he's surrounded by a group of people that's about seventy-five percent female. I watch as he lets out a hearty laugh at something or other McKenna Dantino has said, while Stephanie Hull—Cody's little sister—leans into him on his other side, her hand resting on his shoulder. As the bile works its way up from my stomach to my throat, Kieran turns his attention to Steph, while McKenna—who, as one of the most beautiful girls in school, isn't used to being so easily brushed off—picks at her salad while shooting Steph a death glare that would kill her on sight if she had any idea. Luckily for her, she's too busy staring at Kieran to realize McKenna wants to do her in.

"Impressive," Cassie says as we all stare at Kieran. "He went from zero to popular in under four hours. That's got to be some kind of a record at this school."

I shoot Cass a look and her expression instantly returns to the sad, sorrowful, "So sorry you broke up with your boyfriend" one she's worn all day.

"I'm not surprised at all," Lauren chimes in. "Remember how hot everyone thought he was that first day before we all found out about his narcolepsy thing? But then nobody wanted to hang with a guy who was going to pass out on them all the time."

The guys all snicker—I guess over the thought of Kieran being "hot"—while out of the corner of my eye, I catch Kayla's expression shifting into wide-eyed horror.

"We're talking about my *brother* here, right?" she says, her voice laced with disgust. "You all thought he was hot?"

Kayla turns to me for confirmation and I nod slowly, remembering how most of the girls' basketball team was standing around in the front lobby almost exactly a year ago when Kieran and Kayla entered the school for the first time.

"Well, *you* thinking he was hot, I understand, I guess," she mumbles at me. "But the rest of you, I had no idea."

Lauren shrugs. "Well, yeah. I mean, *look* at him," she says, staring across the cafeteria at Kieran with a dewy-eyed expression. "But as soon as he passed out in first period, everybody except Zip kind of got over him."

I pretend to be very interested in my Beef Whatever-This-Is and French fries as Cassie points out "Never mind half the girls in this school hang with guys who pass out on them all the time. Only most guys save up all their passing out until Saturday night and there's usually beer involved."

"Hey," Cody yelps at her, obviously insulted, and Lauren continues with "All I was trying to say was that I get why he'd be instantly popular now that he doesn't have the narcolepsy thing anymore and now that he's single, okay?"

"Oh, my God, Lauren." Cassie covers her eyes and Lauren, realizing what she's said, turns to me and mumbles "Oh, wow. I'm such an idiot. Sorry, Zip."

"It's okay," I tell her, a note of weariness in my voice. I really *am* okay, or at least I would be if everyone would stop making such a big deal out of the fact that I'm single and my now-ex is eating lunch with other girls.

Kayla, on the other hand, seems anything *but* okay. She stands up from her seat, takes her tray to the garbage, dumps what's left of her food, whispers something to the lunchroom monitor, and walks out without a word to any of us. We all glance around at each other for a minute before I announce, "I'll go check on her. I'm guessing the 'surprise' in the Beef Surprise didn't go over so well."

After dumping the grossness masquerading as my lunch and asking permission to go to the bathroom, I find Kayla on the floor in the girls' restroom, sitting against the wall at the end of the row of sinks.

"Sorry for kind of freaking out in there," she mumbles.

I sit down on the floor next to her, and she rests her head on my shoulder. "I had no idea you'd get so messed up by finding out girls think Kieran's hot," I tell her, and she lifts her head to look at me.

"Well, while I find the topic of Kieran's hotness both gross and baffling, I'm freaking out about other things at the moment," she says. "I'm taking your breakup a lot harder than I thought I would. And I seem to be taking your breakup a lot harder than *you* are."

Her voice has an edge, so I immediately jump in with an explanation.

"Oh, I'm taking it plenty hard—trust me. I'm just putting on a brave face. Inside, my heart's in a thousand pieces. But, I mean, things are what they are, so what's the point of moping around about them in front of everyone, right?"

Kayla pouts, apparently content to mope around even if I'm not.

"You know, it's funny, but what we just saw?" she begins after a brief pause. "Kieran surrounded by people, and they're listening to him, and he's laughing and happy? That's exactly what I've always wanted for him."

"I can imagine."

"But not like this. Not if it means you get hurt. Not if it means *I* get hurt."

"I'm not sure I understand why you're so hurt by this," I say, and because she's still resting her head on my shoulder, I can't read her expression as I continue "I mean, I appreciate the loyalty and empathy and all, but..."

"It's always been Kieran and me against the world. I mean, remember how bitchy I was to you when we first met?"

"Not at all."

Kayla lifts her head from my shoulder so she can take in my stoic expression, but I'm sure her Sarcasm Radar is telling her I'm kidding.

"Anyway," she starts, after rolling her eyes at me before returning her head to my shoulder, "You were a huge threat. And not only because my family had all these secrets we were trying to keep. You were going to come between Kieran and me—I just knew it. And *I'd* always been the one to take care of him. *I'd* always been the one by his side."

"And now you're worried if he becomes Mr. Popular he's going to freeze us both out?"

"Something along those lines, I guess. He doesn't remember you, and he doesn't remember me. He doesn't know we used to take care of him—or, I mean, he *knows* because he's read about it in his journals. But he doesn't really get it. He doesn't understand what we mean to him, and now all these other people are going to take our places and we can't do anything about it."

I think Kayla's panicking a little too much, but on some level, she's right—we're part of a life Kieran doesn't realize he's lived, and he's going to form relationships with new people in the life he has now, however brief his new life may be before his memory returns. But...

"Kayla, new people are going to come into his life whether we like it or not. New people are going to come into *our* lives whether we like it or not. We're all going off to college soon, and he won't be at the same school. The two of *us* might not be at the same school. And after college, we'll get jobs and we'll probably move to different cities..." I shake my head. "Whether Kieran had undergone the treatment or not, everything would have changed eventually, at least to some extent."

Kayla runs her hands through her hair and leans her head back against the wall.

"It's funny," she breathes. "I've spent half my life bitching about having to look after Kieran and wishing he could do things on his own. Now, I've got my wish, but nothing's like I thought it would be because of his stupid amnesia."

I love how Kayla and I are constantly reversing roles—one minute, she's picking me up and the next minute I'm picking her up. I guess that's what friendship's all about. And so I elbow her in the ribs and proceed to pick her up once again.

"Hey, it's only a few weeks, right? I mean, pretty much the only thing keeping me from being a mopey mess right now is

41

reminding myself Kieran's amnesia is a temporary situation. Just a few weeks and his memory will come back. And all the new friends in the world aren't going to replace the memories he has with us."

"Just a few weeks," she says with a hint of resignation to her voice. "Yeah, I know. I keep saying it to myself, too. But I have such a hard time believing things will ever go back to normal after seeing what we saw today. Girls don't just throw themselves at my brother like they were. And I don't even pretend to understand what goes on in guys' heads half the time, but I would think that even when his memory does come back, he'll have a hard time forgetting about girls hanging on him like a cheap suit."

I try to shake thoughts of McKenna and Steph vying for Kieran's attention out of my head so I can point out some realities to Kayla. "Girls never threw themselves at Kieran before you moved here because you and your parents kept him pretty isolated from everyone. And after you moved here…well, Lauren was right. Kieran's always been the 'weird narcolepsy kid,' remember? And everyone thought Kieran and I were dating right from the beginning anyway."

Kayla shrugs. "Either way, I get this feeling he's moving on— from both of us," she says.

"You're his sister, Kay. Whether or not he ever remembers, you two have a bond tying you together forever." As I'm speaking, I'm reminded of a story that might make her feel better. "When we were in New York, the morning I left the Hallorans' to go back to the hotel before flying home?"

"Yeah?"

"Victor was telling me this story about how his dad was in the military when he was little, and so they weren't around each other much until he came home for good. And even though things were awkward because they didn't really know each other, they had enough of a natural bond as father and son to build a relationship. He said that experience was what convinced him Cooper was going to learn to trust him again eventually because they had sort of a brotherly or pseudo-nephew/uncle thing or whatever. He said he and Cooper were already growing closer before he got his memory back."

When I've finished the bulk of the story, I let the words hang in the air without a tidy conclusion because I think Kayla can understand the implications for her relationship with Kieran.

"Maybe Kieran and I will have a relationship no matter what," she begins. "But I want the two of you to have a relationship, too."

I elbow her in gratitude as I tell her "We'll always have some kind of relationship no matter what, I guess. I mean, you're my friend and our parents live next door to each other. At the very least, I'll always be somewhere on the sidelines of his life."

"I don't want you to be on the sidelines, Zip. I want you to be in the game," she insists, carrying my sports analogy further than I intended. "I want you and Kieran to have a real relationship like the one you've had for the past few months."

"I can't even tell you how funny it is to hear you say that considering a year ago, you hated my guts and didn't want me anywhere near him."

"I've evolved," she says with a hint of a smile. "I got over it once I realized you were kind of an okay person."

"Thanks," I grumble, giving her a little push in the shoulder.

"And I got over it once I realized how good you and Kieran are for each other." She turns serious. "I want you two to make things work. If you guys can get through this, then I have hope Brad and I can get through all the little stuff that comes up with us."

"Are you and Brad okay?" I ask, pulling my head back a little in surprise.

43

"Don't worry—we're fine, but…long distance relationships are hard, you know? You get used to seeing each other every day, and then suddenly you're only together every few weeks." She pauses. "If you and Kieran can get through everything you're going through right now, then I know for sure Brad and I can make it through the next few months until I get to Northwestern. Does that sound dumb?"

"No, I get it." I tell her, although I think she's putting way too much emphasis on my relationship—or current lack of one at the moment—as a model for whether or not hers is going to last. "And for what it's worth, I think you and Brad are going to be fine no matter what happens with Kieran and me. You guys balance each other out. Brad's Mr. All-American Nice Guy Future Doctor and you're…"

I pause long enough for Kayla to sit up from my shoulder and finish my sentence.

"A raging All-American psycho bitch?"

"I was going to say 'an All-American weirdo,' but, sure, I'll go with 'raging All-American psycho bitch,'" I say, and then smile so she's sure I'm kidding. Well…sort of kidding, anyway. Kayla's definitely the craziest person I've ever met next to Frank Dozier, and saying I *met* him is probably overstating things a bit.

"But I think the overall point is that we can't control the future, you know?" I continue. "Even when Kieran was seeing the future, he could never see it completely enough for any of us to *really* know what was coming, much less change it. And regardless of when Kieran's memory comes back, there's still a chance we could end up in a long distance relationship, too—for a lot longer than you and Brad."

"I guess I need to stop obsessing about everything, huh?" Kayla sighs.

"You can still obsess," I tell her because I know I'm going to as well. "Just maybe not as much. Or maybe try a little harder to hide that you're obsessing. Like, you could stop dramatically running out of cafeterias, for instance."

"Sure thing." She smiles, pulling her phone from her jeans pocket to check the time. "Looks we've still got a few minutes before the bell. Guess we can grab some ice cream for lunch since we didn't get to eat whatever that was they served us today."

Titusville High's much-maligned soft-serve machine was almost a casualty of a small group of parents who wanted to get rid of ice cream and sodas at school in favor of healthier options. The Titusville School Board promised to make lunches more nutritious if the parents agreed to compromise and keep the soda and ice cream machines, knowing full well they'd have a student revolt on their hands if they got rid of the good stuff completely. The mystery sludge we were served today proves the board isn't exactly living up to their end of the bargain because there's no way that stuff could be healthy for anyone.

"Hooray," I mumble in a less than enthused tone. "Empty carbs. But I need to eat something to get me through the rest of the day and practice after school, I guess."

"Better than having food poisoning from actually ingesting today's lunch," she says, standing up and offering me her hand to help me off the floor.

"Good point."

We head out of the bathroom, and once we're about halfway back to the lunchroom, Kayla slips an arm around my shoulders. "You're the best female friend I've ever had, you know?" she tells me.

"If I'm not mistaken, until this past year I was pretty much your *only* female friend, right?"

"Yeah. Whatever. Minor details," she says, shrugging her shoulders, and we're both laughing as we reenter the cafeteria.

CHAPTER 5

At least I still have basketball—Kayla's suggestion from the night we had dinner at her house has been playing on a near constant loop in my head during this first week without Kieran. I'm thinking about printing up t-shirts, maybe having some bumper stickers and signs made, because *At least I still have basketball* is a pretty good life mantra for me right now. Playing basketball, on top of keeping up with schoolwork, takes up so much time and requires so much focus I almost don't have the brain space to miss Kieran.

Almost. Unfortunately, we're still in English class together at the end of the day.

Kieran and I first met when we had to partner up in English class last year. He remembers this now, of course, only thanks to reading his journals, and we both agreed that even though we're not a couple anymore, we'd remain partners in class in part to preserve our friendship and in part because trying to change partners now would impose on the rest of our classmates, who only need to switch or triple up with other people when their regular partners are sick. Plus, we're hoping by remaining partners as we were last year, one of us will do or say something to jog his memory—it's a long shot because we're in a different classroom with a different teacher reading different books and doing different assignments, but at least we're working together.

Today's class is all about peer reviewing essays according to a checklist designed by Mrs. Rossdale, our teacher, so we can enter the finished products in the county's Martin Luther King, Jr. essay contest. I'm about halfway through the first page of Kieran's essay on *Letter from Birmingham Jail* when he whispers "So, this class is supposed to be for college credit and all, but if *this* is as exciting as college gets, I might need to seriously rethink whether or not I want to go."

"Somehow, I don't think college is the non-stop party you always see on TV shows and in movies," I point out. "Showing people writing papers and cramming for tests probably wouldn't make for a very exciting viewing experience."

"Probably not," he says, with a hint of his usual grin. "Unless, of course, the plot was something about a student having to write a paper for the son of a mobster who goes to the same school. Let's say the student...no...wait...the student's *father* owes the mob a gambling debt or something, and if the student doesn't write an A paper, Daddy gets it. But the student can't write well under pressure, and so he only gets a B and the whole things snowballs. Now, the mobster's son won't get the grades he needs for law school or med school or whatever, and the student and the father go on the run so they don't get snuffed out. While they're on the road, they rebuild what had previously been a strained relationship because of the father's gambling and blah, blah, blah." Kieran sits back and holds his hands out in front of him, index fingers and thumbs poised in the air as if he's framing a shot in a movie. "Go back and imagine that paper-writing scene now—the student at his computer, sweating, knocking over a glass of water on his desk and almost wrecking his keyboard, giving in to the pressure of knowing his life and his dad's are on the line. There's narrative tension there, even more than in some of the books we've read this year when we were *supposed* to be looking for narrative tension. I'd totally watch that movie."

"*Writing for the Mob*—coming to a theater near you this Christmas," I whisper in a dramatic voice, and we both crack up silently but loudly enough for Mrs. Rossdale, a wisp of a brunette in a stylish wrap dress and three-inch heels, to *clomp-clomp* over to us and ask "Everything okay over here?"

"Great," I say.

"Couldn't be better," Kieran chimes in.

"Any questions about the checklist?" she chirps.

We both say "no" in unison. The checklist is pretty self-explanatory—mark awkward sentences, check for grammar errors, point out instances of faulty logic, and so on, and so on—so there's not much to question.

"Good. Then you two won't have any problem finishing your peer reviews before the period is over," Mrs. Rossdale says before *clomp-clomping* off to passive-aggressively scold Kayla and Ashley, who are giggling to themselves about something.

"Your imagination is amazing," I tell him. "The way you write and draw...I could never come up with ideas like you do."

Kieran flips through the three pages of my paper and says, "Based on what I've read so far, you're a good writer. I bet you have an amazing imagination, too."

"Analytical writing, I can do," I say, nodding at my paper. "I can't write creative stuff for anything, though. My brain doesn't work like that for some reason."

"And I can't write about something that's already been written," Kieran says, tilting his chin toward his essay on my desk.

"From what I've read so far, you've done a pretty good job."

Kieran shrugs off my compliment and tells me, "I'd rather create than analyze, I guess. I don't know much about myself, but I think I know that already. Writing this thing for the essay contest? Painful. But I love art class, and coming up with that mob story just now? Totally awesome."

"It was."

"And it had the added effect of making you laugh, which was pretty cool," he says, giving me the grin that will forever melt my heart.

Pleasestopflirtingwithme. Pleasestopflirtingwithme.

I shrug and suggest "Maybe we should get back to reading our essays before Mrs. Rossdale comes over here and non-threateningly threatens us again."

"Sounds like a plan."

I put my head down and try to focus on Kieran's essay, but the words blur together in a cloudy haze on the page. While I realize being flirty and funny is his default setting—and I'm glad this new version of Kieran still has some of the old Kieran's default settings—watching him behave like his old self when the new self isn't my boyfriend anymore is a little hard to take.

But I only need to survive for twenty more minutes and the period will be over. Only twenty more minutes and I can turn my attention to my basketball game tonight.

Because at least I still have basketball.

Our game doesn't start until five, so I'm able to run home for a quick bite to eat and to rest up for a while before I'm due back at school. Tonight's opponent is Brownsville, who hasn't won a game all season, so we're more than prepared because we've been facing tougher opponents all season. But Brownsville is the type of team who's dangerous because they're easy to overlook, so we need to guard against playing down to the level of our competition and getting outclassed. I'm not too worried, though—we've had solid practices this week, and I've almost mastered the no-look pass to Cassie on the perimeter, which should add a whole new dimension to our offense. And we're still undefeated, so if we lose our focus or intensity, we lose our unbeaten season, which should be enough to keep us motivated.

We trot out onto the court to the cheers of our usual paltry gathering of fans and go through our warm-up routine—stretching, shooting, passing—and then we head to the bench for a last-minute pep talk from the coaching staff before the tip-off. Back out on the court, Ashley wins the opening tip and tosses the ball to me, and I raise my left hand in the air, signaling our first offensive set by flexing my middle and index fingers. Brownsville's point guard smothers me, but in my peripheral vision, I notice Cassie's shaken her defender and is free on the wing. Shifting my eyes back to my own defender, I figure there's no time like the present to find out if I can pull off the no-look pass.

Dribbling back and forth as if I'm trying to decide in which direction I want to drive to the basket, I make sure my defender's eyes are fixed on mine and in a flash I pick up the ball with both hands and throw it to Cassie without looking, holding my breath and hoping I didn't just screw up the first possession of the game.

I run to the basket with Brownsville's point guard on me like a shadow, but I'm able to glance over to see Cassie's caught the ball and she's squaring up behind the three-point line. As I'm jockeying for position in the lane, Cassie's shot sails over my head.

Swish. Three points.

The rest of the game doesn't get much better for Brownsville. We're up ten points on them when we head to the locker room at the half, and rather than coasting through the second half, we maintain our ten-point lead throughout the third quarter and step up our intensity in the fourth, ultimately beating them by fifteen points, which is our largest victory margin of the season so far. As we line up to slap hands with the Brownsville players and tell them "Good game," I notice the crowd has increased, but that's probably because the boys' game—the main attraction on a winter Friday night in Titusville—starts in forty minutes.

Now that there are more people here, my post-game ritual of trying to find my parents and grandparents in the crowd is a little harder to accomplish, but since they usually sit somewhere behind the bench, it only takes me a few seconds to find them sitting about four rows up in the bleachers, waving at me and smiling like loons. I wave back and scan the crowd for Kieran, Kayla, and Brad. Kayla and Brad are in the same row as my family, only they're closer to the gym doors and they're sitting with a group of Brad's friends, guys who are also nearing the end of their winter breaks from college. But Kieran's not with them—maybe he decided not to come after all even though he was so vocal about coming with Brad and Kayla earlier in the week.

I'm about to turn and jog off the court when I finally catch sight of him, sitting nowhere near his sister in the dead center of the home team bleachers.

And he's not alone.

He's clapping along to the recording of the marching band's version of the school fight song being played over the gym's speaker system and leaning in close to Stephanie Hull, saying something directly into her ear over the noise. Before I can stare too long and risk looking like a total idiot, I feel an arm slip around my shoulders, turning me away from the crowd and in the direction of the exit to the locker room.

"I take it you hadn't heard," Cassie says to me as we cross the court, her arm still around me.

"I think we've been friends long enough for you to know I'm the last person to find out anything that goes on at this school," I yell back over the swelling noise in the gym. The crowd cheers for the boys' team as they run into the gym from their locker room across the hall for their initial warm-ups. I slap hands with several of them as they pass, as does Cassie.

"Cody told me after school, so I just found out myself," Cassie explains as we exit the gym through the big double doors and cross the hall to the girls' locker room. "Don't ask me how *he* found out because he acts too embarrassed to be related to Steph half the time to even talk to her. But I guess Kieran and Steph are in the same study hall, and she asked him yesterday to go to the game with her tonight."

Yesterday. So the whole time we were working together in English this afternoon, he had a date to the game and didn't tell me. Not that there was a logical opening in our conversation for him to share that information, but still…

"I didn't want to say anything until the game was over," Cassie tells me as we pull our gym bags from our lockers. "Figured you didn't need the distraction."

"I appreciate that," I reply, debating whether or not to ask my next question and going ahead and asking it anyway. "So, are they, like, *dating*?"

"Well, tonight was a date, but I don't have any idea whether the two of them are going to be a thing or whatever. But I told Cody no matter what, we are *not* double dating with them under any circumstances. Not that he'd double date with his little sister anyway, but I told him there's no way I would do that to you. Sisters before misters, you know what I'm saying?"

I can't help but laugh as Cassie holds her fist out to me and I bump knuckles with her.

"Absolutely, Cass. Sisters before misters."

We hit the showers, and as the always-lukewarm water washes over me, I try to think through what I've just seen and what Cassie's told me. The thing is, I *like* Stephanie Hull. A year behind me in school, Steph's the third of the four Hull children behind Cody and their older sister and my former teammate Candace, who's now off at college on the other side of the state. After having three children in three years, Mr. and Mrs. Hull took a few years off from their childbirth frenzy before completing their family with another boy,

Sam, who started seventh grade this year. And same as with everyone else in this town, I've known all the Hulls for as long as I've been alive—I even remember when Sam was born because Cody's grandparents came and pulled him out of school when his mom went into labor right before snack time back in Kindergarten. And while Stephanie and I aren't remotely close in the way I am with Cody and Candace, even though my closeness with Cody is mostly about the fact he's gone out with Cassie off and on since eighth grade, I certainly don't have anything against her. She's the president of the Junior Class, she's smart enough she'll probably be in the running for valedictorian when the time comes, and she's been a seventh grade mentor since freshman year. And if I'm remembering correctly, she also volunteers a few times a week at the animal shelter in Sumner.

In other words, she's an all-around solid citizen. And she's cute, too. Unlike Candace and Cody—who are basketball-player tall and football-player broad, respectively—she's slender and petite, probably even shorter than I am, with a little stub nose dotted with freckles and straight red hair falling to the middle of her back. Between her good looks and her good works, she's exactly the kind of girl I would want dating Kieran.

That is, if I wanted him to be dating another girl—which I totally don't.

Everything's so confusing—in less than a week, I've gone from devoted girlfriend to devastated ex-girlfriend to...what? Jealous former girlfriend? Is that what this feeling of possessiveness is? Jealousy? Envy?

I step out of the shower, towel off, and slide back into the clothes I wore to school, the noise of my teammates talking to each other as they shower and get dressed nothing more than a buzz at the back of my brain. Once everyone's ready, I follow my teammates out of the locker room and onto the stage at the north end of the gym where we all take in the boys' game with our legs dangling over the edge several feet from the floor. I try to keep my focus on the action—which is easy to do for the most part, as the guys are engaged in a back-and-forth contest with Brownsville—but every once in a while, I sneak peeks at Kieran and Stephanie sitting in the stands. They appear to be focused on the game as well because every time I look over at them, they are staring straight ahead at the action and not talking to each other.

As the game draws to a close and our guys start to pull away, Cassie leans over to me. "Hey, did you drive yourself tonight?" she asks.

"Yeah."

"Well, everyone's going to the Downtown Diner once the game's over if you want to come."

I could probably use a night out with my friends, so why not?

"Sure," I tell her, "You need a ride?"

"Yeah," she says, nodding over at a section of the bleachers where Cody and the rest of the football guys who aren't also on the basketball team are sitting. "Cody's been texting me and it sounds like he and the rest of the Testosterone Brigade are heading to the park for a while after the game."

Now I understand why she needs a ride. The only reason people go to River Bend Park at this time of night is to fight, and I'm guessing Cassie doesn't want to stand around and wait for Cody and his buddies to get up to whatever trouble they're going to get up to when she could go straight to the Diner with her friends.

"So, who's fighting this week?" I ask.

"Who knows? Who cares?" she says, as Cody and his buds slip into their letterman jackets and exit the gym with a minute still left on the clock. "I get so sick of those guys and their macho crap sometimes. I hope college guys are a little more grown-up."

The boys pull out a five-point victory, and I lose my mom and grandparents in the crowd so I text Mom that I'm headed to the Diner and she texts back that she'll grab a ride home with Gram and Gramps. A few minutes later, I'm chauffeuring a full car to the Diner—Lauren, Ashley, and our backup point guard Tori Sandowsky pile into the car with Cassie and me for the two-minute trip. We park across the street from the Diner in front of my mom's darkened store, and as we cross River Avenue, I catch Cassie squinting over at the park, obviously trying to catch a glimpse of Cody and the guys.

"Come on, Cass," Ashley admonishes her. "You know they're going to be down by the river where no one can see them acting like a bunch of idiots." She rolls her eyes and turns to me. "Billy McCaffery was flirting with me in foods and nutrition class yesterday, so Rick's going to kick his ass to defend what's left of my honor, I guess."

Cassie reaches the restaurant first and holds the glass door open for the rest of us. I head inside ahead of Ashley, pointing out over my shoulder "But you and Rick aren't even a real couple."

And then there's poor, poor Billy McCaffery, grandson of the McCaffery family who once owned the Laniers' house and son of my mom's high school boyfriend. Billy's not an athlete and he's practically doll-sized next to Rick, so he doesn't stand a chance unless he's got some friends who are willing to help him fight. Billy was technically my first kiss, but only because he ambushed me in Cassie's basement in eighth grade, an experience that wasn't traumatic enough for me to be happy over the guy getting his face rearranged by Ashley's not-boyfriend. Billy freaked me out so much that night four years ago I kneed him in the balls, so he's already suffered more than enough punishment for the kissing incident anyway.

"I know," Ashley grumbles about Rick as she leads us to a booth in the back corner of the restaurant. "I keep telling him if he's going to beat people up over me, then he needs to go ahead and

55

admit I'm his girlfriend. And he keeps pointing out I'm only a *friend* who happens to be a *girl*, but I'm not his girlfriend. And then I point out that since I'm not his girlfriend, maybe we should stop hooking up all the time. And hearing that just pisses him off."

"Boys are so dumb." Tori states the obvious as she slides into the booth and molds herself to the wall so Cassie and I have enough room to slide in next to her.

"Amen, sister," Lauren chimes in as she and Ashley slide into the seat across the table from us.

Morgan comes over to the table to take our orders, and since I'm the only one he knows by name, he greets me with a "Hey, Zip."

"Hey, Morgan. You're waiting tables tonight?" I ask. Morgan's been working here as a cook since shortly after he moved to Titusville last summer, but to my knowledge, he's never waited tables.

"Yeah. Dewayne and I switched duties for the night, so he's in back cooking. He wants me to get familiar with all aspects of the restaurant so I can run the place if he's ever not here."

"Cool."

"So, you guys ready to order?" He sweeps all of us up in his gaze. "I can come back if you need a few more minutes."

We've all been coming here since we were toddlers and the menu hasn't changed much over the years, so we put in orders for different varieties of burgers, fries, and sodas while Morgan scribbles furiously on a notepad. Before he leaves to get our drinks, he asks me "Your mom at home tonight?"

"No, I think she's out clubbing. About ten really big, big guys came to pick her up before my game," I say, but he sees through my fake seriousness.

"Of course she'd be at home." He scratches his head with the end of his pencil, seeming slightly embarrassed. "Guess there aren't too many places to go around here on a Friday night, huh? Anyway, I was asking because I've got a break coming up here in a little bit and I thought I'd give her a call if she's not busy."

"She got a ride home from the game with my grandparents, so she's either over there or at home. Either way, she's got her phone with her—I just texted her before we came here."

"Thanks," he says, and, nodding at the rest of the girls, tells us. "I'll be right back with your drinks."

Once Morgan is behind the counter and safely out of earshot, Tori asks in a low and mildly horrified voice "Is that guy *dating* your mom?"

"Sort of," I mumble, not wanting to try to explain something I don't fully understand myself, and, thankfully, Cassie shifts the topic slightly.

"That guy looks so much like Kieran it's scary," she says, glancing back at Morgan as he fills our drink cups. "They're, like, what? Cousins or something, right?"

"He's Kieran's mom's cousin, so sort of," I lie, and we quiet down again as Morgan places our drinks on a tray and carries them over. As he sets a plastic cup in front of each of us and leaves straws in the middle of the table, I think for the millionth time about how glad I'm going to be to leave this town at last in a few months. Guys picking fights at the park, everyone being in everyone else's business, and—most of all over this past year—my having to lie all the time to cover up the weirdness of Kieran's family...I'm not going to miss any of it. I think I'm ready for a whole new life, and maybe Kieran moving on is the first step.

I'm so inside my head, I don't notice Brad and Kayla sliding into the booth behind us until Cassie turns around and says, "Hey, guys," and I take a quick glance over my shoulder to find out who's arrived.

"Hey," Kayla says back to Cassie before lowering her voice and whispering in my ear "We need to talk. Now."

CHAPTER 6

Kayla practically yanks me out of my booth and drags me to the tiny hallway at the back of the Diner that separates the bathrooms from the dining area. I prop myself against the wall next to a pay phone that probably hasn't been used in years and she leans in so she can whisper "Kieran's on a *date.*"

"I already know," I tell her at normal volume. "I'm cool with it."

"You're *cool* with it?' Kayla shrieks as Jake Tomlinson strolls by, shooting her a look while massaging his hand and licking his split lip—guess the fight between Rick Matthews and Billy McCaffery must have escalated to the point Rick had to call in reinforcements. Jake disappears into the men's room as I say to Kayla "I guess we're not whispering anymore?"

"How can you be cool with Kieran dating someone else?" she whisper-shrieks.

"Because I like Stephanie and because I don't have much of a choice, now do I?" I whisper back, even though I have no idea why I'm doing so.

"And neither of those things is anywhere near the point right now," Kayla hisses, and she's about to say something else when our little area starts filling up with people. Cody enters with his arm around Rick, whose face is a tapestry of red splotches, and the two of them hobble past us to the men's room, with Jason Moberly trailing them and muttering "McCaffery's a dead man."

"Oh, great—it's an idiot convention," I mumble to Kayla, and just as the words are out of my mouth, Cassie flies into the hallway and stops on the other side of the phone.

"Are the guys in the bathroom?" she asks in a panicked tone.

"Yeah," Kayla and I answer, and Cassie barrels past us into the men's room because that's just totally what Cassie would do in this situation.

"Oh, my God," Kayla huffs at me, grabbing my hand. "We're never going to get any privacy back here."

She pulls me through the Diner and out the door so violently my shoulder almost separates from the socket. After whipping her head around for a second, she turns in the direction of the park, and we walk around to the side of the building and lean up against the concrete, staring into the dark expanse of River Bend Park, where apparently Billy McCaffery *didn't* get his face rearranged this evening.

"Kieran can't date anybody else," Kayla says before I get the chance to ask her what the hell is wrong.

"Well, apparently, he can." I shrug. "And, anyway, the world loves a good love triangle, right? So much drama."

"Stop being such a smart ass," she snaps. "I don't think a love triangle technically exists when one of the triangle's legs doesn't remember he's supposed to be in love with one of the triangle's other legs."

"Good point," I mumble.

"And, besides, you *know* why he can't date anyone else. I mean, think about it—what happens when he's in the middle of getting all hot and heavy with Stephanie Hull and suddenly his memory comes back and he realizes he's in love with you?"

"Thanks for *that* image, by the way, but, yeah—I get the idea," I grumble. "I guess Kieran's amnesia gets a little more complicated once other people are involved, huh?"

"Just a little," Kayla spits.

"I like Steph, though. I don't want her getting hurt because she has no idea what she's dealing with here. But what are we supposed to do? Tell her the truth? It's not like she'd even believe us if we could."

"No, of course, we can't tell her. But at least I got Kieran to agree not to say anything to her about the amnesia," she assures me. "I mean, he doesn't totally understand the whole thing himself, so he was willing to stick with the whole 'Hey—guess what? I'm on narcolepsy meds now' explanation. But he was trying to act all innocent about going out with her to begin with. He was like 'What was I supposed to do? *She* asked *me* out.' And I tried to emphasize to him he was running the risk of hurting two different girls here, but he didn't really seem to understand."

"I'm not hurt," I say, and I sort of mean it. Until—*unless*—Kieran gets his memory back, seeing him with other girls is my new reality and I might as well get used to it, no matter how sick to my stomach the idea makes me.

"That's crap," Kayla challenges. "Stop acting like you're some big tough girl. This whole thing is *killing* you—just admit it."

"No—I'm serious." I stand up from the wall and wrap my arms around myself because it's cold out here and our coats are inside. "Kieran and I aren't together right now. We're just friends. Are we supposed to expect him to sit around and act like a monk until his memory comes back?"

"That's almost exactly what he said," Kayla grumbles. "You two really *are* perfect for each other."

"So, have you known about this whole date thing with Steph since yesterday and you conveniently forgot to mention it to me?"

Kayla shakes her head. "He didn't say a word about it until about an hour before the game, when he sort of casually mentioned he had a date with Stephanie Hull and did I think Brad would mind if we picked her up on our way to school?" She smirks. "And I told him Brad would mind, I would mind, and everyone on the planet would mind, and whatever he thought he was doing with Stephanie Hull, he couldn't do it. We went back and forth for a while, and then Mom heard us fighting and got involved."

"And then what?" I ask. I can only imagine what Carlie must think of Kieran dating someone who isn't me given that she took awhile to come around to Kieran and me hanging out in the first place.

"Well, you know Mom—she tried to calmly, rationally explain how maybe dating other people wouldn't be a good idea right now since we don't know what's going on with his memory. And that's when he made the comment about how he wasn't going to stop living his life and just sit around and wait for his memory to come back. So I told him if he wanted to go to the game with Stephanie, he could call her and tell her to come pick him up because I didn't want any part of his plans." Kayla wraps her arms around herself, but I'm not sure if she's doing so from the cold or from sadness or frustration or from some combination of all three. "Dad hadn't gotten home from work yet when all this happened, but I'm sure he and Mom are home right now trying to come up with ways to keep this…*whatever* is going on with Stephanie from going any further than tonight."

"Do you think they'll be able to talk some sense into him?" I catch the note of hope in my voice and I hate myself. On the one hand, I'm trying to be the level-headed ex-girlfriend who doesn't care who my ex dates. But, on the other hand, if Jim and Carlie can do something to stop the relationship in order to keep both Stephanie and me from getting hurt…

"Probably not," Kayla says, bursting my bubble. "If one thing hasn't changed about Kieran since he underwent the treatment, it's his stubbornness. I can almost hear how that conversation's going to go." She lowers her voice, pretending to be Kieran. "'I'm almost nineteen. You can't tell me what to do.' He'd make the same argument whether they were telling him not to date someone or whether they were telling him not to wear a certain t-shirt to school. And it's not like they can follow him around all day to make sure he's not talking to her. I mean, I guess they could take away his phone or something, but..." She shakes her head. "It'll be like when he started hanging out with you and we saw you two were probably going to end up dating. There was no way to stop things once they got started. You're a good person, and there was no argument against dating you that would have made sense to him."

"And Steph's a good person—great reputation around school, everyone in town loves her," I add. "So, yeah—there's no argument your parents can make to talk him out of dating her if he really wants to."

"Except for the obvious argument that he could hurt her when his memory comes back, but I don't think that's a line of reasoning he completely understands. His whole life right now is the present. He doesn't remember his past, and none of us can predict the future."

"Well, not anymore anyway," I point out.

Kayla ignores my comment, her attention on something happening over my shoulder.

"What?" I ask her, before turning to follow her gaze to a car that's just pulled up and parked in one of the few remaining spaces left between the Diner and the park. In the low light from the streetlamps lining the sidewalk and the park, I can't make out the type of car, but I learn who the car belongs to soon enough as Kieran exits the passenger side and waits on the sidewalk for Stephanie to get out and join him. Once they're on the sidewalk together, I can't help but notice Kieran placing his hand on the small of her back as if he's trying to protect her and guide her toward the Diner's entrance.

So, in addition to his stubbornness, his chivalry hasn't disappeared, either, apparently. I'm almost sick to my stomach

63

watching them together, and then my nausea fades into anger—anger at myself for feeling sick in the first place.

Kayla and I watch in silence until they are gone from our sight and, at a loss as to what else to say in this moment, I tell her "Well, we should go back. It's freezing, and I'm sure my food's probably at the table by now."

"You're not seriously going back inside," Kayla says. "Not now."

"Kay, we can't pretend this isn't happening, so we might as well face it. Even if I didn't think I could stay and eat, I'd need to go back for my coat and my car keys eventually. And your boyfriend's still inside, remember? I'm sure he's wondering where you are by now."

She nods in resignation. "I don't understand how you're being so rational about all of this," she mumbles as we start walking toward the Diner's front door. "If I saw Brad with another girl, I'd...well, I have no idea what I'd do."

"Well, knowing you, you'd have some pretty twisted homicidal thoughts, at least at first," I tell her, and she pouts at me. "But then you'd figure out how to move on, just like I'm trying to do right now." I pause for a second, remembering I may not *need* to figure out how to move on, and I continue with "Besides—this whole thing with Steph is only a bump in the road, right? A glitch. In a few weeks, Kieran will remember how everything's supposed to be."

"Right," Kayla says perking up a little as she reaches out for the door handle and allows me to enter the Diner ahead of her. Kieran and Steph are sitting with a bunch of her friends in a large booth at the far end of the restaurant, and I realize my table is at the opposite end. Unless Cassie's kicked me out of the booth in favor of babying Cody, I'll be sitting with my back to the new couple, which should make things much easier—even if I'll be thinking about Kieran and Steph the whole time, I won't have to watch them.

Kayla and I make our way back to our respective booths, and I find my burger and fries waiting for me.

"Where were you?" Cassie asks between bites of her hamburger.

"Kayla and I needed to talk about some stuff," I tell her before quickly changing the subject. "So what was the deal with the fight?"

I'm not interested in the fight, of course, but I need something to keep from focusing on Kieran and Steph sitting behind me. So I listen to Cassie and Ashley give a second-hand blow-by-blow account of how Billy McCaffery was waiting at the park with a bunch of his friends to take on Rick, Cody, and most of the football team, all because Billy *might* have a thing for Ashley. I down my food as quickly as possible without giving myself indigestion, and as the conversation about the fight winds down, I ask everyone at the table "Hey—do you guys think you can get home okay without me? I'm a little worn out from the game and stuff. I think I'm just going to head home."

They all nod at me since they all live within a block or two of the Diner, and I'm guessing they understand why I want to leave. I say my goodbyes and bundle up into my coat before waving at Kayla and Brad and paying my part of the bill up at the cash register, all while avoiding any glances at the back corner of the restaurant.

At home, I find Mom on the couch in her pajamas watching a movie. "You're home earlier than I expected," she says, tucking her legs up under her.

"Yeah. I was kind of tired. Didn't really feel like staying out."

"Well, *Footloose* is on—the original." She pats the space next to her on the couch, but I shrug my shoulders.

"Thanks, but I think I'm going to go to bed."

65

I trudge down the hall to my room, dropping my gym bag next to my dresser and flopping down on my comforter, the stress of the evening and everything I've been holding inside catching up with me. Before I fully realize what's happening, I'm crying into my pillow—crying harder than I've probably ever cried—and hoping my mom doesn't hear me.

Whether she hears me or not, she's in my room within seconds of my breakdown starting. And instead of asking a thousand questions, she sits down on the bed next to me and rubs my back until my sobs die out. Eventually, I pull myself up and put my arms around her.

"What's wrong?" she asks, rubbing my back again.

"Who says something's wrong?" I mumble, trying to be nonchalant and failing miserably.

"Well, other than the crying, you mean? You passed up a chance to watch *Footloose* with me," she points out. "Something's definitely wrong."

I give up the worthless pretense of toughness I'm clinging to at the moment and take a deep breath. "I don't know if you saw anything tonight at the game, but Kieran was on a date," I inform her.

Mom sits back so she can look at me, keeping her hands on my shoulders. "Okay. That's...*weird*," she says. "Are you sure?"

"Yeah. Cassie and Kayla both confirmed it. Stephanie Hull asked him yesterday to go to the game with her."

"Wait—Stephanie's old enough to date?" Mom asks, and I have to laugh.

"She's only a year behind me in school, Mom. You keep forgetting we're not all still five years old."

Mom ignores my making fun of her and wonders aloud "So, how do Carlie and Jim feel about this, given Kieran's situation?"

66

"Carlie found out tonight before the game and Jim didn't know yet," I explain. "Kayla said Carlie's not very happy."

"And I guess the more important question is, how do *you* feel about it? Or do I already know, given the crying?"

I squirm backward out of her grasp so I can lean against my pillows, and Mom scoots onto the bed to sit against the pillows on my other side.

"I love Kieran," I state emphatically. "And somewhere inside him, Kieran still loves me, too. He just doesn't know he loves me back. So, I shouldn't be surprised this is happening, I guess. I mean, Kayla made the point tonight how right now Kieran's whole life exists in the present. He doesn't remember his past at all and I get that he doesn't want to wait around to see if the past comes back to him before moving on with his life. So I can't really blame him for saying 'yes' to Steph when she asked him out."

"But..."

"But, well, I love him," I say again, shrugging my shoulders in resignation. "And seeing your boyfriend with someone else completely sucks, even if he's technically not your boyfriend anymore and even if he doesn't remember that he ever was your boyfriend."

Mom sits up next to me and gathers me into her arms again, which makes the pain lessen a bit for the minute or two that she's holding me.

"Can I ask you something?" I begin when we part, knowing she's a little more experienced in the breakup department than I am.

"Sure."

"And if you don't want to talk about this, just tell me, okay?"

"Zip?"

"You still loved Dad when you two split up, right?" I ask through a breath and quickly, as if I'm ripping off a bandage. My parents have been divorced for so long, I almost can't remember them being together. And they're both in good places in their lives, so I don't want to upset my mom by digging around in an old wound. But at the same time, I'm trying to get a handle on how I should behave in my current situation with Kieran, and my mom is the closest person to me who's been through anything remotely similar.

Mom licks her lips on hearing my question, and she looks away from me. "I did. And to some extent, your dad loved me, too—even then. But sometimes, life gets in the way and love isn't enough." She takes a deep breath. "Your dad and I were young, you know? And I'm not suggesting people can't make a go of things when they start out young, but we didn't have much in common besides being attracted to each other and having a good time together, and there was a lot of practical daily life stuff we didn't really talk through like we should have before making a lifetime commitment. And then we had you right away after we got married. And don't get me wrong—you're okay and all…" Mom pauses and gives me a smile.

"Thanks," I mumble, returning her smile.

"But what I'm saying is that sometimes, rushing into having kids isn't the greatest thing for marital stability when you're not on solid ground to begin with," she continues, getting serious again. "Your dad and I took on a lot of responsibility before we were really ready, and he was never happy living in Titusville but he knew I wanted to come back here and open a store and be close to my parents. We made a go of things for a while, but you can only pretend everything's okay for so long." She shrugs. "And that's that, I guess."

"Okay, but where did you put all of those feelings?" I ask. "You said you still loved him. So, how did you get over it and move on?"

"Well, in some way, you *don't* get over it—"

"Not what I wanted to hear."

68

"Don't interrupt me when I'm trying to make a point," Mom scolds, but her grin tells me she's not mad. "What I was going to say is that you don't exactly get over it, but you do move on. You realize you have other things in your life clamoring for your time and energy. Gramps and I were trying to get the store off the ground, and I had you to worry about, so a lot of my time was taken up with other things."

"So you're telling me I need to go out and get a kid?" I say with a smile.

"Ha! No." She leans over to rumple my hair. "I'm saying that while my marriage was definitely the biggest part of my life at the time, I had other things in my life to fill the void, and eventually, I realized I had an incredibly full life I could build on when I had to start over without your dad. And now, your dad and I have a friendly enough relationship that we can finish raising you without damaging you too badly."

"That's still up for debate," I say, smirking, and she smirks back before continuing.

"Look, I know you love Kieran, and I still think the two of you are going to get through this once he gets his memory back, but you have so much else going on—playing basketball, going to school, choosing a college. I know it doesn't seem that way right now, but your life is already so much bigger than this one relationship. And once you go away to college and start focusing on your future, your life is just going to get bigger."

"I know." I sigh. "Deep down, I already know everything you're saying and I've already been reminding myself that I have other things going on. I guess I just need people to keep telling me I'm going to be okay if Kieran doesn't come back to me. And I've said it over and over, to myself and to other people—even to him, although he doesn't remember it now. But sometimes I have these moments—

like tonight, seeing him with somebody else—when I wonder whether or not I'm going to make it. And then I'm afraid I'm going to turn into some mopey, vacant loser. I'm trying so hard not to be *that* girl, you know? I don't want to be the girl who cries all the time like I was doing tonight."

Mom leans in and touches her forehead to mine, whispering, "Sweetie, in a million years, you will never be *that* girl, okay? Trust me. You've already been through so much more than I could have ever imagined at your age, and yet somehow, you still keep moving forward. You've never once curled up in a ball and given up. You're basically my hero."

"Mom, cut it out." I pull back from her and roll my eyes. "Now you're just going overboard."

"Maybe. But you're so strong, Zip. One good cry isn't going to wipe that out. In fact, I think you're allowed several good cries in this situation, so if you need to bawl, don't hold back. And even when you're bawling your head off, remember you're still ten times stronger than I ever was at seventeen and eighteen years old. Never forget that, okay?"

"Okay."

"Now are you *really* tired, or do you think you can stay up for a little while and help me find a cheesy movie to watch?"

"I think I could be up for a cheesy movie. Do we have popcorn?"

"Didn't you just get home from the Diner?" Mom asks with wide eyes.

"You know, I played a game earlier and I'm a growing girl," I remind her before admitting what's closer to the truth. "And I didn't have much of an appetite at the Diner—Kieran and Steph showed up."

Mom reaches out to ruffle my hair.

"We have popcorn. I'll go get some started while you change into your pajamas."

Mom slides off the bed and leaves me alone so I can change clothes, but I take a few minutes instead to glance around my room, a relatively small space holding nearly eighteen years of memories. Up against the wall opposite my closet is a low shelf displaying all the trophies, medals, and plaques I've earned playing basketball over the years, and in the corner on the same wall, closest to my bed, is a pile of stuffed animals, most of which were presents from my dad, some of them given to me long after I'd outgrown stuffed animals. As I look around, my eyes return over and over again to one of the more recent additions to my room—a simple sketch of a rose hanging above my desk. Kieran gave the sketch to me for Valentine's Day not long after we met, and I responded with a "thank you" and nothing more because I had—*have*—no idea what I'm doing where boys are concerned.

The rose drawing has had an honored placed on my wall for nearly a year, but now, it needs to come down—at least until Kieran's memory comes back.

I scramble to the edge of my bed and on over to my desk, leaning over and sliding my thumb under the tack attaching the sketch to the wall. Once I've freed the paper from its place, I slide it into my desk drawer atop a mess of office supplies, greeting cards, and school assignments. My charm bracelet bumps the drawer and for a second, I'm tempted to put the bracelet in the drawer as well.

But I'm not ready to part with the charm bracelet. Not yet. I finger the band and the charms that have become such a part of me I almost don't feel fully dressed off the basketball court without them around my wrist. So, rather than hiding the bracelet away, I take it off and set it in its usual place atop my dresser before changing into my pajamas for a late night movie marathon, hoping some goofy make-believe can help me forget the weird state of my real life, at least temporarily.

CHAPTER 7

Our undefeated season is tested in a big way the following weekend when we travel to Rockford to take on one of the big public schools. Coach Denton explained to us at the beginning of the season that she had scheduled this game so we could go up against some tougher competition than what we normally face in order to better prepare us for postseason play, when we'll be facing teams from outside the three-county radius in which we normally travel. Chicago and Rockford are the two largest metropolitan areas in the state, so the girls on these teams, in some cases, play basketball year-round for traveling teams and have attracted attention from major colleges. Win or lose, playing a city team gives us a much-needed chance to find out how our game stacks up against a bigger program.

The minute we walk into the gym at Rockford South, which is at least twice the size of our gym back home, I'm terrified that we're in over our heads. Everything about this school is bigger, from the players—everyone on their starting five is at least six feet tall—to the crowd, which make sense considering this school's enrollment is over fifteen hundred students. The gym is half-empty here just as it is for girls' games back home, but even with a ton of empty seats, there are probably more people on the Rockford side of the gym alone than are enrolled at Titusville High School.

"Everybody remember to breathe," Coach Denton tells us on the sidelines before tip-off as she takes in our nervous faces. "This is just basketball, a game you've played thousands of times. Tonight is no different than any other time you've been on a court. Just go out there and play Titusville basketball like you know how to do."

"I'm not sure 'Titusville basketball' is going to be enough against these Amazons," Cassie grumbles in my ear. "'Pro basketball,' maybe."

"Well, we *are* near Chicago," I say, snapping her with my towel as the huddle breaks up. "Maybe we should call in some reinforcements."

Cassie snorts, and I tell her "You heard Coach. We just need to go out there and do like we do and believe it's going to be good enough."

And, sure enough, we stick to our game and manage to be competitive, losing by only five points on the strength of our outside shooting since South was way too big for us to get much action under the basket. Cassie and I both have amazing nights from the three-point line, and I put up a personal best of six three-pointers. Performance-wise, we had a stellar game overall. I only wish we could have walked away with a win and preserved our perfect season.

The trip back from Rockford takes an hour and a half, so I go home and straight to bed when we get back and don't get up Saturday morning until nearly eleven. When I do, I find a note from Mom in the kitchen:

Hi, Sleepyhead,

Great game last night! You'll want to check out this website.

And below her looping handwriting, she's printed a web address that I don't recognize. Figuring that my own mother wouldn't be directing me to check out porn or spam online, I make some coffee and take the note back to my room, where I boot up my laptop and type the address into a browser. What pops up is the sports section of a Rockford newspaper, and as I scroll down, I find what my mom wanted me to see—a headline that reads "Rockford South Girls Struggle against Titusville." The article that follows is

74

very complimentary of our team's talent overall, and I read the line "Titusville point guard Zara McKee was blistering from behind the arc, with eighteen of her twenty-six points coming from three-point range" about twenty times before I finally close my laptop.

Weird. I'm not used to seeing full-length articles detailing one of our games. The most we usually get is a paragraph or two in a "round-up" article of girls' games around the county in the *Sumner Statesman*. I never expected I'd read my name in a newspaper for a place the size of Rockford, which is an *actual* city with multiple high schools and real fast food places and a mall and TV stations.

And, after the Rockford South game, things change at home, too. More and more people start showing up for our games instead of waiting until our game is almost over to come and find seats in order to watch the boys, which is a good thing in general but also for me personally—more people in the stands means I have to search harder and harder to find Steph and Kieran sitting together, and some nights, I give up looking completely. By the end of the regular season, a few weeks after the Rockford game, the whole school has caught Lady Titans' fever to the point the school sends two busloads of fans *and* the varsity cheerleading squad to our regional game at Tusculum, and combined with all the people who make the trip up on their own, we have almost enough fans to fill up the visitors' side of the gym for the first time I can remember.

Although Tusculum is hosting the regional as they did last year, our first opponent is Sumner, who should be ready to take us down after losing to us twice this season. Fortunately for us, we're more than ready to take them down once again, beating them by eight points to advance another round, one round further than we went last year.

As we line up to slap hands and say "Good game" to the Sumner team, I'm struck with the thought that this is the last time I will ever play against these girls, some of whom I've played against—and with, in the case of county summer leagues—since grade school. Instead of high-fiving as usual, most of us slap each other on the back, and Brynne Lostrand, who's been a thorn in our sides in so many games over the years, surprises me by gathering me into a hug.

"We're pulling for you guys," she says into my ear over the crowd noise. "Go all the way, okay?"

"Thanks, Brynne. We're going to give it our best shot."

Two days later, we face St. Thomas Aquinas, a Catholic school in the next county that finished third in our conference this year. Aquinas definitely comes to play, and we trade the lead back and forth with them throughout the first two quarters. We go into the locker room down three points, and as I glance around while Coach is reviewing our first half play and setting strategies for the second half, I see that everyone appears to be worn out. Lauren sits with her head down, a towel around her neck, and Cassie leans into me almost as if she's going to fall asleep from exhaustion.

This isn't good.

"Look, guys," I say, slipping into team co-captain mode and standing up from the bench once Coach finishes her review and pep talk. "This is it—our whole season could end tonight if we don't step it up. Do you want to go home and say to ourselves and everyone else 'At least we went one game further than we did last year?' Well, I don't." I pause and watch as droopy heads start rising, chins lifting from chests. "We were almost undefeated this year, and we let another team get the better of us once." I stop again for effect. "*Once.* We can't go back and change what happened now because it's in the past. And it should stay in the past. But let's be undefeated from here on out, okay? Our season starts over again right now."

Cassie sits up a little straighter and says, "I don't want to go home, either." She stands up from the bench and joins me in facing the team, two co-captains presenting a united front. "Zip's right. We lose—we go home. There is no future beyond tonight. There is no tomorrow. There's only now. And Zip, Lauren, Ashley, and I aren't going out with a loss. These Aquinas girls are nothing. *Nothing.* They're lower than nothing…"

I stare at Cassie in open-mouthed amazement. This is some action movie inspirational speech-level stuff she's dishing out right now, and it's freaking me out. Part of me wonders if this vicious streak hasn't come from hanging out with Kayla too much.

"So, let's put this thing away, okay?" she continues. "Like Coach said, the first five minutes back out on the floor are crucial. If we can win the first five minutes, we win the game. So, let's do this."

Cassie's speech seems to re-energize the team completely as everyone jumps up as soon as she's finished and gathers in a tight circle.

"Are we ready to win this game?" Coach yells.

We all put our hands in the middle of the circle and yell "One…two…three…Titans!" before jogging back to the court.

Cassie and I probably need to work on our pep talk skills a little, but apparently we've said enough to pull us through. By the end of the game, I'm able to read the Aquinas defense well enough to burn my defenders and end the game with a season-high thirty points while Cassie finishes with a career-high five three-pointers.

We're going to sectionals, the first basketball team in Titusville history—boys' or girls'—to do so.

After the final buzzer, once we've said "Good game" to the Aquinas team and have returned to our bench, I take a moment to search the crowd. My eyes only search for a few seconds before I find my mom, Morgan, my grandparents, and—to my surprise—the Laniers all sitting together on the other side of the gym in a section close to the double doors leading to the main lobby of Tusculum High School.

The Laniers—Jim, Carlie, Kayla, *and* Kieran. And Stephanie isn't with them.

Cassie drapes an arm over my shoulder, and I half expect some kind of reverse replay of the night of the Brownsville game, when Cassie first told me Kieran and Stephanie were together. But instead of saying, "Hey—Kieran and Steph broke up," she says "Zip, you were an absolute beast out there tonight. You keep playing like that, we're winning a championship for sure."

"Thanks, Cass. You looked pretty good out there, too." I tell her, casting a final glance over my shoulder before we leave the gym for the locker room.

Since we have to take time for a team meeting and to get cleaned up a little before we get back on the bus, all the fans who travelled to the game easily beat us back to town, where what seems like the entire population of Titusville has gathered to welcome us home, cheering and waving at the bus as we pull into the parking lot at school.

"Wow," Tori Sandowsky says over my shoulder as we gaze out the windows at the crowd. "It's like we're celebrities or something."

I laugh at the thought of us being famous, but as we get off the bus, we get a small taste of what rock stars must go through sometimes when they arrive at or leave an arena. People swarm us, pressing in and patting us on the back and yelling "Way to go" and "Good game, girls," and other forms of congratulation. Someone starts yelling out the words to the Titusville fight song and the crowd gradually joins in as I make my way to the edge of the parking lot, where my mom and grandparents are standing as I thought they might be, probably realizing I'd have an easier time finding them there than if they were milling around with the rest of the town's citizens. The Laniers are with them, Kieran kind of skulking around behind the entire group in the darkness

"Imagine what this place'll be like when you win a championship," Mom says, gathering me into a hug. Gram and Gramps take their turns hugging me, and Jim and Carlie do as well. Kayla steps to me next, saying her typical Kayla way "So, you get that you guys still have some work to do before you even *make* the state finals, right?"

"I'm well aware of that. But thanks for the reminder," I say, giving her a final squeeze.

Morgan, who has never struck me as the hugging type, reaches out while I'm still in Kayla's embrace and gives me closed-fisted tap on the shoulder. "Nice work, kid," he says, and I'm in such a good mood, I can't help making fun of him a little.

"What? No hug?" I let go of Kayla and hold my arms out in front of me in an invitation, which he grudgingly accepts, putting his head down and reaching around me with both hands. Our hug, on his part anyway, is really more two people giving each other pats on the back than actually hugging. Over his shoulder, I catch my mom biting her lip to keep from laughing.

I release Morgan from this tiny bit of torture and glance over at the one person I haven't made physical contact with yet. Kieran also apparently realizes his turn at congratulations is up as he moves toward me and stops right next to Morgan.

"Good game, Zip," he says. He takes a step, I take a step, and we sort of stare at each other for a moment before I give an awkward laugh and hold my arms out. We move toward each other at the same time, and the two of us sort of awkwardly crash into each other like bumper cars at the fair.

"Thanks," I mumble into his shoulder, feeling the intensity of everyone's eyes bearing down on us—nothing like having your families staring at you while you're trapped in the middle of an uncomfortable moment. We step away from each other and I wipe my hands on my warm-up pants while Kieran looks away at the dwindling crowd.

"So," Kayla begins, sidling up next to me. "I heard a bunch of people talking after the game about heading to the Diner once the team got back. You up for it?"

"Just you and me?"

"Me, too," Kieran says, adding quickly, "If that's okay."

I shift my eyes back to Kayla, and she answers my question before I can ask. "Yeah. Just the three of us," she says, her eyes sparkling.

Kieran nods and I say "Sure. Sounds good."

Just the three of us. No Stephanie. I'm not sure what the rules are for a guy hanging out with his ex-girlfriend without his new girlfriend present, but I can't imagine Steph would be too happy about this.

Unless maybe they're not together anymore.

We turn to our parents to secure the necessary permissions for a trip to the Diner, assuring all of them we won't stay out too late and we'll call if we decide to go anywhere else. And then we make our way to the Diner, where everyone in Titusville who isn't still in the high school parking lot has evidently gathered. The restaurant is so crowded, people—including a group of juniors headed up by Stephanie Hull—are spilling out the front door and crowding the sidewalk. I immediately stiffen as she and her friends approach us on the sidewalk and I notice Kieran, who is walking so close to me our coat sleeves are almost touching, has the same reaction.

"Hey, Steph," he says before Kayla or I can greet the group.

"Hey," she replies, immediately shifting her eyes to the pavement. An eternity of seconds passes with all of us standing here like a bunch of morons before I focus my attention on Abbie Winthrop, a wisp of a blonde who's on the dance squad.

"What's going on?" I ask her.

"It's insane," Abbie says, her eyes widening. "I've never seen the place that packed before. It's like everyone in town is in there. I didn't even think that many people *lived* in Titusville." She pauses, shifting her eyes back and forth between Kieran and Steph before setting them on me once again. "Nice game, by the way."

"Thanks," I say, peering over her shoulder to see more people give up and leave the Diner. "So, there aren't any tables at all?"

Abbie shakes her head. "Dewayne said it would be a while, and, I mean, they close at eleven," she tells us, shrugging and glancing at the other girls in her group. "We were thinking about going up to the Burger Barn instead."

As soon as the words leave her mouth, Abbie's nose wrinkles and she casts a sideways glance at Stephanie as if she's wondering whether or not she should have revealed their destination.

"Well, maybe we'll see you there," I tell Abbie, trying to gauge Kayla's and Kieran's reactions from the corner of my eye, but they're both maintaining pretty neutral expressions at the moment.

Everyone mumbles goodbyes at each other and the group with Abbie and Stephanie heads off to a sedan parked down the street from where we're standing. And I know I probably shouldn't say anything at all, but once the group is out of earshot, I turn to Kieran and start "Well...that was...sort of..." but I can't bring myself to spit out the word he ultimately speaks.

"Awkward?" he suggests. "Yeah, well, Steph and I broke up today right after school."

On Kieran's other side, Kayla leans forward and raises her eyebrows at me, and I imagine she knows the full story, at least some of which I will probably get through a series of texts later on tonight.

"I'm really sorry, Kieran," I tell him, and I hope I sound sincere.

And I hope I sound sincere because I *am* sincere.

Well…in actuality, I feel like I'm about ninety percent sincere. The other ten percent of me, however, is crying out for joy right now.

"It's no big deal." He shrugs, and once again, Kayla raises her eyebrows at me as he continues. "You know, sometimes things just don't work out, I guess."

I think I know that better than any of us, but I definitely don't say so aloud. And while Kieran seems a little down in the dumps, he definitely isn't coming off as devastated that things "just didn't work out" with Steph. After all, he came out to my game tonight instead of staying locked up in his house moping around, and he also didn't run away screaming at the mere sight of Stephanie. Regardless, I don't think pressing Kieran for further details about their breakup would be a good idea right now, so I'm kind of relieved when Kayla changes the subject.

"So, should we head up to the Burger Barn or…"

She's interrupted by the blare of a horn behind us, and we turn to see my mom's car coming toward us on River Avenue. All the parking spaces are taken, so Mom stops in the middle of the street and Morgan exits the passenger side before Mom honks again and drives off.

"Hope you weren't wanting to grab a bite to eat," Kieran says as his father jogs up to us on the sidewalk. "We just heard the place is a madhouse."

"I just heard that, too," he tells us. "Dewayne called and asked if I'd be willing to come in and help."

"On your night off," Kayla comments. "That sucks."

Morgan hitches up his shoulders toward his ears. "Eh, I could use the cash and it looks like he could use the extra staff right now," he says, glancing past us at the crowd gathered around the Diner's front door. "I'm guessing you guys couldn't get in?"

"We didn't even try," I respond for all of us. "We're thinking about heading up to the Burger Barn instead."

"Oh, no," Morgan says, shaking his head. "I'm not letting you get away to the competition. Follow me."

He tilts his head toward the dark expanse of River Bend Park and starts walking off behind the Diner, the three of us following suit after exchanging puzzled glances. I realize Morgan's letting us in through the back door, but I'm not quite sure what he's hoping to accomplish by doing so—regardless of which entrance we use, there still won't be any tables available once we get inside.

Morgan holds the heavy metal door open for us and we enter the Diner's storage room, shelves lining both walls piled high with giant cans of soups and vegetables, which I find surprising since all I ever eat here are burgers and fries. "Head through that door to the left," he tells us, and we do as we are told, arriving at what must be a break room, a drab, low-lit space with a square table and four folding chairs but no room for much else.

"Your table," Morgan says, sweeping his arm out to welcome us inside. We ease past him, Kieran and Kayla inching along the wall toward two seats in the inner part of the room, while I hang back a little and ask "Are you sure this is okay?"

"Well, I know these aren't your usual accommodations, but I'll check with Dewayne just to make sure," Morgan says. "Trust me— this is probably the only table you're going to get for a while."

I nod and slide into the seat closest to the door as Morgan leaves. "At least we're inside the restaurant," I say shrugging as Kayla huffs "If you call *this* being inside the restaurant. We should have gone to the Burger Barn."

"Nobody's going to the Burger Barn on my watch." Dewayne Masters, his graying hair pulled back in a low ponytail and a pencil tucked behind his ear, appears in the doorway with Morgan at his heels. He looks down at me and says "Nice game tonight, Zip. Me and the guys were listening to it on the radio."

"Thanks."

"It might take a little longer than usual to get your food, but everyone on the team and their guests eat free tonight if you're willing to wait," he continues. "I've never seen this town in such a celebratory mood, and the team's brought me all the business I can handle. I figure I can part with a few meals and more than make up for it."

We all mumble thanks at Dewayne and give him our orders before he and Morgan head back to deal with the crowd in the restaurant.

"So," Kieran begins, "how does it feel to be a celebrity?"

"A celebrity?" I say through a laugh.

"Yeah." He sits back in his chair and crosses his arms over his torso. "Private tables, free meals…"

"Soon you'll be riding around in the back of a limo, getting into all the hottest clubs…" Kayla picks up the joke.

"Yeah. Okay," I say with a smirk. "Somehow, I think a free meal in the Downtown Diner break room is probably as rock star as my life is ever going to get."

"Doubt it," Kieran says. "If you win the championship, people will be falling all over themselves to give you whatever you want."

I smile, but I don't say anything because one of the things I want most of all is sitting right here next to me and has just broken up

84

with his girlfriend. But while Kieran may have broken up with Steph, that doesn't necessarily mean he's getting back together with me.

And it's been nearly six weeks since he underwent the treatment and lost his memories of me and everything else, and as Kayla kindly reminded me in the school parking lot, the team isn't even to the semifinals yet.

So, right now, everything I want still seems pretty far out of my reach.

CHAPTER 8

The day after the regional final—Saturday—is practically spring-like, mirroring my amazing mood. I've put any thoughts of Kieran breaking up with Steph out of my mind, and I'm so hyped up over the team getting to sectionals I can't help but wonder if Mother Nature has jumped on the Titusville Lady Titans' bandwagon, too. After loafing around the house for a while and doing some homework, I decide by early afternoon I can't stay inside any longer. This is the Midwest, and it's still February—with our crazy weather, we could have a blizzard and sub-zero temperatures by tomorrow. So I slip my heaviest Titusville Basketball sweatshirt on over my t-shirt, grab my basketball from the front closet, and head for the hoop in Gram and Gramps' paved driveway to do some outside shooting for the first time in months.

Cradling the basketball against my hip, I set out across the brown, winter-dead grass to my grandparents' house. I'm only a few feet past my house when I can clearly make out Gram's round figure on the front porch, and as I get closer, I can see she's sweeping dirt off the porch and out into the yard.

"I wondered if you might come over here today," she calls out once she notices me approaching.

"Yeah. Homework wasn't doing it for me, so I thought I'd shoot around a little."

I bound up the porch stairs and she stops sweeping long enough for me to give her a kiss on the cheek.

"Gramps out back?" I ask, referring to the art studio in the shed behind the house.

"He's in Sumner today. One of his former colleagues has an art show opening in one of the little galleries downtown, and he went to help him pick out some display pieces." Gram shakes her head a little as she speaks, and she's probably thinking the same thing I am—that Gramps spends almost as much time in Sumner now as he did before he retired from the college.

"I was thinking tonight might be a good night to get the grill out while the weather's warm," Gram continues. "We might not get good grilling weather again for a while. Think your mom would be up for picking up some steaks on her way home from the store?"

"I think Mom would be up for picking up anything as long as she doesn't have to cook it," I point out, smiling, and Gram nods her head in agreement.

"Of course. I'll give her a call. She'll be giving Morgan a ride home from work, so he can help her shop." Gram leans in and ruffles my hair with her free hand. "Well, I'll let you get to practice. This porch isn't going to sweep itself."

Gram returns to sweeping and I head for the driveway, the faint *swish-swish* of her broom against the wood of the porch the soundtrack to my first few layups. She finishes and disappears into the house as I switch to practicing free throws, backing up in the driveway an appropriate distance from the basket and sinking my first two without hitting the rim or the backboard. I back out a third time, but as I'm bending my legs to start my shooting motion, something in my peripheral vision distracts me and I stop before I release, clutching the ball against my stomach.

Some kind of luxury car I recognize as belonging to the Laniers has turned off the county road and is heading up the driveway at about two miles an hour. But as the car gets closer, I'm able to make out that neither Jim nor Carlie is driving.

The car slows to a stop a safe distance from the basketball hoop and after shutting off the engine, Kieran gets out, pushing a pair of sunglasses up on the top of his head. I can't help but smile seeing him slide the keys into his pocket—learning to drive is another milestone on his road to normalcy, I guess.

"Hey," he says, walking towards me. "I was heading out for a drive and noticed you were out here. Thought I'd stop by and say 'hi.'"

He stops in front of me, mere inches from my hands folded around the ball sticking out from my stomach like a growth.

"Last time I checked, you didn't have a license," I point out. "You haven't even taken driver's ed."

"I'm eighteen," he reminds me proudly, flashing his grin. "If you turn eighteen before you have your license, you don't need high school driver's ed. I took a six-hour driving course last Saturday in Sumner, and Mom took me back this morning to take the road test—which I passed with flying colors, by the way."

When he looks at me with his usual grin, I can't help but slip into Flirt Mode—or, what passes for flirting with me, anyway.

"Can you parallel park?" I ask, smiling, "Because if you can, you're firmly ahead of me in the driving department."

"I said I passed with flying colors. I didn't say I got a perfect score," he tells me, smiling back. "Parallel parking is the one thing I screwed up, but otherwise, I'm officially road-ready according to the State of Illinois."

I think back to the awful semester I spent in driver's ed. sophomore year—Mr. Herzmann and his lack of deodorant made being crammed in a sedan with him and three classmates a completely unpleasant experience—and I kind of wish I'd waited until I was eighteen to get my license.

"So, you realize you and your six hours of experience are driving around in a car that's probably worth about a year of college tuition, right?" I point out to him.

Kieran glances over his shoulder as if he'd forgotten the car was behind him, and then he shoves his hands into his hoodie pocket, giving another nonchalant shrug as he turns back to me.

"Kayla's on her way to Evanston to visit Brad and Mom and Dad went back to Sumner with the other car after dropping me off," he tells me. "I really had no choice."

"Because just staying at home and not driving at all wasn't an option?" I ask, my voice taking on a slightly teasing tone.

He spreads his arms out and swings slightly at the hips, his eyes skyward and blinking rapidly in the bright sunlight.

"On a day like today? No—staying home was *not* an option." He shifts his eyes to the basketball I'm still cradling against me and to the hoop behind us. "Looks like staying home wasn't an option for you, either. Mind if I hang out and watch while you practice or whatever?"

I'm certainly not going to discourage any desire Kieran has to be in my general vicinity, especially considering he and Stephanie just broke up.

"Um, sure," I mumble. He backs up a few feet and leans against the hood of the car while I dribble backwards out to my imaginary free throw line, keeping my eyes on him—and he keeps his on me—the whole way. As I turn to face the basket, I catch him flashing me The Grin and I'm nearly undone to the point I need to make myself stop looking at him and dribble a few more times before I'm steady enough to put up a shot.

But when I do put one up, once again the ball sails through the net with a barely perceptible *swish*. Kieran applauds as I retrieve the ball, holding it against my hip and turning toward him to take a bow.

"Hope you're not expecting me to yell cheers or something," he calls out. "I get the sense cheerleading's not exactly my department."

"Applause is fine," I tell him, dribbling out for another free throw and staring at him a little longer than I probably should, his grin threatening to unravel me completely with each passing second. This time, my shot is off and the ball clanks off the left side of the rim, sailing out toward Kieran. He pushes himself off the hood of the car and chases the ball down before it rolls all the way to the edge of my grandparents' gigantic yard. I wait at my free throw post as he carries the ball in front of him, expecting him to toss it to me or to completely close the distance between us and hand it directly to me. And while he does end up stopping beside me, standing so close our shoulders are almost touching, he doesn't hand me the ball but instead rolls it around between his hands a few times, his brow furrowed in serious concentration.

"Mind if I try one?" he says at last, tilting his head toward the basket.

"Sure," I say, trying to keep the skepticism out of my voice. I've seen Kieran attempt one free throw in his life, last summer when he and Kayla came up to school with me to hang out while I shot around, and even then we had to teach him how to shoot, and he promptly started to fall asleep immediately after he put up his shot.

I step aside so Kieran can square his body toward the basket. He once again rolls the ball around in his hands a few times, takes two tentative dribbles, bends at the knees, rises, and releases the ball with enough strength and accuracy that it bounces off the front of the rim. I jog to retrieve the ball before it rolls out into the yard and, holding the ball against my stomach, I turn to face him.

"Kieran, how did you know how to shoot a free throw? I mean, do you remember learning how to do that?"

I study his face as he stares at some unspecified point on the pavement in front of him, his mouth twisted up with confusion.

90

"I don't...I don't know. I don't remember doing that for the first time. I don't remember *ever* shooting a free throw, actually. It kind of felt like some kind of a...like a reflex, you know? Like brushing your teeth or putting on pants—it's something you do every day but you don't really remember the first time you did it."

"Except I'm guessing you don't shoot free throws every day," I point out.

"Yeah," he says, shifting his eyes from the asphalt to my face. "Why do you ask?"

I take a deep breath and say, "Because I taught you how to shoot—well, Kayla and I did, anyway. This was back in June."

After waiting a minute for a flicker of recognition to cross his face that doesn't come, I continue detailing the memory.

"You mentioned something about maybe playing basketball in grade school before your condition kept you from playing sports anymore. But I showed you how to shoot a free throw—we were up at school, in the gym—and as soon as you shot the ball, you started to get kind of unsteady like you always used to when you were about to fall asleep. Luckily, Kayla and I were both there to help you to the bleachers."

His face is blank, so I move forward with the most important part of the story.

"That's the day we met Cooper—and Victor, his assistant. We'd met Cooper briefly in North Carolina, but the day we were up at school was the first time he told us who he was, and that he had the same condition you had. We were outside the front entrance, on the steps..."

I stop talking because I can see from his eyes focused on the pavement and the slightly less blank expression on his face that he's thinking, struggling to pull the memory from some deep pocket within his brain where all of his recollections about his life have gone to hide.

Pleaseremember.Pleaseremember.Pleaseremember, I chant to myself.

"Nothing," he says, shaking his head and looking up at me. "I'm sorry, but the memory's…not there."

I mash my lips together and nod.

"But thanks for teaching me how to shoot a free throw." He gives me his grin once again, and my disappointment ebbs a little. "I'm not sure if that's a skill that's ever going to come in handy for me, but…"

His voice fades away and I suggest "Maybe…maybe you'll have a boss someday who will ask you to play a pick-up game, and you'll need to impress him with your free throw abilities."

"You're really reaching there," he comments, but he's still grinning.

"Yeah, I totally am."

I'm smiling at him, and he's still smiling back. This feels good. This feels natural, the two of us hanging out and bantering back and forth. It's almost like the good old days, which really aren't all that old. And he must sense something, too, because he asks me, nodding back at his car, "So, you want to go for a ride?"

"With you and your six hours of driving experience?"

"Mom let me drive home from Sumner this morning, so it's really more like seven hours," he points out, his grin in full effect.

"Well, I'm not much of a risk-taker," I begin, struggling to keep a straight face, "but I'm willing to live on the edge just this once."

"Good." He's trying to keep a straight face as well, and a long minute of the two of us staring at each other passes by.

"Um, let me go tell Gram I'm leaving and I'll be back out in a minute, okay?" I ask him, turning to run toward the house without waiting for his answer. By the time I return after saying goodbye to Gram, Kieran's in the car, revving the engine at me as I approach.

"Again, I remind you we're in a luxury vehicle," I tell him as I get in the passenger side and buckle up as he continues revving. "And if you destroy the transmission on our little excursion, I'll deny any knowledge of this trip to your parents. Just so you know."

"Got it," he says, reversing and pulling forward in the driveway a few times so the front of the car is pointing toward the county road. And just as when he drove up earlier, he barely presses the accelerator and we move down the driveway so slowly I'm squirming forward in my seat as if doing so will make the car go faster.

"So that thing I just said about you destroying the transmission?" I begin as he stops at the end of the driveway. "Never mind. Gram drives faster than you do."

"Hey, I'm a little inexperienced, remember?" he says with a laugh.

"But I thought you had *seven whole hours* of driving experience," I tease, and he rolls his eyes at me as I continue, "So, where we headed, Speedy? Downtown Diner? Burger Barn? Paulie's Pizza?"

"You think about food a lot," he points out. "But there's too much traffic in town."

"*Traffic*? Titusville isn't exactly a bustling metropolis, you know."

"I get that, but I've also had my license for less than four hours. I'm not ready to do a ton of driving around other people yet."

"So, where are we going then? I know you don't remember much about Titusville, but there's not really anywhere to go out in the country."

"Then I guess you're going to have to tell me where we're headed." He grips the steering wheel and stares ahead into the expanse of grassy nothingness ahead of us, land not owned by anyone stretching out to the four-lane highway leading to Sumner. "Is there anywhere out here in the middle of nowhere that might jog my memory? Like, anywhere we used to go?"

"Oh, I can think of a couple places," I tell him, my tiny smile masking the fact that I'm inwardly thrilled he wants to go somewhere that might mean something to us. "Take a right."

Kieran looks both ways and taps the gas pedal, easing out onto the county road. We pass his house at about twenty-five miles an hour—ten miles an hour below the speed limit—and still haven't sped up about two miles later, where the speed limit goes up to forty-five.

"Hey, what's that?" Kieran asks me as I'm resisting the urge to yell at him to floor it. He's nodding out his side of the car at an opening in the tree line. "Is that a road or something?"

I glance behind me after we pass. I'd intended to take us there on the way back from our first destination.

"It's a narrow gravel road," I tell him. "Leads to a boat launch at the river."

He must read something in my face or voice because he asks "And we've been there before?"

"Several times." I squirm in my seat and try to diffuse any awkwardness I'm feeling with some humor. "But that's not the first destination on the Kieran Lanier Memory Recovery Tour. We're headed a few miles up the road, which, by the way, would go by a lot faster if you drove the speed limit."

He shoots me a look and speeds up to about forty miles an hour—I'm not going to complain. Once I see the Stanley house sitting on a slight hill in the near-distance, I tell Kieran to slow down and let him know we'll be turning into their driveway.

I've only been here once since Prom night, and I was nervous then, too, thinking about everything that happened out here on that night last May—thinking about everything that *could* have happened. But Kieran doesn't have the same problem, calmly making the right off the county road onto the gravel drive and heading up the slight hill.

"Are we going to the house?" he asks.

There aren't any other cars in the driveway, so I'm assuming the Stanleys aren't home, which is good because I hadn't worked up a reasonable excuse for why we're trolling around their property if they were.

"No. Stop right here," I tell him.

He shuts off the engine, and I get out of the car.

"Does anything look familiar?" I ask him once he's exited the driver's side. He takes in the house, the barn, and the field, which right now is nothing but dirt to the naked eye but this summer will yield rows and rows of corn stalks taller than both of us.

"No. What am I supposed to be remembering?"

I walk over to his side of the car and stand next to him, pointing up the hill.

"Prom night. The Stanley family holds an after-party in the barn every year."

"And we were here."

"We were." I nod. "We were only in the barn for about a song or two, and then a fuse blew, so we were going to leave. But we ended up in my mom's car…"

95

I pause for a moment. Do I tell him we were doing some hardcore making out? Would that help him remember?

"…not the car she owns now. She had this vintage Camaro then. And Frank Dozier ambushed us and pulled you out and ran off with you that way."

Kieran follows my gaze across the cornfield to the county road that intersects the one we travelled to get out here.

"And then he and Morgan chased us to the river," he says, and my heart leaps at the thought he might be remembering things, a thought that is quickly reversed by his next statement: "I think I remember reading about that night in my journal."

Of course. The journal. I was with him when he wrote about Prom night, and so I didn't need to skip the part about us being all over each other in the back seat of the Camaro because he already knows—in graphic detail.

"Seeing it isn't helping any more than reading about it," he says, shrugging his shoulders in resignation.

"Well, it was nighttime," I offer as a way to make him feel better. "Everything probably looks a little different."

"And I'm guessing the road to the river we passed on the way here is where Frank Dozier met his untimely end?"

"Yup."

"Well, let's go to destination number two and see if I remember anything there."

We get back in the car, but Kieran pauses with his hand on the ignition before starting the engine.

"What is it?" I ask, buckling up. "Are you remembering something?"

"No," he mumbles, looking at me and giving me a little smile. "Just…thanks, you know? For taking me out and showing me stuff like this to try to help with my memory. And for sticking by me through this whole thing. You're a good…"

He catches himself, and my heart breaks a little although I try not to let my disappointment show.

"I know," I tell him. "Don't mention it."

CHAPTER 9

Kieran and I ride back to the river in a silence broken only by my telling him "The road's right up ahead—the break in the tree line there."

He nods, slows the car, and turns down the narrow gravel road. Once again, I'm nervous, but Kieran calmly eases off the accelerator at the bottom of the hill and rolls over the rut that launched Morgan and Frank Dozier into the river in the car they stole from Cody Hull. I give Kieran a sideways glance and he comments before I can ask "I remembered the rut in the road from my journal, too."

"Of course," I mumble.

Kieran pulls over to the right side of the boat launch, sets the parking break, and kills the engine. I wait a minute or so for him to look around and take in the scene before I start what's become my normal interrogation.

"Anything?" I ask.

"Nope."

He releases his seatbelt and gets out of the car, walking forward until the gravel meets the water. After watching him kick at the rocks for a minute, I get out and join him at the river's edge, the two of us standing side-by-side and letting the water lap up against the toes of our shoes.

"I'm trying, you know?" he says, staring out at the river. "I've read all my journals until I've almost got them memorized, I go places all the time that are supposed to be familiar to me, and...nothing."

I can't say anything to help him, so I don't say anything at all.

"So, Cooper says he had amnesia for about three weeks?" he asks.

"Yeah."

"So, I guess I'm just screwed then." He kicks at the rocks again. "It's been nearly six weeks for me."

"Kieran," I begin, but I stop my attempt at comforting him before it begins as he keeps jamming his toe into the gravel at the water's edge. "I do that all the time, you know."

"What?" he asks, moving his eyes from the river to look at me.

"The kicking thing. Whenever I get nervous or upset, I jam my toes into stuff—rocks, carpet, hardwood floors, whatever…"

"I remember," he interrupts. "I mean, I remember reading about that in my journals. I've probably read about it so much I'm doing it unconsciously now myself."

"Well, I'm pleased to share one of my weird habits with you," I tell him. "And we can't give up on your memory coming back. Your mom's always said the amnesia isn't predictable."

"I like how everything with you is always 'we,' like we're in this together," he says, smiling at me.

"We *are* in this together."

Kieran punts a few more rocks into the river and looks away from me.

"I broke your heart and started dating another girl, and yet you're still here."

"Of course I am," I insist. "I promised you. I promised your family."

"But hanging out with me isn't only about obligation, is it?"

His eyes meet mine again, his expression deadly serious, and I sense I have no choice but to meet his question head on.

"What do you want me to say, Kieran? I miss you. I miss *us*. I…"

I want to say those three little words that used to roll off my tongue, but I catch myself. Now isn't the time.

The time may never be right again.

"I'm your friend," I say, right before the pause in the conversation heads into "totally awkward" territory. "It's hard for me to watch you be so confused about your life, so I just want to help. I can't imagine what it must be like to read in your journals about all these things you've lived through, but you can't remember living through any of them."

He lowers his eyes to the rocks and keeps kicking at them. "Yeah…and speaking of my journals," he begins, "I've been meaning to ask you something. But it's kind of personal, if that's okay."

Um…

"Anything," I tell him after a brief pause. "Ask me anything."

Still refusing to look at me, he shoves his hands into his hoodie pocket before mumbling "Did we ever…? You know."

I think I do know, but I don't want to assume what he's getting at and end up totally embarrassed.

"Did we ever…?" I prompt.

"Well, I've read all the journals, and I've read how close we were, and we knew each other for almost a year but I couldn't find any mention of us…" *Kick, kick, kick* goes his toe against the gravel as he sighs and closes his eyes. "It just seems weird to me that we never had sex, or that I wouldn't have written about it if we did."

If a giant wave wanted to rise up from the river and drown me right now, I'd be totally cool with that.

"We did," I tell him after a deep breath. "The night before you underwent the treatment when we were staying with the Hallorans in New York. You wouldn't have had time to write anything."

Or to draw pictures, I say to myself, and I bite my lip to keep myself from laughing at the thought.

"Makes sense." Kieran opens his eyes and gazes across the river at the naked trees on the opposite bank. "Was I…did you…" His face screws up in frustration. "I guess what I'm trying to ask is, was it okay?"

That giant wave I was hoping for? Yeah—it can go ahead and suck me under any time now.

"Let's just say I didn't complain," I tell him.

A tiny version of his usual grin forms and his cheeks redden as he continues looking downward.

"Guess talking about this is a little awkward," he points out.

"A little." I shrug. "But I understand why you'd be curious. I mean, I would be too if I were in your shoes."

"Well, I just thought it was weird, you know? There's so much detail in those journals about everything else, but not about that. And I sure as hell wasn't going to ask Kayla. That's not exactly something you want to talk about with your sister."

I almost want to remind Kieran that he and Kayla have had any number of strange conversations just in the brief time they've lived in Titusville, but since the reminder probably wouldn't do any good, I stop myself.

"It's not exactly something I wanted to talk to your sister about, either," I say, although I'm not quite sure why I chose this particular thought to fill our uneasy silence.

"You never told her?" Kieran sounds surprised. "I thought you two were pretty close."

"We are," I tell him, realizing that I'm just now grappling with the events of that night at the Hallorans' for the first time—so much has happened in the meantime, I haven't really thought much about our first time together since the morning after. "It kind of never came up. We've all sort of had a lot of other things to deal with since then, you know?"

"Guess so," he says with a hint of a smile. "I just assumed you and Kayla probably talked about that kind of stuff."

101

I think back to Kayla telling me about how she lost her virginity to Brad on Prom night, and I can't help but wonder if things were a little less chaotic whether I would have shared my loss of virginity story with her at some point.

"But thanks for being willing to talk about it with me," Kieran continues. "I mean, I had no idea until right now if I was still a virgin or not. It's kind of a weird feeling not to know that kind of information about yourself."

We are quiet for a moment as I think through the implications of what he's just said, and my curiosity gets the better of me.

"So you and Stephanie never…"

"No." He cuts me off before I can finish my thought and angles his body so he can look at me. "We were only together for a few weeks, and, I mean, a few weeks is way too soon as far as I'm concerned. And Steph's a great girl and all, but we didn't really have that kind of relationship. We were never really serious, and I don't think we ever would have been."

"Is that why you two broke up—because things weren't too serious?" My voice sounds small and tentative.

"Sort of," Kieran starts, shrugging. "Like I said, she's a really great girl, but…I don't know…there wasn't much there, I guess. No chemistry or whatever. And conversations with her were always kind of surface-level and not really very natural—not like…"

He pauses, his eyes flitting away toward the river and then back to me and my heart pounds, waiting for him to finish his thought. But he doesn't, or at least not in the way I want him to.

"Anyway, being with someone doesn't seem fair if you're not feeling the whole thing," he continues. "And, besides, I'm leaving for college at the end of the summer and she'll still be here, and so we didn't really see the point in keeping things going. I mean, maybe if I go to Sumner we could make a relationship work since I'd only be forty-five minutes away, but I'm not sure the whole thing even meant enough to both of us to try."

I bob my head in understanding, even though I'm not really sure I understand, and Kieran shifts the subject slightly.

"Speaking of college, I'm going to Chicago tomorrow with my parents. I've got admissions interviews at a couple of places on Monday, so there's a chance I might be living further away from home than I thought."

"Kayla mentioned you'd be going up there over Presidents' Day," I tell him. "Do you have a frontrunner right now, or are you still weighing your options?"

"No clue. Going to school in Chicago would be cool, I guess, but Sumner's got a good art and design program, too." He gives me a sad smile. "It seems kind of bizarre to be planning the next stage of my life when I can't remember anything that's come before."

"It's weird planning the next stage of your life no matter what," I assure him. "I kind of can't get my mind around the fact that this time next year, I won't be in Titusville anymore. And don't get me wrong—not being here is a totally a good thing. But it's just strange to think that in just a few months, everything's going to be so different than it is now."

"Are you still going to Northwestern? Kayla had told me you'd applied there."

"Maybe," I say, hitching my shoulders up with uncertainty. As Coach Denton had predicted, thanks to our stellar season so far both Cassie and I have started to get some attention from schools regarding basketball scholarships, although most of the schools are smaller Division Two schools and not ones most people have ever heard of. "I won't hear until April whether or not I got in. And Sumner's expressed some interest in me as far as basketball, so I applied there, too. I think I can definitely get an academic scholarship there even if the team doesn't make me an offer."

"Would you want to stay that close to home?"

"Probably not," I say with a little smile. "Part of the point of college—for me, anyway—has always been getting out of here. Going down the road doesn't really seem a whole lot like getting out. But there are some Division Two schools in Wisconsin and Indiana showing some interest, too—I just don't know if I'm interested in them. I'm planning to take some college visits once the season is over, so we'll see how everything works out."

Now I'm the one kicking at the rocks out of nervousness. Conversations about college were never easy even before Kieran underwent the treatment because we knew we could possibly end up far away from each other. Now, these same conversations are awkward on an entirely different level. What if we both end up at Sumner but Kieran still doesn't remember who I am?

"What about you?" I ask him, shaking off my fears. "Would you be okay with staying so close to home?"

"I don't know," he says, and then lets out a tiny laugh. "I guess this isn't really 'home' to me, so I kind of don't care if I go to Sumner or not."

"Good point."

I can't believe, even after everything that's happened over the last few weeks, Kieran and I could still end up in the same town or city, and may end up at the same school. Six months ago—two months ago, even—nothing would have made me happier. Now, given Kieran's condition, the prospect fills me with a strange mixture of excitement and dread.

"At any rate, sounds like we both have some decisions to make," he says.

"Guess so."

I lift my left hand up over my ear to smooth back some hair that's come loose from my ponytail, and as I'm lowering my arm, Kieran catches my wrist, just above my charm bracelet.

"I have really good taste in jewelry, apparently," he says, bringing my arm to my side, but not letting go of my wrist. He slides his thumb underneath the silver chain, and the sensation of his skin against mine makes me die a little inside.

"You do," I murmur, barely able to form the words.

He slides the bracelet around my wrist, fingering each of the charms.

"So, if I'm remembering correctly from what I read in my journals," he starts, "each one of these charms means something, right?"

"Yeah." My mouth is so dry, I could drink straight from the river without a second thought.

"And I gave you this one because I thought you were going to be the key to my memory coming back, right?" He rubs his thumb along the grooves and indentations in the tiny silver key.

I don't speak, but only nod my affirmative.

If this were a cheesy movie, all I'd have to do is kiss him and he'd remember everything. He'd come back to me—just like that. And he's practically offering me an engraved invitation to kiss him, right? After all, *he's* the one fiddling with my charm bracelet right now. *He's* the one who brought up the key.

What the hell—let's find out what happens.

I step to him, my hand reaching for his free hand, and as my lips meet his, his other hand slides from my wrist and he laces his fingers together with mine. Our lips part to deepen the kiss, and as he moves his hands to my waist, my hands creep upward, finding his cheeks, trying to hold him against me as firmly as I can.

105

Oh, man, I think. *This is amazing. This kiss is like Christmas and New Year's and my birthday and the Fourth of July all jumbled up together in one beautiful, glorious mess...*

But after a few seconds, I can sense him pulling away, and as much as I don't want to, I step back as well. But instead of seeing the happiness of recognition in his face, instead of watching him smile as all our memories together come flooding back to him, I see...what? Anger? Confusion? Regret?

I've never seen this expression on his face before, his eyes narrowed and his mouth twisted up in a way I don't recognize, and all I know right now is that I want out of this moment and never to see that look—whatever it is—again.

"Um..." he begins, but I don't let him finish.

"Um, yeah." I tilt my head back behind me at the car. "Maybe we should..."

"Yeah. I should probably get you home, I guess." He pinches the bridge of his nose. "I'm starting to get a little bit of a headache for some reason, anyway..."

A headache. Cooper got a blinding headache when his memory first started coming back at Homecoming.

"Are you okay to drive?" I ask, setting aside for the moment the fact I'd almost be too uncomfortable to drive his parents' car if he isn't, and setting aside the fact I want to yelp out loud with happiness.

A headache. He has a headache. I did it. His memory's starting to come back.

"Yeah. Yeah—I should be okay." He shuts his eyes tightly as if trying to squeeze the pain out of his head, and when he opens them up again, he finds me standing in front of him, probably staring at him like some weird expectant moron.

Obviously, his memory isn't coming back right this minute, so I gather myself together and tell him "Um...I'm having dinner at my grandparents' house, so you can just drop me off there."

"Okay."

We march to the car in silence, and we don't say a word to each other until a few minutes later when he's parked in my grandparents' driveway.

"I had fun today," he says, and instantly cringes, maybe wondering if he's said the wrong thing.

"Me, too," I mumble, grabbing up the basketball from the floorboard and getting out of the car. "See you later."

"Yeah. See you," he says, and I shut the door and turn toward the house, the dull ache trying to take over my stomach battling with the sense of hope rising in me—

He's starting to come back. I did it. I'm the key...

CHAPTER 10

…Except I'm not—not the key, that is. Not yet, anyway. When I run into Kieran at school Monday, everything's just as it has been for almost two months, only maybe a little more awkward on my end since I planted that kiss on him. Luckily for me, Kieran doesn't say anything about what happened at the river once we've settled into pairs discussion time in English class—the topic today is Virginia Woolf's *Mrs. Dalloway*—and instead wants to focus on my sectional game coming up tomorrow night. And once I'm sure he doesn't want to confront me about our surprise lip-lock from the other day, I'm able to relax a little.

"So, let me make sure I have this straight," he begins, "if you win tomorrow night, you go to the finals, right?"

"We go to the *sectional* finals."

"And then you go to *finals* finals?"

I shake my head. "Then we go to the super-sectionals," I tell him.

He taps his pencil on our discussion question sheet and laughs as quietly as he can so Mrs. Rossdale doesn't come to the back of the room to give us a hard time. "The *super*-sectionals?" he asks, his voice full of doubt. "Really? And do you go to the super-duper sectionals after that?"

"No, we don't," I fire back, laughing a little myself.

"The super-cool-awesome-fun-time sectionals, maybe?" he suggests, and I press my lips together to keep from laughing out loud and getting us both in trouble.

"After the super-sectional game, we go to the state final tournament," I tell him after I calm down. "If we win both our games there, then we've won everything and we're State Champs."

"This is all very complicated," he informs me, sitting back in his chair and folding his arms over his stomach.

"You know what's going to be complicated?" I say, pointing to our discussion questions. "Mrs. Rossdale calling on us to share what we've discussed when we haven't even started talking about *Mrs. Dalloway*. Call me crazy, but I get the impression she wouldn't be remotely interested in the finer points of the girls' basketball playoffs."

He heaves an exaggerated sigh. "Fine," he says. "I just wanted a rough estimate of how many games I was going to have to go to before the end of the season."

I rest my chin on my knuckles and blink. "You know, you don't *have* to go to any of my games for the rest of the season," I tell him, pretending to be annoyed, but I can tell from the grin on his face he knows I'm kidding around. Flirting with him feels good—natural, even. And flirting with anyone, Kieran included, is about the last thing I ever expected to feel natural to me. Guess I really have changed a lot since last year.

"I may not *have* to go to any of your games, but I *want* to," he says. "Now let's talk about boring Mrs. Dalloway and her boring dinner party."

True to his word, Kieran shows up along with Kayla to both our first sectional game and our sectional final even though the sectional site is nearly two hours away. We plow through our first opponent, Newton Catholic, on Tuesday night, winning by twelve points. But we have a little more trouble with our Thursday match-up against Linville Central, squeaking out a three-point victory.

But a three-point victory is still a victory, and it puts us in the super-sectional game in Decatur the following Monday night against Cohler City. Because of the distance we have to travel to get to the game, the team leaves school early and I miss English class, so I don't get a chance to ask Kieran if he's coming to the game. But I shouldn't have wondered—during warm-ups, I search the crowd and find him sitting next to Kayla in the top row of the bleachers near the gym's entrance. Scanning further, I'm shocked to discover my dad sitting next to my mom in the center of the stands with my grandparents right behind them, a sight I've been waiting for since my parents split up so long ago. I wave up at my dad and he waves back, my happy moment only broken by Lauren hissing in my ear, "Zip, go!" as it's my turn to catch a pass from one of the coaches and go in for a practice layup.

Dad's been promising to attend one of my games for pretty much my entire life, and he's never once kept his promise until tonight. Having him watch me play for the first time should make me more nervous than I already should be, considering we're playing a team we've never played before in a gym we've never seen. But, oddly, his presence seems to increase my focus and I play one of the best games of my career, equaling my three-point total from the Rockford South game. We're up by seven as the clock ticks down and Cassie inbounds the ball to me. I dribble slowly up the court to run out the clock, and, sensing there's no hope, Cohler City's point guard backs off from defending me. As the buzzer sounds, I toss the ball to the referee and my Cohler City counterpart, a girl who is at least three inches taller than I am and who probably outweighs me by thirty pounds, comes up to shake my hand.

"Good game," she says into my ear over the crowd noise. "I've never seen a player as fast as you."

"Thanks," I yell back. "You guys played a good game, too."

"Thanks," she says as she drops my hand and gives me a pat on the shoulder. "Good luck at State."

Hearing someone else say the words makes our accomplishment sink in.

Oh, my God. We're going to State.

Cassie, who had jogged up the court just a few feet away from me, runs over and throws her arms around me.

"We did it!" she shrieks into my ear. "We're going to State! Can you believe this?"

I want to yell back how I can't believe it, but we're smothered by our teammates as they rush over from the bench and from their positions on the floor to envelop us in a group hug. Eventually, the circle widens so we're all standing with our arms at each other's waists, jumping up and down in unison and screaming, one giant happy mass of girls in ponytails.

Just two more wins—two more wins and we're State Champions.

After a post-game team meeting in the locker room, we all get cleaned up and try to wind down a little before getting back on the bus for the long trip home to Titusville. Coach tells us we can take a few minutes before the bus leaves to check in with our families, and so I run back out to the gym and search the people still wandering around, finding my parents and grandparents talking to each other underneath the south basket.

"Dad!" I yell out as I approach the group, dropping my gym bag on the floor once I've reached them. He turns and scoops me up in his arms.

"Zipperoo," he says into my ear. "Great game. I'm so proud of you."

"Thanks, Dad." I pull back from him. "I can't believe you drove all the way here. Aren't you supposed to be at work tomorrow morning?"

He shrugs his shoulders. "I have some vacation time coming to me," he says. "I'll definitely be at your games this weekend, too. I can't wait to be there when you win the whole thing. My team never did that when I was in high school."

I can't stop smiling, but my enthusiasm dies down a little as I catch sight of Kieran and Kayla over Dad's shoulder. I turn in his arms until I'm standing at his side as he twists around to find the Lanier siblings coming up to our little group.

"Hello, guys," Dad says with booming enthusiasm. "I didn't know you were here. How are you?"

I shoot a panicked look back at my mom. Between the two of us, we've gotten Dad up to speed on the state of Kieran's memory, but I can't tell, as Dad stands here beaming at the Laniers, if he's forgotten Kieran may have no idea they've met before or if he's ignoring the facts and choosing to pretend everything's normal.

Kayla tells Dad "We're great. Good to see you again, *Mr. McKee*," putting an exaggerated emphasis on *Mr. McKee* that seems to make Kieran's shoulders hitch as if someone's startled him. A tense moment passes as we all wait for whatever Kieran's going to do. Part of me expects him to step forward and repeat Kayla's greeting, except it would be a lie—he can't exactly say "Nice to see you again," when he doesn't remember ever seeing him in the first place.

Just as the moment is about to pass over into being excruciatingly awkward, Kieran looks at me, obvious panic in his eyes over not knowing how to address my father. I nod at him slowly, hoping my action is enough to convey to him that my dad knows all about his situation and however Kieran decides to approach this moment is going to be okay with all of us. He flashes me a tiny smile and steps forward, holding his hand out to Dad.

"Mr. McKee," he says, shaking Dad's hand with the same level of enthusiasm he did the night they first met in North Carolina. "Good to see you."

I sense the tension draining from our little group like a slow leak in a dam. *Good to see you*—a statement that's polite yet relatively neutral, leaving off any reference to the past.

"Good to see you, too, Kieran," Dad responds, giving Kieran's hand a final pump before letting go, and now Dad's the one who seems a little nervous, not adding anything else to his greeting for a few seconds. He mashes his lips together as if thinking of the right thing to say, finally settling on "You're looking well."

"Thanks, sir," Kieran says, smiling. "And I'd be even better if I could remember anything that happened to me before January."

I give Kieran a grateful smile for going ahead and confronting the elephant in the gym, and I can feel my Dad relax a little as I still have my arm draped across his back.

"Wasn't Zip awesome tonight, sir?" Kieran asks, and I'm further grateful that he changes the subject from him to me, even though being glad over anyone changing the subject to me usually isn't my default position.

Dad looks down at me and gives me a little squeeze. "She was amazing," he says, not looking back at Kieran.

"Thanks, Dad," I say before glancing at Kieran and telling him "Thanks" as well.

Kayla, perhaps deciding to save us all from any further discomfort, steps forward and tugs on Kieran's coat sleeve. "Well, we should get going. The team's probably going to need to leave soon," she says. I glance past Kayla to see some of my teammates breaking away from their families and heading toward the back entrance, where the team bus would be parked right outside. Kayla moves toward me and I step away from my dad so she can gather me into a hug.

"Good game," she whispers in my ear. "You're so close to getting everything you want."

"Thanks," I say, pulling back from her and glancing at Kieran while thinking I'm not *that* close to getting everything I want, particularly when we're not talking about basketball. But I don't get to wallow for too long because Kieran steps in as Kayla moves aside, drawing me to him in a hug. The action surprises me and comforts me all at the same time, and I have to stop myself from overanalyzing the significance of the hug and let myself relax in Kieran's arms.

"So, *now* you're going to the finals, right?" I can hear the smile in his voice.

"I think you're starting to get the idea," I tell him. "Thanks for coming."

"Wouldn't have missed it."

He lets me go, and he and Kayla say goodbye to my family and head off across the gym as Dad slides his arm around me once again.

"Walk me to the bus?" I ask him, and he nods. I hug my grandparents and my mom, and Dad and I walk off toward the back entrance.

"I know you and your mom have tried to keep me up to date on the whole Kieran situation, but seeing him is something else," Dad says. "I mean, I had no idea. He didn't remember me at all, did he?"

"Don't feel bad. He doesn't remember me at all anymore, either. All he understands is what he reads in his journals and his notes, and I'm not sure if any of that means much to him."

Dad steps ahead of me to push open the door, allowing me to walk out into the parking lot before him. "Zip, I'm so sorry. I can't imagine how hard this must be for you," he says.

"I'm dealing with it." I shrug and put on my brave face. "Luckily, I've got other things to worry about right now."

We stop a few feet from the bus, and Dad turns to me and puts his hands on my shoulders. "About those other things," he begins, "I

114

can't even begin to tell you how proud I was watching you tonight. You're an amazing ball player, Zip. I guess somehow I've always known from how you looked when we've played together in my driveway and from things you've told me about your games, but now that I've actually seen you play…" He pauses, his brow wrinkling. "I want you to know how sorry I am."

"Sorry? For what?" I ask, although I think I can guess where this moment is headed. If there's one thing Dad's good at doing, it's rambling on about his Absent Parent Guilt. And even though I don't want his attitude ruining my good mood, I can't exactly walk away from him right now. After all these years, he's finally come to one of my games, and so I don't want to storm off and risk making him feel even worse. So I stand in front of him, his hands gripping my shoulders, and prepare to accept his apology for whatever it is he's apologizing for this time.

"I'm sorry for not coming to one of your games until now. And I'm sorry for not doing more to help you get a scholarship to a big-time school. I kept sitting there tonight thinking if I'd been more involved, or if I'd had you live with me in Chicago, you could have played ball year-round on traveling teams and maybe gotten some more attention from scouts…"

"Dad, I'm fine." I interrupt him because I don't want to hear anything else he has to say about what he *could* have done for my basketball career. "A few schools are interested in me. And maybe if I get into Northwestern, I can try out for a walk-on spot or something. It'll all work out."

But I know he's right. If I'd lived in the Chicago area, I probably would have gotten more attention as a recruit because I could have played on year-round teams in addition to my high school team. And if he'd paid attention to me as a player in addition to paying attention to me as the daughter he only sees on holidays and

115

in the summer, he could have guided me through the whole college recruiting process and I might have some bigger schools looking at me right now.

If, if, if. Maybe, maybe, maybe.

I'm tempted to get mad, but I swallow down the bile working its way up my throat from my stomach. Now isn't the time to hash out our father-daughter issues—and I don't know when that time will be—but here, in these few minutes before I have to get on the bus, all I can do is pretend his lack of attention hasn't impacted my basketball career at all.

"Really, Dad," I say, calmly. "You'll see. Wherever I go to school, everything will be okay."

Dad nods, seeming a little put out that I interrupted his moment of detailing his regrets about me. "Well, anyway," he starts, changing the subject, "I'll be at State—Kathy and Liv, too. I called them while you were in the locker room, and Liv's so excited to go to one of your games she can hardly contain herself."

I'd almost forgotten—my little sister's never seen me play anywhere other than her driveway, either.

Someone taps me on the shoulder and I glance behind me to find Coach Springfeld—one of our assistant coaches who, by day, is *Mrs.* Springfeld, the Titusville French teacher—nodding toward the bus.

"Sorry to interrupt, but we've got to head out."

"Okay," I tell her before turning to hug my dad one last time.

"Thanks for being here, Dad," I say into his shoulder, and I mean it. Despite whatever mixed feelings I'm having right now about what my dad could or couldn't have done for my basketball career, I'd rather have had him here watching me tonight than not.

"See you Friday, Zipperino," he replies, giving me a final squeeze before letting me go to get on the bus. I hitch my gym bag up on my shoulder and jog up the stairs, stopping in my tracks next to the bus driver once my teammates break out in applause and cheers.

"Ladies and gentlemen," Cassie bellows from the back of the bus even though there are no men—gentle or otherwise—anywhere in the vicinity, "Our fearless leader, the highest-scoring player in Titusville High School history, and my friend and yours, the amazing Zip McKee!"

The team continues hooting and hollering as I make my way to my usual seat at the back of the bus across the aisle from Cassie, slapping high-fives with my teammates the whole way.

"Okay—*that* was completely unnecessary," I grumble at Cass.

"Well, I did it because I know how much you like the attention," she teases back. "When I realized you were the last one on the bus, I couldn't resist messing with you a little."

"Thanks. You're a real friend," I say, sarcastic and honest all at the same time. As I put my headphones on and start blasting music, I realize that after two more games, Cassie and I will never play basketball together again. I lift my chin and can see the backs of Lauren's and Ashley's heads a few seats ahead of me, Ashley's head bobbing up and down as she laughs about something.

Two more games, and I'll never play basketball again with them, either.

I settle into my seat, a satisfied smile crossing my face.

This is my life, and I don't need to think about the life I could have had living in Chicago with my Dad because those thoughts are irrelevant. I can't picture my life as anything other than the life I've lived in Titusville with Mom, and at the moment, I can't imagine trading a shot at playing Division One ball for all the movie marathons and talks I've had with her over the years.

So Dad can go ahead and have his regrets about my not living with him and playing ball for some big Chicago school, because right this minute, I'm not sorry about how everything worked out. For better or worse, Titusville is my home. My team is my team. And I don't think I would have wanted things any other way.

CHAPTER 11

Given that basketball sometimes seems like the most normal thing in my life right now, I've had to laugh several times over the last few days at the fact that the Girls' Basketball State Championship will be played at Illinois State University in Normal, Illinois. But as we pull into the parking lot at Redbird Arena for our Thursday afternoon shoot-around, I'm not laughing anymore.

Now, I'm all business. Now, it's time for me to help my team do what we've come here to do.

We all change into our practice gear in a locker room that's bigger than the Titusville boys' and girls' locker rooms combined, and once we're ready, we make our way to the tunnel that leads to the court, Cassie and me in front of the rest of the team. And like something out of a bad movie, Cassie stops right outside the tunnel and Lauren, who's busy looking around and not paying attention, crashes into her.

"Whoa." Cassie croaks out what we're all thinking right now. Our dinky gym in Titusville holds about six hundred people. Redbird Arena, on the other hand, holds over ten thousand. And even though I know the basketball court is regulation size, here in this vast cavern complete with chair back seats, wide sidelines, and press tables, it seems like the biggest basketball court in the whole world.

The rest of the team moves in slow motion toward the sideline, but I've got something I need to do first. After taking a second to get my bearings, I decide I'm headed in the right direction as I walk toward the basket closest to the tunnel from which the team emerged. I press my right knee against the padded stanchion holding the backboard, rim, and net aloft, and then I back out to where the baseline meets the court and lie down.

I've heard the story enough times to know I'm probably lying in the exact place my dad landed after he crashed into the stanchion and tore both his anterior cruciate ligament and medial collateral ligament, more commonly known as the ACL and MCL. While I'm not normally a superstitious person, for some reason I need to do what I'm doing right now—I need to make one of the first things I see in this arena as a player be the *last* thing my dad saw here as a player, as if the cosmic connection will bring me some sort of good luck.

"What are you doing, you total freak?" Cassie calls out as she jogs over to the baseline and sits down next to me.

"This is where my dad got hurt. I've told you that story, right?"

Cassie joins me in gazing at the ceiling that looks far enough away it could be on another planet. "Yeah. Wow. Right here, huh?" she asks, her voice nearly a whisper.

"Yeah."

"Remind me not to step here, then."

I sit up and bump shoulders with her. "Well, if you step here, you're out of bounds, so there's that." I point out.

"True." Cassie glances around. "And, anyway, you might want to get up. Coach said there could be college coaches here scouting the practices. You don't want some assistant coach saying 'You know, we'd love to offer that McKee kid a scholarship, but she seems like a total head case.'"

I don't get the chance to respond as Coach's voice booms from the sideline since she's just now noticed her co-captains have separated themselves from the rest of the team and are sitting on the floor under one of the hoops.

"If you ladies are done relaxing over there, I'd like to get to work."

Without a word, Cassie and I get up and jog to midcourt, where the rest of the team is heading over from the sideline to begin our pre-practice stretches. We all flop down where in a few hours the game will tip off, stretching our legs out in front of us and reaching for our toes almost in unison, as if we're doing some sort of weird interpretive dance routine. As Ashley releases her toes and sits up straight, I notice her eyes drifting over my head to focus on something near the sideline.

"Hey, who are those people?" she asks through a breath as she reaches again for the toes of her shoes and pulls back. I follow her gaze to a table full of people sitting parallel to the sideline, some typing away on laptops while others talk in pairs and small groups, all of them with a laminated card hanging from their necks on a lanyard.

"I don't know. Media, maybe?" I say.

"Or maybe scouts from college teams?" Cassie suggests.

Scouts. Media. A wave of nerves washes over me, nerves that only intensify when I take in the wide-eyed expressions of my three fellow seniors.

This is the Big Time. Win or lose, our names—and possibly our faces, too—will be in every newspaper in the state by tomorrow morning. In some cases, the mention might not be more than a box score somewhere in the sports section. In other cases, such as the *Sumner Statesman*, we'll likely be front-page news regardless of what happens tonight. I swallow hard and refocus on the task at hand, as Coach Springfeld tosses us exercise bands so we can finish with our leg stretching routine.

Since we're in the first semifinal tonight, we run through a light shoot-around before heading back to the hotel to rest. Coach practically has to force us to eat dinner before we leave to return to the arena since we're all too nervous to eat, but by the time we've piled back onto the bus for the five-minute trip to the arena, we're starting to loosen up a bit, singing the Titusville fight song and running through some of the standard school cheers that are probably best left to the cheerleading squad. In the locker room, we all retreat into whatever individual pregame routines we've established to get ourselves psyched up. In most cases, pregame rituals consist of listening to a certain playlist of tunes, but I prefer to sit quietly, staring ahead or down at the floor—I guess some people might call what I do "meditating." In my mind, I'm replaying every missed shot, every bad drive to the lane, every blown pass, and I'm mentally correcting them all so they don't happen again. By the time the coaching staff tells us we need to hit the court, I'm in the perfect headspace.

It's go time.

We come out for our pre-game warm-ups, and while the arena is nowhere near completely full, I know I've never seen this many people at one of our games before. The Titusville section is completely full and as I scan the crowd, I see more than a few people from town who I'm pretty sure haven't set foot in the high school for one of our games or anything else since they were high school students themselves.

"Hope the last person to leave town locked everything up so the meth heads don't steal it all while we're gone," Cassie says, surveying the crowd.

"No kidding," Lauren says, her wide-eyed gaze also on the Titusville section. "I bet there's no one left in Titusville right now."

"Except the meth heads," I point out.

"Well, yeah," Lauren says, before the coaching staff yells at us to line up for layup drills.

Everything about this game exists on a bigger scale than any of us have ever seen before. Even the team introductions are more drawn out than normal. Rather than the public address announcer introducing the starting five as we assemble for our final team huddle at the bench, here, after each one of us is announced to the crowd, we're expected to jog to midcourt and shake hands with our counterpart on the other team before rejoining the rest of our team on the sideline.

Our semifinal opponent is Harvest Light Christian Academy, a school from some town in the northwestern part of the state I've never heard of. And right from the opening tip, they prove themselves to be our equals, matching us shot for shot whether we're driving the lane for layups or shooting from outside. But they're taller and more physical than we are, to the point that one of their players accidentally pops Ashley in the nose with an elbow when the two of them are on the floor struggling for possession of a loose ball. Ashley ends up on the bench with a bloody nose, and when we all head over two minutes later during a time out, she's still pressing a cloth to her nostrils.

"You'd think girls from a Christian school would be a little friendlier," Cassie harrumphs, reaching down to tug on Ashley's ponytail.

"It was an accident," I remind Cass. "And I'm guessing no matter what religion they are, they want to win as badly as we do. These girls are *tough*."

"No kidding," Ashley mumbles through a face full of towel.

Coach huddles us up to talk strategy for the rest of the time out, and by the time we return to the court, Ashley's nosebleed has stopped and she's able to go back in. But even though our starting five is once again back on the court, we still can't get an edge on Harvest Light before halftime and end up falling behind, heading into the locker room down by five, the most we've been behind all season since we lost to Rockford South.

After the coaches break down the first half, Coach Denton turns to Cassie and me and says, "Any words of wisdom from our co-captains?"

Cassie and I look at each other and stand up before the team. "Look, these girls are good," I begin. "But we've faced good teams all season..."

...well, we've faced good teams for the most part, anyway. We've also faced a few teams, like Brownsville, who haven't been so great, but I brush the thought away. I'm supposed to be inspiring my team here.

"And we've *beaten* good teams all season. Harvest Light is just another good team we're going to beat, right?"

"Right," a few members of the team yell back in response.

"So we need to stay focused and remember what we came here for. We came here for a championship, right?"

"Right!"

"And I don't know about you, but I'm not leaving without one. How about you, Cass?"

I'm kind of out of things to say, so I'm hoping Cassie picks up where I've left off. Public speaking is definitely not my strong suit.

"Me, neither," she says. "And I'm *not* losing to these Harvest Light brutes. Nobody jacks one of my teammates in the face and gets away with it."

Cassie reaches out and slaps hands with Ashley, and Coach Denton mumbles "Um...girls..."

"I don't care if these girls are bigger, and I don't care if these girls are taller. *We're* the better team, am I right?" Cassie yells.

"Yeah!" we all say in unison.

"Now, we're going out there in the second half, and we're taking this team down. And whoever we end up playing in the finals, we're taking them down, too," Cassie continues, getting more fired up by the second. "Nobody gets in the way of what we came here for, got it? I'm talking killer instinct, ladies. Killer instinct. I want to smell blood out there."

"Yeah!" Ashley yells, jumping up out of her seat. "These girls are going down!"

Coach shoots me a look and I shrug at her as the team and coaches gather in a circle. We all put our hands in and yell "One, two three...Titans!" and head back to the court. I fall in next to Cassie and bump elbows with her as we jog toward the sideline.

"I think we need to work on our halftime speeches a little," I tell her over the rumbling of the crowd and the music playing over the arena's public address system.

"Did I go overboard with the whole 'killer instinct' and 'smelling blood' stuff?" she asks, giving me a smile that tells me she doesn't really care if she went overboard or not. I hold up my thumb and forefinger, leaving almost no space between the two.

"Maybe a little," I say. "But I don't think anyone's going to ask *me* to go on an inspirational speaking tour anytime soon, so..."

Cassie drapes an arm around me as we get in line for our second-half layup drill. "Well, hopefully, we'll have one more halftime tomorrow night to get our speeches right," she says.

"We *will* have one more halftime to get our speeches right," I assure her, and she takes off, catching a pass from Coach Springfeld on her way to the basket.

While our halftime speeches may kind of suck, they—combined with some adjustments in our defense—are enough for us to even the score by the end of the third quarter. We head back to the bench with our confidence high and the game momentum on our side, and Coach Denton gives us a new plan of attack as we huddle up next to the bench.

"They're getting tired, so I want everyone to run on them as much as possible. Up-tempo offense and drive the lane whenever you can—especially you, Zip. Their point guard is no match for your speed, and she definitely won't be toward the end of the game. Drive on her whenever possible, okay?"

"Got it, Coach," I tell her, and we all put our hands in before heading back out to the court.

Just as Coach ordered, we drive on them whenever we can, and I can almost feel them—and their point guard, in particular— getting more gassed by the moment, as if we're getting stronger and faster and they, already a bunch of bulky girls, are getting bigger and more sluggish as the clock winds down. I drive the lane repeatedly, as if I'm leaving my defenders standing still after draining the energy from them. Before I know it, we've started pulling away, and I'm totally feeling it—this game is ours.

We're going to win, I think to myself, running back onto the court after Harvest Light takes their final time out. *We're going to the final game.*

But as soon as the timeout ends and I'm back out on the court, I put any thoughts of having the game already wrapped up out of my head and get down to business. Behind by ten with time running out, Harvest Light has no choice but to foul once we gain possession of the ball in order to put us on the free throw line in an attempt to extend the game. Because the clock doesn't run when a team shoots free throws, the team that's behind often fouls in the hope the shooter misses. If the losing team gets the rebound, they can drive the ball down the court and attempt a quick two points—if the strategy works enough times, the team that's down can close the gap and possibly even tie the game. If the team that's ahead hits their free throws, however, then the other team ends up even further behind. Luckily for us, we're a good free throw shooting team all around and so fouling to stop the clock probably isn't going to work in Harvest Light's favor, but fouling us is their only hope to catch up with us at this point in the game.

Harvest Light inbounds the ball from the sideline, and their shooting guard puts up a quick two points from the top of the lane despite Cassie's hand being right in her face as she shoots. Ashley takes the ball out of bounds under Harvest Light's basket and one of Harvest Light's tallest players runs down to defend the inbounds pass. Their point guard is on me immediately, ready to foul as soon as the ball is in my hands, assuming Ashley throws the ball to me, that is. On the other side of the court, Cassie is jockeying for position against her defender, and Ashley will have five seconds once the referee blows the whistle to get the ball in to either her or me, depending on which one of us is in a better position to catch the ball and avoid a Harvest Light steal.

The ref blows the whistle and Ashley raises the ball above her head, pump-faking a few times to get her defender off balance as I run around, trying to stay in front of my defender in order to prevent her from stealing the ball and driving for an easy basket. I'm faster than Cassie, so I'm able to get around my defender and head for the baseline, but Ashley still has to pass high in order to clear her gargantuan defender even though I'm running toward her at the same time. Pulling up a few feet from the baseline, I bend my knees to jump and catch the ball, noticing my defender closing in so she can foul me as soon as I hit the floor. My plan—which is less of a plan and more of a split-second determination—is to plant and spin almost simultaneously, hoping my speed will get me around her before she can touch me. The move will be incredible if I can pull it off, but even if I can't, my defender will foul me and I can earn my points at the free throw line.

I jump up and snatch the ball out of the air, pulling it to my chest as I plant my feet on the court, pivot, and prepare to dribble toward our basket.

And that's when I hear the snap and feel a burning sensation in my right knee as my shoulder meets my defender's chest. I collapse in a heap, Harvest Light's point guard landing on top of me, her weight forcing my knee into the hardwood court just as I'm trying to roll over and grab my leg, some weird instinct telling me if I could only get my hands around my knee, the pain will go away. The weight on my legs disappears—because my defender has rolled off me, I suppose—but I can't turn over. I can't move, panic and fear paralyzing me, keeping my face pressed against the hardwood.

I've watched this scene before—never live, always on television—so I can imagine what's going on around me. The quieting of the crowd, the coaches rushing over from the sidelines, the players on both teams standing around watching in horror while at the same time secretly relieved *they're* not the person lying on the floor in pain right now...I've seen it all, and I know that if I can force myself to roll over so my face isn't pressed against the floor, I'll be watching it from the position of participant rather than spectator. And I'm pretty sure I won't like that particular view.

So I keep my face to the floor and close my eyes, willing this moment to pass as quickly as possible.

CHAPTER 12

I awake from a sleep so intense, my brain needs a few minutes for the fog to clear in order to function properly. At first, I think I'm at home in my room, but after I blink a few times and rub some sleep from my eyes, I realize I'm clearly somewhere else—the generic landscape paintings on the wall, the lingering smell of pine-scented dusting spray, the scratchy sheets, and Cassie snoring away next to me are enough clues for me to realize I'm in a hotel room.

My brain still full of fog, I decide to get up and stumble to the bathroom. But as soon as I attempt to move, the pain shooting through my right leg wakes me up completely.

Oh, yeah. My leg. I'm hurt. With one game left in the season—the most important game of my high school career—my season is over.

I won't know the full extent of my injury until I can undergo an MRI in Sumner once the weekend's over, but I don't need a medical procedure to tell me whatever's happened to my knee is pretty bad. Like "end-my-college-basketball-career-before-it-starts" bad. Like "brings-tears-to-your-father's-eyes" bad, because all I had to do was stare at him as he and my mom sat with me in the emergency room to understand the likely diagnosis of the pop and burn I experienced on the basketball court will be every bit as awful—if not worse—than his diagnosis after an injury on the same basketball court over twenty years ago.

"Hey." I hear Cassie's voice next to me, and I angle my head to look at her. She's giving me the same sad expression she was giving me in the days after Kieran and I broke up.

Wonderful. I'm an object of pity once again.

"How are you doing?" she croaks, her voice shredded from all the yelling during the game last night.

"Well, I need to get up to pee and I'm not sure I can, but other than *that*, I'm great."

Cassie props herself up on her elbow. "Want me to get your crutches?" she asks.

"Wasn't aware I had crutches, but sure."

"Your mom brought them up last night when we were getting you settled," she says, jumping out of bed and crossing to the corner of the room to grab a set of titanium crutches—really nice ones with gel underarm pads and grips, like the ones pro athletes use—leaning against the wall. "You were kind of out of it and there was a lot of commotion. You basically passed out as soon as you hit the bed, so I guess you had no idea when she brought them in."

The last moments I clearly remember begin with my crumpling like a rag doll on the court and Harvest Light's player struggling to pull herself off my leg. Then I closed my eyes and kind of blacked out for a few seconds, and I vaguely recall hands helping me roll over. And I sort of remember staring up at the ceiling as my coaches and teammates gathered around me and the crowd fell silent. Everything after being helped from the arena floor—going to the hospital, sitting with my parents in the emergency room, coming back to the hotel—is just bits and pieces of time shrouded in a haze of pain and confusion and tears, probably more tears than I've cried since the night I learned Kieran and Stephanie Hull were a couple.

So, yeah—the crutches are kind of a surprise.

Lauren and Ashley both mumble and stir in the other bed as they start to wake up while Cassie carries the crutches over to me. I sit up and take them from her, putting my weight on the gel underarm pads in order to pull myself up from the edge of the bed. Looking down, I take in my knee for the first time, which really doesn't seem like a knee at all at the moment—it's so swollen, it resembles a giant alien growth in the middle of my leg, the skin pulsing with angry warmth. After taking a few seconds to let my new reality sink in, I turn carefully on my crutches and try to gauge how much weight I can put on my right leg—which turns out to be not very much—and I end up performing this sort of stumble-hobble-walk combination towards the bathroom.

Part of me knows I'll get used to using the crutches eventually. The other part of me is completely sickened by the fact that I have to get used to using crutches to begin with.

Cassie follows me to the bathroom, Lauren and Ashley both mumbling "Hey," at us as we pass their bed. When I turn to shut the bathroom door, Cassie is already over the threshold and leaning against the sink.

"Um…do you need any help?" she asks sheepishly.

"With peeing? Thanks for the offer, but I think I mastered that one a long time ago."

She smirks at my joke. "I meant with…you know…holding your crutches or getting to the toilet or…"she mumbles, her voice trailing off as if she's unsure how exactly she's going to help me. And, frankly, I'm not sure what kind of help I need.

"I think I'll be okay," I tell her, unsure if I'm going to be okay at all. "Maybe you could stand outside the bathroom door and listen for me to fall over. Then call for help."

We both laugh a little. This situation is utterly ridiculous.

"I'll be right outside," she promises, shutting the door.

I manage to do my business and get myself back up with a little bit of a struggle, but once I'm standing upright again, leaning on the edge of the sink, I realize my crutches are on the floor next to the toilet. After wasting a few seconds trying to bend over and being thwarted by the pain in my knee every time, I give up.

"Cass," I say loudly. "You still out there?"

Cassie opens the door just enough I can see only her eyeball peeking in at me. "Yeah?" she squeaks.

"Come on in. I need to you to help me get my crutches."

She swings the door open and crosses behind me to pick my crutches up off the floor. "Thanks," I mumble at her as I settle into them and hobble back out to the bed, kind of at a loss as to how to get dressed and go about my day, so I instead check my text messages, finding a steady stream of condolences from people at school who heard about—or, given the fact most of the town is here, *saw*—my injury. Finally, I run across a text from my mom, telling me to text her when I wake up so she can come to my room and help me get dressed.

I turn on the TV and aimlessly flip through channels while the other girls get dressed. Once I'm alone, I text my mom and in a few minutes, she's knocking on the door. I hobble over on my crutches and am able to reach out to the door handle to let her in without toppling over, so *that's* a victory.

I suspect my victories are going to be pretty small and infrequent from now on.

Mom steps inside and lets the door shut behind her, taking my face in her hands.

"Oh, Zip," she says sadly.

"Mom...please don't, okay? Just help me shower and get dressed."

She ignores my grumpiness and helps me into the bathroom, where she reaches through the shower curtain and holds on to me while I do something in the bathtub that approximates showering. Luckily, getting dressed is a little easier since I can do most of the work sitting down. Jeans are out of the question given the size of my knee, but Mom finds a clean pair of basketball shorts in my bag and

132

so I put those on along with a Titusville Basketball sweatshirt, allowing her to help me into my socks and shoes since I don't think I can get into them on my own. She sits down on the other bed across from me and I nearly have to fight to stay upright to talk to her—the struggle involved in showering and getting dressed has made me want to go back to sleep.

"Everyone's downstairs in the atrium when you're ready for breakfast," Mom says. "Or we can call room service and eat up here, just the two of us. Whatever you want."

This morning was going to be about the only time I'd get to hang out with Dad, Kathy, Liv, and my grandparents before the team meeting and before we'd have to leave for the arena, so I don't want to skip out just because I'm having a crappy day. Granted, I'm having one of the crappiest days of my young life, but still...

"Going down to breakfast is fine," I say looking away from her, my eyes falling on the crutches on the bed next to me. "Mom, did they give these to me at the hospital? Everything about last night is kind of a blur, but these don't exactly seem like the kind of crutches they'd hand out in the emergency room, if they even hand out crutches at all."

Mom gives me a teasing smile. "They didn't come from the hospital," she begins. "They came from the one person you know who has a fortune in disposable cash and wouldn't hesitate to spend some of it on titanium crutches for you."

I narrow my eyes because I can think of only one person in my life fitting that description.

"*Cooper*? Cooper had crutches sent to the hospital?" I'm so confused. "But how did he even...did Kieran and Kayla text him or something?"

Mom smiles, shaking her head. "They didn't have to," she says. "He's here."

133

My mouth drops open as Mom continues with "I know—I was surprised, too. Apparently, he and Victor flew to Chicago yesterday and drove down for the game. They came to the hospital along with…well…pretty much everyone." She pauses, reaching over to smooth my bangs off my forehead. "I went out to the waiting room for a few minutes while the doctors were checking you out, and the place was full of Titusville people, the team included. I don't know if you realize how much people care about you."

I just shrug because I have no idea what to say. I'm kind of overwhelmed.

"Kieran was there, too, by the way," Mom adds. "He stayed until we brought you back here."

I don't know what to say to that, either, so I don't say anything.

"Anyway," Mom continues, "Cooper brought the crutches to me after you were released and we'd gotten you back to the hotel. No idea how he managed to find titanium crutches at eight o'clock at night, but…"

"Cooper's magical," I say, joking.

"I'm guessing it's easy to be magical when you're worth billions."

I snort, and Mom finishes detailing the events of last night that I don't remember. "I brought the crutches up so you'd have them to help you get around this morning, but you were already so out of it I couldn't tell you," she says.

"Well, remind me to thank Cooper when I see him," I tell her.

"You can thank him right now," she says. "He's downstairs with everyone."

"Guess we might as well head downstairs, then." I rub my stomach. "I'm kind of hungry now that I think about it."

Mom and I take the elevator to the first floor, and once we've passed the check-in desk in the lobby, I see Kieran trotting around the atrium with Liv on his back as Cooper and Victor stand off to the side near a miniature waterfall, laughing at them.

"I'm going into the restaurant to find Gram and Gramps," Mom says. "You'll be okay on your own?"

I nod at the activity in the atrium. "Looks like I won't be alone for long," I tell her. "I'll catch up with you later."

She heads off for the restaurant as I push myself forward into the atrium. As soon as she notices me, Liv slides off Kieran's back and rushes forward to meet me.

"Hey, Zip." She goes to hug me but stops, looking at the bulbous welt on my leg where my knee used to be. "Wow, your knee is really gross."

I love little kids and their unlimited capacity for honesty.

"Yeah, it is pretty gross. I'll probably need to ice it some more later."

"How are you?" Kieran asks me as he comes up behind Liv, his voice full of concern.

"I'm okay," I tell him, mostly because I don't have the words to convey how I really feel. In fact, I'm not even *sure* how I really feel because since I was so out of it last night, I've only been fully conscious of my injury for a little over an hour. At some point, I'm going to have to think through what shredding my knee means for my present and my future, but right now, standing here in front of the love of my life, isn't the time. So I continue our conversation with "So, I see my sister's been keeping you busy."

"I was actually third in line," he explains. "She's worn Victor and Cooper out already."

"Liv," I say, my voice scolding, but I'm smiling to let her know I'm kidding.

135

"I'm not wearing them out," she insists. "They *wanted* to play. Honest."

"And your dad wanted us to meet him in the lobby at nine-thirty so you could eat breakfast," Kieran says to her. "Want a piggy-back ride to the elevators?"

Kieran bends at the knees and Liv responds by molding herself to his back.

"Have fun," I say to him, laughing as the two of them trot off toward the lobby. I turn toward the waterfall, and both Victor and Cooper wave at me as I crutch myself over.

"Hey, Zip," Cooper says, reaching out to squeeze my shoulder as Victor nods and says "Ms. McKee."

"This is a nice surprise," I say to them. "You two are about the last people I expected to find here."

"What can I say? I'm a huge fan of girls' basketball." Cooper shrugs and I arch an eyebrow, which prompts him to admit, "Yeah—who am I kidding? I'm just a huge fan of girls in general."

"Thought so."

"And, seriously though, what is up with those baggy shorts you guys wear when you play?" he asks, his brow wrinkling with near disgust. "You could make parachutes out of those things they're so big. Totally not sexy."

Victor and I roll our eyes at each other. "We're going more for comfort than fashion," I explain, although I'm sure Cooper already understands that.

"Well, anyway, once Kieran texted me about your team making the state finals, I decided I wanted to watch you play for once, even if your uniforms aren't very hot," he says. "Good game last night, by the way." He pauses and nods down at my knee. "You know, until *that*."

"Yeah," I begin, tilting my head toward my right crutch, "I understand I owe you some thanks."

"You mean for the crutches or for getting Kieran to break up with his girlfriend?"

"Um...excuse me?" I ask, blinking. Other than what Kieran told me at the river the day we went out driving around, I realize I'd never heard much more about Kieran and Steph's breakup. Kayla's never said anything to me, which I took to mean Kieran didn't share any details with her.

"I think I'm going to let you handle this one, sir," Victor says, patting Cooper on the shoulder and turning in the direction of the pool.

"Where are you going?" Cooper demands.

"Just going to take a walk, sir," Victor tosses back. "You're on your own with this one." He glances more toward me than Cooper as he makes his last statement—"I had nothing to do with it."

Victor starts walking off as Cooper calls out at his back "You know, you're supposed to be my personal assistant. I could use an assist here, Laughlin," but Victor doesn't turn around and instead raises his hand up near his ear and waves back at us. "Un...believable." Cooper shakes his head. "You get cured of a sleeping disorder and suddenly the guy thinks you can do *everything* for yourself. I mean, what am I even paying him for?"

"Cooper," I say, a note of warning in my voice, and he sits down on the rock wall lining the pool in front of the mini waterfall, patting the space next to him. Using my crutches to bear my weight, I lower myself to the rock with Cooper's help and lean the crutches next to me.

"So, Carlie called me about a week after Kieran started dating...Stephanie? Was that her name?"

I nod.

137

"Well, anyway, as soon as Carlie told me about Kieran breaking up with you, I was ready to fly to Illinois and smack some sense into him. I mean, breaking up with you was *not* an option."

I laugh. "You sound like Kayla," I tell him. "I appreciate the loyalty, but the two of you seriously underestimate what Kieran can and can't do."

"I just meant that he obviously had no idea what he was doing breaking up with you." I open my mouth to add to what he's said, but he raises a hand, cutting me off before I can get anything out. "And I know he *literally* has no idea what he's doing as far as anything's concerned right now. Trust me—I get that better than anyone else. But somebody needed to tell him what he was walking away from. And somebody needed to tell him this other girl was only going to get hurt because she had no idea what she was getting herself into, and then he'd end up hurting *two* girls for the price of one."

"I think Kayla and their parents made the same arguments," I point out. "So how come he was willing to listen to you and not them?"

Cooper pats me on the shoulder and gives me his lizard-like grin. "Oh, Zip, Zip, Zip," he begins, his voice dripping with condescension. "You're forgetting I'm the only person on the planet who truly understands what Kieran's going through right now. Remember what I was like after I underwent the treatment?"

"A zombie?" I can't help myself.

"I'm talking after the zombie period," he says, smirking at me. "Remember how I kind of wanted to do everything all at once? I wanted to leap tall buildings in a single bound, I was so happy to be free of that stupid sleeping disorder. And that's all this thing was with Kieran and this other girl. He doesn't remember anything about you and he doesn't want to hurt you, so he sets you free because he

138

thinks he's doing you a favor. But then this other girl asks him out, and he doesn't want to stop living his life, so he takes her up on it."

"So, all you said was basically the same stuff the Laniers said to him, only he believed it more coming from you?" I ask, wanting to make sure I understand.

"Sort of. I mean, I'm just more credible." Cooper pauses, shifting his eyes away from mine. "Plus, I think I kind of led him to believe I'm really into you."

Cooper's eyes meet mine again, and he allows his usual lizard grin to take over his entire face.

"Oh, my God," I mumble, lowering my head to my hands. I'm still covering my face when Cooper's arm slides around my shoulders, pulling me closer to him. I drop my hands from my eyes and try to force my body in the opposite direction, but Cooper's sheer size and strength draw me into an awkward sideways embrace, my head resting on his shoulder.

I realize a lot of girls would find my current situation to be pretty awesome, but I've never been attracted to Cooper as anything more than a friend. And even being friends with him took some time and effort, all of which he's about to erase with his little routine here.

"Um…Coop…I…"

My awkward mini-protest is cut off by Cooper's laughter. "Calm down, sweetheart. I'm not hitting on you," he insists. "Don't flatter yourself."

He relaxes his grip and I sit up, punching him hard in the shoulder, which only makes him laugh even more because he's so solidly built that a punch from me probably feels like nothing more than a love tap.

"You're such an amazing ass, you know that?" I tell him.

"I'm well aware," he says before sobering up. "But, seriously, though—in some parallel universe where Kieran doesn't exist, or

139

where Kieran exists but you're not in love with him? I'd totally try to hook up with you."

"Thanks?" I say, and Cooper smirks at my refusal to accept his compliment, which seems like less of a compliment coming from him and more like a bad pick-up line.

"Come on, Zip. I know you don't believe this because it's coming from me, but a guy would be crazy not to want to hook up with you. Why do you think I hit on you that night in Asheville when all I really needed to do was make contact with Kieran?"

"Because you're an amazing ass?"

"Because you're *you*," he says, ignoring my repeated insult. "I realize you don't get this because you've been going to school with the same group of losers since Kindergarten, but you're totally hot. That's apparent on first sight. And then I started talking to you and you immediately called me on my bullshit? Girls don't understand how that's pretty much like throwing gasoline on a fire. Tell a guy he can't have something and he'll want it even more."

I open my mouth to say something—I'm not sure what—but it doesn't matter as Cooper holds up a hand to stop me.

"But now, I've been around you and Kieran enough to know you two are meant for each other," he continues. "And Kieran's one of the best friends I've ever had. Even though he doesn't remember he's in love with you right now, hitting on his girl wouldn't be a cool thing to do."

"So why make him believe you have a thing for me?"

Cooper reaches out to put his hand on my shoulder again, but this time, I brush him off.

"I'm not sure if you're aware of this," he starts, ignoring my hostility, "but guys are kind of dumb."

Gasping, I say, "Get out. Seriously?" with mock surprise, and he just glares at me.

140

"Like I said, tell a guy he can't have something, or tell him everyone else wants something he wants, too, and he'll only want that thing—or person—even more. I could tell he was only into this other girl because *she* asked *him* out, and he was curious. But you...he's been reading about everything you two went through together. He knows on paper how great you are, and he's starting to get a sense of that in person. So, now he's curious about *you*, so I think hearing me go on and on about you—plus begging him not to hurt this other girl—is what's keeping you in the game right now." He glances down at my knee. "Sorry—bad analogy."

I roll my eyes at him. "So, you basically manipulated him into breaking up with Steph and being interested in me," I say, sighing. "Just what I want—a guy who's been tricked into wanting to be with me."

"Don't think about it like that," Cooper encourages me, his voice softening. "Think about it as me buying you some time."

"Buying me some time?"

Cooper nods, angling himself toward me. "I'm not telling you anything you don't already know when I say that at this point, we have no idea if Kieran's memory is ever coming back," he says. "It's been over two months, and he hasn't remembered anything. And I'm assuming you're still in love with him anyway."

"Of course," I say quietly.

"So, like I said, I bought you some more time. Hang in there and don't give up on him, okay?" Cooper implores me, and I feel like I'm in the locker room getting a pep talk, an experience I suddenly realize that, given the current state of my knee, I may never have again. "He's still Kieran. The guy you fell in love with is still in there somewhere. Let him fall in love with you again. Whether his memory comes back to him or not, you two are going to find your way back to each other somehow—I just know it."

141

"I never would have guessed you to be such a romantic," I tease. And "romantic" definitely isn't a label I would have hung on him after his attempt at a real relationship with Maisie Baker, America's favorite red-headed pop star and Cooper's partner-in-crime in a pairing manufactured for the tabloids, didn't quite materialize when she returned from the Japanese leg of her current world tour.

Cooper runs a hand through his sandy brown hair and stares at me intensely. "I'm not a romantic. I'm a realist," he pronounces. "And—whether I like it or not—I'm supposedly a future businessman, so I like things that make good sense. And I've been around you and Kieran enough to know you make good sense. You balance each other out—yin and yang, peanut butter and jelly, you get the idea. Where he's going off half-assed and doing crazy stuff without thinking about it—especially now that he can—you're more level headed and you think things through. You're both smart, but he's more creative and you're more book-smart and sports-smart— you know, analytical."

I think back to my discussion with Kieran in English class the day we were going over our Martin Luther King, Jr. essays, and I have to laugh to myself that Cooper's observed the same thing in us— the creative versus the analytical.

"In investment terms, you and Kieran are what I'd term an 'acceptable risk.' In other words, you're a safe bet, and I'm betting whether or not Kieran ever remembers anything about the relationship you had before January, he's going to end up falling for you all over again." Cooper pauses and lowers his voice, looking at me up and down in a way that, for once, doesn't feel to me like he's a reptile sizing up his prey. "I mean, how could he not?"

Cooper and I stare at each other for a few seconds before I blink to break the spell, saying "Thanks, Coop. I hope you're right."

"Oh, I'm right. I'm always right." A pause. "Well, I'm right, like, eighty-five percent of the time, anyway. Remember what I said about acceptable risks."

I laugh. "And thanks for the crutches, too, by the way," I tell him. "Unfortunately, I think I'm going to be needing these for a while."

"My pleasure. I figure if you can't play like a pro, you might as well be injured like one, right?"

"Oddly enough, Coop, hearing that makes me feel better somehow," I tell him, and I'm being serious.

Cooper laughs and puts his arm around me again, but this time, I'm not creeped out. We sit close together for a few minutes until we see Victor approaching us.

"Vic, what do you say we take this poor girl to breakfast?" Cooper suggests once Victor's close enough to hear. "She's going to need some fuel if she wants to help her team win a championship tonight."

"Cooper," I say, a sad note to my voice.

"Hey," he says, squeezing my shoulder. "You're still part of the team, right?"

"Yeah."

"And you're still going to be at the game tonight, right?"

"Yes," I say, mildly annoyed.

"Then you're going to be helping your team. Maybe not in the way you're used to, but still…" I roll my eyes at his pep talk, but that doesn't stop him from continuing. "Even if you're on the bench, you're still a part of the team. And no matter what happens, you need to eat, right? I mean, I know *I* can't go for more than a few hours without food, so…"

"I get the point, Coop," I say, cutting him off. "And I'm totally starving, so I'm not going to argue if you guys want to buy me breakfast."

Victor leans over and offers me a hand so I can get to my feet and, with his arm around me, he reaches down to the rock wall to retrieve my crutches. Once I'm steady under my own power, the three of us head for the lobby restaurant, where as soon as we walk in, we see Kieran dining with his parents. We all exchange waves and Kieran doesn't stop staring at me and smiling, and I do the same until the hostess comes up to direct us to a table. The restaurant is crowded enough that she has to seat us on the other side of the room from the Laniers, and I can't even find my dad, Kathy, and Liv, nor can I find my grandparents and my mom. I take the seat facing away from the Laniers because it's the only one at the table that offers enough room for me to stretch out my legs and put my crutches on the floor without tripping anybody. I feel like I've turned into a giant speed bump, at risk of slowing down the rest of the world until it's hobbling right alongside me.

A perky blonde ponytailed waitress comes up to get our drink orders, and a lizard grin immediately settles on Cooper's lips and doesn't leave, even after the waitress walks away and he turns his grin on me.

"Sizing up your next conquest?" I ask him with a sugary smile.

"What?"

"The waitress. I figured she's the reason for that look on your face."

Cooper somehow manages to smirk and lizard-grin all at the same time—he's talented. "Whatever look I have on my face, it's because I've been watching Kieran," he informs me. "And Kieran hasn't stopped staring at the back of your head for a second since we sat down."

"Really?" I say to Cooper before glancing at Victor for confirmation.

"Really, Ms. McKee," Victor responds. "Mr. Lanier has kept his eyes on you this entire time."

I'm tempted to turn in my chair and stare at Kieran, but I realize that would seem pretty nerdy and not very subtle, and so I stop myself, focusing my attention on Cooper instead. Cooper's still working the lizard grin while he uses his spoon and fork to drum out a tune on the tabletop.

"It's just like I said, Zip," he begins, tapping out a staccato rhythm. "Acceptable risk. Remember that."

CHAPTER 13

Losing Kieran has been hard—one of the hardest things I've ever been through—but I've only known him for a little over a year. I've been playing basketball practically since I could walk, and sitting here on the bench while my teammates play for a championship, something I've worked and wished for ever since I knew what a championship was, well...

Well, I'll be totally honest. It's killing me. I've watched hundreds, maybe thousands, of basketball games over the years, but I've never had the emotional investment in a game that I do in this one. Every other time I've been a spectator, whether watching a pro game on TV or watching the Titusville boys play in our gym, I've been able to view the game with a sort of detachment, the thrill disappearing after the final buzzer just as quickly as the anticipation mounted before tip-off.

But tonight, this team I'm watching is my team. These players are my girls. I'm supposed to be their leader, their co-captain, their floor general.

Instead, I'm sitting at the end of the bench in my uniform—which I insisted on wearing rather than street clothes so I would still feel like part of the team. My leg is slightly elevated and I have an ice pack strapped around my knee, but instead of holding a basketball, I'm wielding a clipboard and a pen so I can help keep game stats.

I'm utterly heartbroken. And for once, my broken heart has nothing to do with Kieran.

Shortly after tip-off, I become even more heartbroken because this game is evidently going to be a cakewalk, and the old, healthy Zip McKee could have put up some amazing stats. We're up against St. Elizabeth Ann Seton, a small Catholic school just outside Chicago who spend most of their season playing against some tough city competition. But they quickly prove to be no match for our size and speed, and as the clock ticks away the last seconds of the first quarter, we're up on them by fifteen points. When the buzzer sounds to end the quarter, the team huddles up at the bench, and before they head back to the court, Tori Sandowsky comes down to talk to me.

"Any suggestions, Coach?" she asks, smiling and breathing heavily. Since she's not used to playing as much as I am, her in-game conditioning isn't as good.

"Yeah. First of all, breathe. Deep breaths. In, out. In, out."

Tori smirks and whips me in my good leg with her towel.

"Seriously, though, you guys look like world-beaters out there. So for the most part, just keep doing what you're doing," I tell her.

"For the most part?"

"Well…" I hate to be critical, but I did promise her in the locker room I would watch her and give suggestions on her game. "Seton's point guard is left-handed, and it's obviously her strongest side, so she's going to try to drive that way as much as possible. But when she switches to her right, she doesn't protect the ball too well." I try to mimic a dribbling motion as best I can sitting down, and I mime letting the ball drift away from my body rather than dribbling close into the body as one is supposed to. "She lets the ball get away from her a little. Cut off her left side to make her switch and try to drive right, and you should be able to get a steal on her every time until she figures you out."

"Thanks," Tori breathes, reaching down to slap hands with me.

"Go out there and bring it home," I yell at her back as she tosses her towel on the floor near me and heads to the court.

My strategy for Tori works for most of the second quarter, as she's able to score six points off turnovers she forces on Seton's point guard. Seton will probably readjust at the half, making Tori's stealing strategy obsolete. But unless Seton's other halftime adjustments include transforming into the Chicago Bulls, I don't think we're going to squander our lead, which has swelled to thirty points.

When we take the court again for the second half, Cassie stands with me at the bench for a moment before heading out to shoot around.

"Sucks our crowd is getting such a crappy game," she says to me.

I survey the collection of Titusville humanity and assorted non-Titusville team relatives. Most people are bopping around and clapping along to the rap song being played over the arena's public address system. Considering a good chunk of the crowd is made up of parents, grandparents, and teachers, the display is pretty hysterical, and I hope somebody's recording all of this because the footage would make some good blackmail material once we're back in Titusville. The under-thirty crowd, meanwhile, is yelling out cheers, led by our cheerleading squad on the floor and by the boys' basketball team in the stands, the boys all painted navy blue and gold and dressed only in skimpy navy swim trunks.

"Somehow, I don't think anyone minds," I tell her. "But I think we're all going to be wishing we could unsee what the boys' team looks like right now."

Cassie laughs and points at them in the stands where Jake Tomlinson, who's definitely built more for football than basketball, waves back at her, his gut spilling over the waistband of his barely-there trunks.

"I think I'm going to have nightmares about Jake until I'm well into my twenties," Cassie says, still waving at Jake. I start

148

laughing so hard tears spring to my eyes as Cassie takes the court with the rest of the team.

While Seton definitely adjusted to Tori's defense for the second half—mainly through the tactic of switching point guards—the Lady Titans have already inflicted too much damage. No matter what players Seton subs in against us, we're able to score at will, and our defense holds them to eight points in the third quarter. As the buzzer sounds and the team jogs to the bench, for the first time all night, my sadness is replaced by anger. I'm pissed I'm not playing. I'm pissed I'm not putting up the best stats of my career—I bet I could have hung forty points on this team. I'm pissed that any college scouts here aren't seeing a dazzling display of my basketball skills and won't be dropping to their knees after the game, begging me to come play for them. I'm...

The fourth quarter begins, and while Coach keeps Tori in to run the point, she subs out all of our starters, playing the girls who are likely to be on the starting five next year. I realize Coach is doing this to show some mercy toward Seton, but they're so outmatched they aren't able to do much better against our second string. Coach puts Lauren, Ashley, and Cassie back in for the final minute of the game so the team can run out the clock with the seniors—except for me, of course—on the court. The Titusville side of the arena counts down with the clock from ten seconds, and as the buzzer sounds and Tori throws the ball up in the air, the entire place seems to explode with noise. My teammates all rush to the center of the court, dogpiling on top of Tori in a celebration I want to be a part of more than anything.

But I can't.

I push myself on my crutches out to the edge of the pile and start hoping on one foot next to the coaching staff, who are exchanging hugs. The pile breaks up and the tears and hugging start, the first person to throw her arms around me being Cassie.

"We did it!" she screams at me, and my heart plunges to my toes.

"I didn't do anything," I yell.

She breaks our hug and stands back from me far enough to look me in the face. "You did *everything*," she tells me, her hands gripping my shoulders. "You're the greatest player in Titusville history. We're not here right now without you, got it? Don't ever forget that."

I choke down the sob working its way up my throat at her words right before Ashley jumps on Cassie's back, nearly causing all three of us to topple over. Thankfully, my crutches keep me upright, and the coaching staff starts herding us off the court so the arena staff can set up for the trophy and medal presentation.

After a few minutes, the staff has moved a raised platform to the middle of the floor, and the team and I sit on the bench, listening and clapping politely as the Seton players receive their second-place medals and as their head coach collects the second-place trophy. After a brief pause while Seton's coach makes her way back to the bench, the public address announcer introduces us as State Champions, and the arena erupts in cheers. One by one, the announcer calls out our names in alphabetical order so we can go up to the platform and receive our medals. The first of my fellow seniors announced is Ashley, and she jogs up on stage, bowing her head to the state official so he can hang the medal around her neck. Before she walks off, Ashley waves at our crowd with both hands high in the air.

Next alphabetically is sophomore guard Andie Loring, and then it's my turn. "Zara McKee," the public address announcer booms, and I hobble up the two stairs to reach the platform and swing myself over to the state official she can place my new hardware

150

around my neck. The medal is heavier than I expected, and I almost forget where I am for a moment, keeping my head down so I can study it where it rests just below my breastbone. But the cheers from the crowd pull me out of my head, and I want to wave to everyone as Ashley did, but I realize I can't if I want to avoid falling flat on my ass. So, instead, I lean all my weight on my left side and swing my right crutch out to my side in a kind of wave, but I only have the strength to do so for about a second before I have to pull the crutch back in close to my body. Feeling like a fool, I make my way to the other side of the platform where Andie's waiting to help me down.

Once each girl on the team has received her medal, Coach Denton heads up to the stage to claim the championship trophy, the first of its kind in any sport in the history of Titusville High School. She holds the trophy, which is as long as her torso and about half as wide, high above her head as the crowd erupts in cheers and applause. After she makes her way back to the floor, the team and the coaching staff practically maul her, everyone trying to touch the trophy.

Everyone but me, that is. I stay on the outside of the scrum so I don't risk getting pushed over by accident. Once the frenzy dies down a little, we're subjected to what seems like an endless round of team pictures with the trophy, and for once in my life, I'm standing in the back row because I have to instead of kneeling or sitting in the front because I'm one of the shortest girls on the team. After both the professional and parent photographers have had enough, the team heads off to the locker room for our last post-game debriefing of the season—and, for four of us, of our high school careers. I take a seat in a folding chair in the front row of the vast locker room so I can stretch my leg out, and I'm shoving my crutches underneath the seat when someone taps me on my shoulder.

"I think you're the only one who hasn't spent any quality time with this yet," Coach says to me, holding the championship trophy out with both hands. "Why don't you hang on to this for me during the team meeting."

I take the trophy from her and clutch it to my chest. The trophy's heavier than I thought it would be, and not too easy to hold—with the trophy resting in my lap, I can barely peer over the top of it—but this thing is something I've worked for my entire life and I'm thrilled to have it in my possession, if only temporarily, and even if I believe I played no part in the game that brought the trophy to my team.

Cassie bumps me in the shoulder and smiles as I hang on to the trophy for dear life, and I zone out during most of Coach's speech, thinking about how we, this exact group of fourteen girls sitting here right now, will never do this again. We will never take the court together again as a team, and we will never compete for another championship.

My Titusville basketball career is now nothing but memories, along with a bunch of plaques and trophies for the glass case in the school's main hallway. And my basketball career in general is probably over, thanks to my stupid knee.

After Coach finishes her speech and takes the trophy back from me, my teammates start yelling and celebrating and goofy dancing, and I make a good show of having fun, even getting into the dance circle and hopping around on my crutches and good leg for a few seconds, but I'm not really in the mood to celebrate. Now that everything's over and done with, I sort of just want everything over and done with for good because despite what Cassie said to me on the court, I feel like I have nothing to do with this victory at all.

Everybody finally calms down, and we head to the team bus to go back to the hotel, the mess of Titusville humanity still in the parking lot honking and waving and cheering at us as we pull away. At the hotel, team relatives swarm the lobby, but I don't need to search for long to find my family, particularly since adding in the Laniers, Brad, Morgan, Victor, and Cooper means I have nearly an entire fan club here with me.

"I want to wear your medal," Liv demands before anyone else can descend on me, and I bow down as best I can on my crutches so she can slip the medal over my head. She puts it on, its weight bouncing against her stomach.

"This is so cool," she tells me.

"I know, huh?"

"Liv, make sure you give that back to Zip in a few minutes, okay?" Kathy says to her, casting an apologetic glance my way.

"She's fine," I tell Kathy, as Liv bounds off toward my dad so she can show him my new treasure. Meanwhile, everyone else gathers around me for hugs and congratulations, neither of which I deserve right now.

It's after eleven, which is late for most of the adults, and gradually, the horde of people in the lobby thins out. Liv gives my medal back to me before heading upstairs with Dad and Kathy, and as I bend down as much as I'm able to give her what passes for a hug on these crutches, I notice Cassie, Lauren, and Ashley heading off for the elevators, probably on their way up to our room. I'm guessing not much sleeping will go on tonight given how wired they—and everyone else on the team, for that matter—have all been since the game ended. The thought of staying up all night celebrating something I wasn't a part of exhausts me and I'm tempted to go upstairs and ask if I can spend the night with my mom.

"So, what now?" Kayla asks, looking at the group of us who are left—Brad, Kieran, Victor, Cooper, and me. "Everything's closed."

Cooper shrugs. "I guess Victor could pick us up a couple of six-packs and we could party upstairs in our suite," he suggests.

Victor, ever unflappable, rubs the stubble on his tan domed noggin and answers with "I don't think that would be advisable, sir, since you're all underage."

"Vic," Cooper begins, patting him on the back. "I meant six-packs of *soda*, and by 'party,' I meant 'hang out in our room and watch movies.'"

"Of course you did, sir," he replies, exchanging glances with me, and I can't help but laugh.

"Guess hanging out upstairs sounds as good as anything," Brad says with a shrug, putting his arm around Kayla. The rest of the group, resigned to the fact that there's not much else to do, turns toward the elevators, but I don't move.

"You know, I think I might stay down here for a while," I say, and everyone turns around.

"By yourself?" Kayla asks.

"There are still people around," I point out, although the atrium is nearly empty. A group of older people I don't recognize, probably among the few non-Titusville people staying in this hotel, is sitting at a table outside the pool area, but otherwise, no one else is on the first floor.

"You're sure?" Brad asks, and the look of concern on his face is similar to the look on everyone else's faces right now. They all think I'm crazy.

"Yeah…I'm just going to…." I'm going to *what*? "I'm going to hang out by the waterfall and relax for a while."

Wow—that sounds really stupid, but I want to be alone and I can't think of any other excuse.

"Okay," Cooper says, his expression softening into understanding. "Well, text or call or something when you're ready to hang out. We'll all be upstairs in my suite."

"I'll be up in a little bit—I promise," I assure everyone. "I think I need to clear my head for a while and be somewhere quiet, and I'm pretty sure my room would be anything *but* quiet right now. Tonight's been a long night, you know?"

"Yeah," Kayla says, patting me on the back. "We'll see you in a while. Text me if you need anything, okay?"

I nod and take off toward the fountain, carefully lowering myself to the rock wall surrounding the pool and setting my crutches on the carpet next to me. Stretching my leg out, I find I can still lean over and run my hand through the water, but I can't reach far enough to scoop up any of the pennies resting on the bottom. I'm so mesmerized by the sensation of my hand gliding through the water and the sound of the waterfall crashing against the pool's surface over and over that when Kieran comes up behind me and says "Hey," I nearly lose my balance and keel over.

"Sorry," he says, grabbing my shoulder to steady me. He steps over my crutches and sits down next to me on the rock wall. "Didn't mean to scare you."

"It's okay," I assure him. "I didn't hear you coming."

He nods. "I know you said you wanted to be alone, but I thought I should check on you. If you want me to go, just say the word," he says, leaning forward as if he's expecting I'll tell him to leave and he'll need to get up.

I'll take being alone with Kieran over being alone with myself at the moment, mostly because any time I spend with Kieran could put us closer to being back where we used to be. And where we used to be seems a whole lot better than where I am right now.

"Stay," I tell him. "I could use the company, I guess. I just didn't want *tons* of company, you know? Especially tons of loud, boisterous company, which is probably the mood everyone else is in."

"I know. And I think I kind of get what you're going through right now." He glances down at my knee. "At least some of it, anyway. I watched you a lot during the game and after, and in the lobby just now, and…well, you're kind of acting like how I feel most days."

"Depressed?"

He shrugs. "*Depressed* might be too strong a word," he says, rubbing his knuckles along his chin as he thinks. "*Lost*, maybe? I'm lost most of the time."

"Sounds about right," I say as I start to think through the implications of the word *lost*. "It's kind of like I don't know what's supposed to happen to me now. And maybe I would have felt this way after the game even if I had been able to play tonight…I don't know. Either way, tonight would have been the end of something. But how it went down doesn't seem like the *right* ending, you know?"

"Because you didn't play," Kieran says more than asks.

"Yeah," I run my hand through the water again. "And I hate myself for thinking that. The team deserves the championship, regardless of whether or not I'd been able to play. But I'd dreamt of winning State my entire life, and I had all these images in my head of how the game would go, what shots I would make, stuff like that. Nobody ever pictures having to sit on the bench with a busted knee not being able to do anything at all."

"And so you're lost because…" Kieran prompts.

I can tell my face is screwing up as I think because I'm not really sure I understand why I'm feeling the way I do, and I'm definitely not sure I can vocalize those emotions. "Because I'm not the person who can't be happy for her teammates because they won a

156

championship—that's not who I am. Because if this injury is as bad as I think it is, I might never play basketball again, and I've always played basketball. Because I don't know where I'm going to college and, again, if this injury is as bad as I think it is, some of my college choices are off the table." I pause for a moment, not sure I should say aloud the next phrase bubbling up into my brain, but everything's so awful already, I decide to go ahead. "Because nothing about my life except basketball has been normal since December, and now even that isn't normal anymore."

He looks away from me and drags his hand through the water. "Well, from what people tell me, nothing about my life has been normal since December, either, so we have that in common, I guess," he says.

"We have a lot in common," I tell him, my voice quiet. "You just don't remember it."

I wish I could take that statement back as soon as it's out of my mouth. Apparently, the evening's events have inspired me to Kayla Lanier levels of bitchery.

"I'm sorry," I whisper. "That was a really mean thing to say."

"No, it wasn't," he says, still raking his hand across the water's surface. "And I'm sorry, too. I'm sorry all this stuff going on with me has been so hard on you." He takes his hand from the water and wipes it on his jeans before standing to reach into his front jeans pocket, pulling out a small handful of change. "Here," he says, sliding a penny forward with his thumb from the pile in his palm. "Make a wish. Maybe the possibility of getting something you want will help."

I give him a little smile and take the penny from him, rolling it over in my fingers as I contemplate my wish and then sliding the penny to my thumbnail before flipping it into the water.

"So what did you wish for?" Kieran asks, his grin overtaking his lips.

"Well, if I tell you, it won't come true."

"That's okay," he says, still grinning. "I think I may already know what it is."

We are quiet for a long minute, listening to the rush of the waterfall behind us and dragging our hands through the water, our fingertips almost touching a few times, but not quite.

"Zip," Kieran says at last. "Don't beat yourself up because you can't be happy right now—for your team, I mean. You'll get over that. Those girls are your friends, and you've been a part of that team for years. I mean, you played with them even before high school, right?"

"Yeah. I've played with some of them since grade school."

"And I went to all those games since January and I saw how good you are and all the points you scored," he continues. "So, when you think about it, the team wouldn't be where they are right now without you, right?"

I remember Cassie saying something similar in the chaos that was the after-game celebration, but her words hadn't really sunk in for me until now.

"Right," I say quietly. "Deep down, I guess I know that. It just kills me to know I couldn't see the season through to the end. That'll take me awhile to get over, I think."

"Understandable," he says, and another long silence settles over us, but Kieran's eyes narrow as if he's wondering about something and so I can't help but ask "What?"

"You said nothing about your life except basketball has been normal since December. So, I was thinking, let's go back to the past for a while. Let's pretend it's December."

I give him a nervous laugh. "Okay," I start, "So, how do we pretend it's December? Ask the hotel to put up a Christmas tree?"

"No, since they probably wouldn't," he says. "I'm wondering, though, if we had been sitting here back in December, what would we probably be doing right now?"

I think back to us sitting on the steps of St. Patrick's Cathedral on Christmas Eve night, kissing each other as the snow started to come down.

I decide not to mention the kissing and take my chances with something a little less intense.

"We'd probably be holding hands," I tell him.

Without a word, Kieran takes my hand in his and rests them together between us on the rock. And we sit next to each other, hand in hand, for a very long time, listening to the waterfall rushing behind us.

CHAPTER 14

I never dreamed I'd spend my eighteenth birthday hobbling around school on crutches and asking my teachers to give me as many future assignments as possible so I can keep up while I'm housebound after my knee surgery, but here I am, living my own personal April Fools' joke. By the time my lunch period starts, I'm so exhausted I just want to get through the rest of the day, go home, and collapse, but Cassie has other ideas.

"Sooo, what are your plans for tonight?" she asks, sliding into the seat next to me and placing a paper plate with one of the cafeteria's dried-out brownies in front of me. Kayla does the same to Kieran and reaches into her backpack and comes up with two candles, wedging one into each of our brownies. Kieran laughs at her and says "Thanks," while Cassie props her chin up on her knuckles and blinks, waiting for me to respond to her question.

"I was going to sit around and watch documentaries about people who wake up in the middle of surgery," I say flatly. Kayla rolls her eyes at me—she's had to listen to me complain non-stop about how scared I am to go under the knife, but I'm sure she's enjoyed every minute of making fun of me for being such a big baby.

And I reserve the right to be a big baby because, for all intents and purposes, my basketball career is over. The MRI on my knee showed damage to the ACL, the MCL, and the meniscus, making my injury even more devastating than the one my dad suffered so many years ago. The tears from turning and pivoting on the court would have been bad enough on their own, but falling and slamming my knee into the floor plus the added insult of having Harvest Light's bruising point guard land on top of my leg was essentially the equivalent of having a linebacker plow into my knee on the football field, according to my doctors. Even if I am able to play ball again, I'm going to be out of commission for a long, long time.

Cassie rolls her eyes on my admission that I'm going to sit around at home tonight and mope. "I know your surgery's tomorrow, but it's your *birthday*," she insists as if I'm unaware of this information, and then she turns to Kieran. "Yours, too. You guys should do something fun. And as it just so happens, Cody's parents are out of town for the weekend. You know what that means."

I glance across the table at Cody, who raises an expectant eyebrow at me.

"Hmmm…let me think. It means you have to get dressed all by yourself while Mommy's away?" I tease, and he throws a tater tot at me, which I dodge and so it lands on the floor against the wall.

"*It means*," Cody begins, giving me a sharp look, "I'm having a big blowout at the farm. Two kegs, a bonfire, the whole deal."

"Oh, well, if you're having *two* kegs, I'm in. Just one was going to be a total deal breaker," I say.

I think I've been to maybe three parties in almost four years of high school, mostly because I'm not into the whole drinking scene, and also because I've never found sitting around in someone's basement or standing around a bonfire on someone's farm to be all that exciting—maybe that's why heavy drinking is a necessity at these things.

"Don't worry. I bought soda, too, for all the lightweights, so you won't have to risk any Demon Liquor crossing your lips," Cody assures me with a sugary smile, which I mimic in response.

"Careful, Cody," Rick starts, "I think if Zip McKee actually shows up at a party, it means the Apocalypse is coming."

"Well, far be it from me to hold back the Apocalypse," I say through a breath. Today *is* my eighteenth birthday after all, and hanging out with people would probably be a lot more fun than spending the first night of my adult life sitting around obsessing about my surgery.

I glance over at Kieran, who's picking at his brownie. "What do you say?" I ask him. "Are you up for helping me jump-start the Apocalypse on our birthday?"

Everyone else at the table seems to be leaning forward and holding their collective breath, as if they're expecting Kieran to say "Yes," and the two of us will immediately get back together and start making out on the tabletop in the midst of all their trays and cellophane wrappers.

"Why not?" Kieran shrugs. "Bring on the hellfire and damnation." He glances at Kayla and then back at me. "I'll even drive all of us."

"No way." Kayla shakes her head so swiftly she practically leaves vapor trails in the air. "You are not driving *my* vehicle."

Kieran ignores her. "We'll pick you up. Driver to be determined," he says to me.

Kayla, just as I had figured, ends up driving, honking for me from my gravel driveway as the sun is going down. I hop outside on my crutches, and Kieran immediately exits the passenger side to help me into the backseat.

"Thanks," I tell him, as I push myself up onto the leather seat with my good leg as he places my crutches in the floorboard. "I promise I'll try not to be too big of a buzz kill for you guys tonight."

"Well, it's *your* birthday." Kayla smirks at me in the rearview mirror. "You get to be as big a buzz kill as you want to be."

"Thanks, Kay."

"Do I get to be a buzz kill since today's my birthday, too?" Kieran asks, and although he's in front of me, I can hear the smile in his voice.

162

"You're always a buzz kill, Kieran," Kayla grumbles. "No reason tonight should be any different."

Unfortunately for me and everyone else, being a buzz kill is pretty easy for me once we get to the Hull farm. Realizing I probably wouldn't be able to stand comfortably for too long, Cody's set up a lawn chair for me in his backyard near the bonfire, which was thoughtful, but leads to the probably unintended effect of my feeling like a queen holding court as people come up to talk to me. And, of course, I can't mingle effectively in my condition, so to avoid my having to sit alone at any point, Kieran offers to sit on the ground next to me and keep me company.

Which was very nice of him to do.

"You know, you don't need to stay here and babysit me all night if you want to go hang out with people," I tell him after a while.

"I'm not babysitting you," he says, looking up at me and glancing around at the people surrounding the bonfire and those who are ducking in and out of the barn, where Cody's stashed the kegs. "This whole thing isn't really my scene, anyway. I'm happier to be sitting here talking to you than doing anything else."

He shoots me That Grin, and my stomach flutters. *Pleasestopflirtingwithme. Pleasestopflirtingwithme.*

"Just out of curiosity," he continues, the grin fading somewhat. "Was this kind of thing ever my scene? I don't remember reading about going to parties in any of my journals."

"No," I say, shaking my head. "I think before you moved here, you always stuck pretty close to home unless you were with Kayla. And here...well, we were kind of a low-key couple."

On my mention of us as a couple, a sort of uneasy silence settles over us. Kieran still hasn't said anything to me about our kiss at the river, and after holding hands at the hotel the night of the state

163

finals, we eventually went up to Cooper's room to hang out and neither of us has mentioned that night since.

"Um…you want some food or something?" he asks at last. "I think Cody said snacks and sodas are in the kitchen."

He nods in the direction of the house, where people are going in and out the back door.

"Yeah—I could use a soda if you're going to get something," I say.

Kieran pulls himself up from the ground and tosses a "Be back in a few" over his shoulder as he heads for the house. I sit alone for about a minute, staring at the groups of people around me I could get up and interact with if the mere act of standing up from this chair weren't such a total pain in the butt. On the other side of the bonfire, I notice Stephanie Hull standing at the edge of a group of girls from her class, the flames almost seeming to lick the side of her face given the angle I'm sitting at and how far away she is in relation to me. Our eyes meet, we both look away, and when I take a chance on another glance, I catch her looking at me again. But instead of breaking our mutual stare, Steph says something to one of the girls in her group and makes her way over to me.

"Hey," she says once she's in front of me. Steph's petite—she's maybe an inch or two shorter than I am and skinny as a weed—but looking down on me as she is while I sit here in this lawn chair makes her seem massive.

"Hey."

"I've been meaning to tell you how sorry I am about your knee and everything." She buries her hands in the back pockets of her jeans and hunches her shoulders up to her ears. "When's your operation?"

"Tomorrow, actually."

"Wow." Her eyes get big. "I had no idea. Hope everything turns out okay."

"Thanks."

And...silence. I haven't been in a situation this awkward since...well...this whole evening so far has been pretty awkward, actually.

"Zip...look. I'm really glad you and Kieran are back together. I mean it," Steph says, looking away from me toward the house and tucking some of her straight red hair behind her ear. Out of the corner of my eye, I see Kieran walking toward us with two plastic cups, so rather than say anything else to Steph, I stay quiet until he hands me a cup of soda and says "Hi" to her.

"Hey," she mumbles back.

"Everything okay?" Kieran asks, glancing back and forth between the two of us and asking the most loaded question in the history of loaded questions.

"Yup," I tell him, smiling as Steph says "Yeah." Still, Kieran seems to sense he's interrupted something important.

"Okay, then. I'm going to head back inside real quick for some snacks," he says, hitching his thumb in the direction of the house. "Be back in a minute."

And off he goes, leaving me here with Stephanie, her last statement to me still hanging in the air as if the words have shape and mass and are waiting for me to confront them.

"Steph, Kieran and I aren't back together. We're just hanging out as friends."

"Oh." Even in the low light from the fire, I can see her face redden. "I just thought...I didn't mean..."

"It's okay," I tell her, smiling in the hope of putting her at ease.

"I just assumed you guys were together again," she explains. "I was actually kind of pulling for you to get back together, if you want to know the truth. You guys are a really great couple. Even

165

when Kieran and I were dating, I could kind of tell he was still into you."

I have no idea where to go with this bit of information. Obviously, Steph doesn't know that Kieran doesn't remember ever being into me to begin with, which makes her statement totally weird in a way only I would understand. And then there's the fact she just admitted to her ex-boyfriend's previous girlfriend that she realized she was second best the whole time—and she doesn't seem to want to strangle said previous girlfriend where she sits.

"Steph, I..." I begin, not knowing what I want to say to her.

"It's okay," she says with a wave of her hand. "I'm not going to lie and say it didn't bother me, but Kieran and I weren't very serious, so it's all...you know...whatever."

She shrugs, taking her hands from her pockets and crossing her arms over her torso.

"Anyway, I just came over to say 'hi.'" She nods over her shoulder at her group of friends. "I should probably get back."

Her eyes shift, and once again, in my peripheral vision, I see Kieran heading back toward us from the house, this time carrying a bowl.

"Yeah. Nice talking to you, Steph."

"Yeah. You, too."

Stephanie turns to head back to her group of friends, giving a little wave in Kieran's direction. He waves back and takes a few more steps to get to me.

"You guys okay?" Kieran asks me as we watch Steph blend in with her crowd of girlfriends.

"Yeah," I say with a wave of my hand. "Steph and I are fine. I think she was just making sure."

He nods and hands the bowl—which is full of popcorn—to me. I rest the bowl on my lap, far enough out so he can still reach up and into it when he sits down on the ground in front of me, his back resting against the edge of the lawn chair. We sit in silence for a few minutes, munching on popcorn and sipping our sodas, while we watch the groups of drunks and social butterflies—most of whom are the same people—circulate around us.

"As exciting as this is," Kieran starts, and I laugh, "would you want to go for a walk or something?"

"I'd love to," I tell him, leaving out the fact that I mostly want to stand up because I think my butt's fallen asleep from sitting in this chair for so long. "Just don't expect me to walk too fast."

"No problem," he says, standing up and retrieving my crutches from the ground to hand them to me.

Once I've struggled to my feet and Kieran's placed our drinks and the popcorn on the ground under my chair, we start walking—or, rather, he walks and I hobble—away from the party and toward the outer reaches of the Hull farm.

"So I've been meaning to ask," he begins, consciously slowing his pace so I can keep up. "I know Sumner was interested in offering you a basketball scholarship. Made up your mind about whether or not you want to go there?"

"I haven't yet, and they haven't decided on me, either. I think they'll want to know what my prognosis is after my surgery."

"Are you scared?" he asks in a low voice.

"About my surgery or about college?"

We laugh a little and he says "Both."

"Well, I've never had surgery, so I'm a little freaked out by the idea. My dad says it's pretty much like going to sleep and waking up, only you go to sleep in one place and wake up somewhere else." I pause, my mind making a connection between my present and his past. "I guess it's sort of how you used to describe the walking blackouts you had sometimes when you used to have your sleeping disorder."

"Only without scalpels, I'm guessing," he says, flashing me his grin, and I shudder at the thought of a surgeon cutting into my skin.

"So are you scared about college, too?" he asks again.

"Of college itself? No." I shake my head, giving his question some additional thought. "Of making a decision about college? Definitely. I haven't heard from Northwestern yet, but it looks like it's going to be down to them and Sumner. Oddly enough, the other schools that were showing interest in me haven't exactly been blowing up my phone since the semifinal game."

Kieran ignores my poor attempt at humor and says, "Yeah— I'm pretty much terrified of making a college decision, too. I'm in at Sumner and at both places I applied in Chicago, so I should be happy. But now I have to choose and I'm completely frozen. I mean, this isn't a decision that only impacts the next four years. It's, like, your whole life, you know?"

"Yeah."

"So, I'm going to put off making a decision as long as I can and hope something magical happens to make things clearer," he says, shrugging.

"And that something would be?" I prompt.

"No idea."

We both laugh, and I survey our surroundings. We are behind one of the Hulls' large grain silos now, completely out of view of anyone at the party. I'm about to suggest we turn around and walk back when Kieran lowers his voice.

"Zip, I need you to kiss me."

Well, *this* is unexpected. I back up against the grain silo, the edges of my crutches scraping the metal.

"What?" I whisper, although no one can hear us.

168

He moves in closer. "I need you to kiss me," he murmurs. "Please."

I certainly don't want to turn a guy down when he's begging, but my condition makes this whole scenario a little difficult. Under normal circumstances, I'd wrap my arms around Kieran and go in for the kill, but if I throw my arms around him now, my crutches will go out from under me. I lean in a little, but he's too tall—usually, I'm able to get on my tiptoes to pull myself up to him.

"Um…" I begin, and wait for him to get the hint, which he finally does, shaking his head.

"Right. Sorry," he says, leaning into me so that my back is almost flat against the metal of the silo. He takes my face in his hands and lowers his lips to mine, his kiss just as warm and soft and comforting as ever. When we part a minute later, he doesn't move away but instead rests his forehead on mine.

"Zip, I'm remembering things."

His announcement is almost enough to make me go slack despite the crutches holding me up.

"Like what?" We're still so close to each other, I can almost feel his heart pounding against mine.

"Just bits and pieces of things, mostly," he says, tracing my jawline with a fingertip. "Things that don't seem to make much sense."

He moves in to kiss me again, dropping his hands to my shoulders, and somewhere in the rational part of my brain, I know we can't keep kissing right now or we're never going to have a serious conversation about this.

"Like what? When did this start happening?" I ask before his mouth can settle on mine.

"Remember the day we drove out to that farm and then to the river?"

Do I ever—I nod vigorously.

"I had a headache that night, so I went to bed kind of early. After I woke up, I had this weird flash of the two of us sitting in English class and talking like it was any other day, except the room was different, and Mrs. Harvey was there instead of Mrs. Rossdale, which I thought was kind of strange, but the whole thing hit me so fast I just kind of blew it off and didn't say anything to anybody. And then a couple of weeks later, it happened again."

"You saw the same thing?"

"Pretty much, only the flash lasted a little longer this time. And we were reading *To Kill a Mockingbird* for some reason."

"Kieran," I start, my voice no more than a breath, "those memories are from the week we first met."

"I'd kind of put that together based on things I was reading in my journals." He nods. "And then the last two weeks or so I've started getting other flashes of things, stuff I think must be from my past because my parents seem younger, or Kayla looks a lot different than she does now."

"Have you told anyone about this?"

"No," he mumbles, his eyes flit away for a moment. "At first I wasn't sure the memories were anything, so I didn't want to get anyone's hopes up. I didn't want to get *my* hopes up. I mean, when Cooper's memory came back, it was like he had a few little memories here and there and then everything started coming back all at once, right?"

"Pretty much. I think there are some things from his distant past he still has trouble with, but for the most part, everything came back within a few weeks of the treatment."

Kieran cringes, and I instantly wish I could stuff my words back into my mouth. Not much about Kieran's response to the treatment has mirrored Cooper's situation, particularly the part about

170

the amnesia lasting only a few weeks. But now he's revealed his headache that night at the river was followed by a memory flash, and now that he's starting to have more frequent memory flashes, I can't help but wish—for the both of us—that a complete recovery of his memory is right around the corner.

"I guess I didn't want to take the risk and get everyone all excited in case these few little episodes were all there was going to be." He shifts his gaze to the ground. "But then tonight, before we picked you up, I had another flash and I knew you were the person I had to tell first." His eyes lock back on mine. "Zip, I remembered us kissing. I didn't have enough time to look up anything in my journals before we had to leave to come here, but everything was so clear in my mind like it all just happened."

Well, *this* is encouraging. My breath catches in my throat as he continues with "We were in, like, this shed or something, and we were sitting on the floor. There were some benches and lots of artwork and this…bear carving."

He seems so confused that I can't help but shatter the seriousness of this moment by laughing.

"I'm sorry," I say once I sober up. "We were in the art studio Gramps has behind his house. He and my mom keep all their art supplies there. And the bear…" I pause, thinking of the bear in his now-finished state, standing guard in the foyer of my grandparents' house. "That's Norbert," I explain, using the silly name Gramps gave his new friend. "Gramps was carving him at the time. You may have seen him inside their house."

Kieran squints as if he's trying to remember whether he's seen Norbert or not, and I realize we have more important matters to discuss.

"The night you're describing was exactly a year ago," I tell him. "Our birthday. Our first kiss."

I dart my eyes away, embarrassed, my gaze falling on my charm bracelet, the links in the silver chain barely standing out where they rest against the metal of my crutches.

"You gave me the charm bracelet as my birthday present," I say, tilting my head to the left since I can't raise my wrist without risking my balance. "Do you remember?"

He moves his head back and forth slowly, his eyes still squinting as if he's trying to squeeze the memory out from whatever dark corner it's run to in his brain.

"And your parents...that was the night they told you all about Morgan and how they adopted you after he went to prison. That was the night they told you your narcolepsy wasn't really narcolepsy."

And Prom. That was the night Kieran asked me to Prom. But I don't mention it—if he can't remember the more earth-shattering, life-changing parts of that night, chances are he won't remember asking me to Prom.

"Nothing," he says, opening his eyes and leaning in. "All I remember is your kiss."

"And Norbert," I mumble, right before his mouth covers mine, my lips parting to let him in. This feels so good, so incredible, one good knee and a set of crutches almost aren't enough to keep me upright. I just want to lie down here in the dirt and dead grass next to the Hulls' grain silo and kiss him until we don't know where we are anymore.

And as his tongue slowly rolls over mine, I realize that while I do know where I am and where I've been for the last year, Kieran doesn't. Everything and everyone in Titusville, including his own family, is brand new, is only part of his present, and the sole physical action that reminds him of what tiny bits of his past he now recalls is what we're doing at the moment—kissing.

So as much as I don't want to, I pull back.

"Kieran, we can't do this," I tell him.

"We can't?" His face twists in confusion.

"Well, obviously we have the physical capability to do so, but I'm saying it might not be such a good idea."

"Feels like a pretty good idea to me," he murmurs, raising his hands to my face and stroking his thumbs along my cheeks. And he's right—this does feel good. All of it. If only I could shut my brain off...

"Kieran." I take a deep breath, because I'm not sure I want to hear the answer to the question I'm about to ask. "Did you bring me back here to kiss me because you *wanted* to kiss me, or because you were hoping kissing me would jar your memory?"

He drops his hands to his sides and pauses a little too long before asking "Can't it be both?"

Given everything he's been through, I can't hold what he's said against him. I really can't. But...

"Yes," I tell him. "Yes, it can. I'm just not sure how knowing that makes me feel."

He reaches out for the charm bracelet, fumbling along its length until he finds the key charm.

"But you're the key, right?" he reminds me, and the flicker of hurt in his eyes makes me want to lose myself in him, but I stand firm.

"Maybe I am. But that's not all I want to be to you. It's not even the biggest part of what I want to be to you."

We stand in an awkward silence for a few seconds before I finally say, "Maybe we should get back to the party."

"Yeah. Guess people will wonder what we're doing back here."

He steps back so I can move away from the grain silo, and we round its side to start walking back toward the house. Ahead of us, people are still stumbling around, but the bonfire is a little lower than when we first left. We don't say anything until we're almost halfway to the fire, and then I force myself.

"You know, you should at least tell Kayla you're getting your memory back," I tell him. "This whole thing has been hard on her."

"She puts up a good front, but I'd gotten that impression." He rubs his knuckles under his chin and doesn't look at me, apparently taking my suggestion as an excuse to examine the different groups standing around the fire. "There she is," he says, pointing toward a group that I can see as we draw closer contains Kayla, Ashley, Rick, Cody, and Cassie.

"And where did you two disappear to all by yourselves?" Cassie asks, arching an eyebrow and standing away from Ashley so we can join the circle.

"We just took a walk," Kieran says, waving his hand in the direction of the grain silos. "Mind if we borrow Kayla for a minute?"

He tilts his head in the direction of the barn. Kayla wrinkles her face in confusion but follows us around to the side of the barn facing the grain silos, her hand still curled around a red plastic cup of soda.

"What's up?" she asks.

Kieran looks at me, I look at him, and neither of us says anything.

"Okay, then," Kayla huffs. "I'm going back to the party."

She starts walking back over to the bonfire, but Kieran grabs her jacket sleeve.

"I'm remembering things."

Kayla snaps back as if Kieran has her at the end of a rubber band.

"What did you just say?" she breathes.

"You heard me. I wanted to wait until I was sure before I said anything." He casts a sideways glance at me. "And now I'm sure."

174

Kayla starts trembling as if she's going to shatter, but she swallows hard and steadies herself before tossing her cup to the grass and reaching out to him.

"Oh, my God. Kieran," she breathes. He gathers her into a hug, and watching the two of them have this moment together almost wipes away my disappointment over my moment with Kieran behind the grain silo.

Almost.

Kieran pulls back from Kayla enough to study her face, but not enough that he has to let go of her. "Think Mom and Dad would still be up if we went home right now?" he asks.

"If they're not, I bet they'd be willing to get up for this," Kayla says, smiling.

CHAPTER 15

We're halfway to my house when Kieran turns around in the front seat to face me. "I want you to be with me when I tell my parents my memory's coming back," he says. "I mean, if it's okay with you."

I'm confused as to why he would want me around. "Are you sure?" I ask. "This kind of seems like a family thing."

"You're family," Kayla says before Kieran can respond. "I don't think Mom and Dad will mind if you're there if Kieran wants you to be."

"Besides, without you, none of this would be happening right now," Kieran points out. I shift my eyes to the rear view mirror and there's just enough light shining up from the dashboard I can see Kayla shoot me a split-second puzzled look before turning her attention back to the road. But she doesn't ask Kieran what he's talking about.

"If you want me there, then okay," I tell him, and he gives me a slight nod before shifting back around in his seat. In minutes, we're rambling up the Laniers' gravel driveway, the porch light on next to the front door welcoming us home.

"Mom? Dad?" Kayla yells once we're all inside. I hang back by the front door as Kayla and Kieran walk to the bottom of the stairs. After a few seconds, I hear the shuffle of footsteps upstairs and then Carlie, in a gray sweatshirt and sweatpants looking almost exactly as she did the night I first met her, appears on the landing.

"You're home early," she points out, her face contorting with concern. "Did something go wrong at the party?" As she asks, she gazes past the siblings to find me leaning against the front door. "Zip—I'm sorry. I didn't realize you were here as well."

I step forward, realizing I probably look like an idiot lurking back here in the shadows, hunched over on my crutches like Quasimodo. "Hope we didn't wake you," I say.

"No, no. Jim and I were upstairs watching a movie." She shifts her eyes back to her children. "I still don't understand why you're home, though. It's not even eleven."

Kayla and Kieran exchange glances as if neither of them is sure which one should break the news. "Can...can you get Dad down here, too?" Kayla finally says. "We need to talk."

The words "We need to talk" have barely left Kayla's lips before Carlie flies down the remaining stairs, taking first Kayla's, then Kieran's face in her hands.

"What's wrong?" she demands, her mother's instinct in full effect. "What happened at the party? Is either of you sick? Hurt?"

"No, Mom," Kieran says, smiling as broadly as he can with his face still in Carlie's hands. "Everything's fine. Everything's fine, and I think things are only going to get better from now on."

Carlie's eyes widen and her expression softens, the fear fading away—she's finally starting to get what's going on here.

"Oh," she breathes, slightly startled. "Oh." Pulling Kieran to her, she wraps her arms around him and kisses his hair over his ear before releasing him and trotting back up the stairs with tears in her eyes. "Jim!" she yells once she's on the landing. "Jim, you need to come down here, please."

As another shuffle of footsteps begins upstairs, Carlie returns to her son, putting her arm around him and guiding him toward the living room. Kayla and I follow them, and about a minute or so later, Jim joins us. He's also in sweatpants and a sweatshirt, more casual than I've ever seen him, and once again, I feel a bit out of place at being here.

"What's going on?" he asks, stopping at the threshold of the living room. Kayla flops down in an easy chair at the far end of the room while I basically fall into the chair closest to the fireplace, putting my crutches on the floor to the side. To my surprise, Kieran slips from his mother's grasp and comes to sit on the arm of my easy chair, and so Carlie sits alone on the couch, waiting for her husband to join her.

"I think Kieran needs to tell us something," she says, slipping her arm through Jim's after he sits down, her eyes practically sparking with anticipation.

Kieran glances at me briefly before turning back to his parents. "I'm starting to remember things," he says. "I'm pretty sure."

Jim's eyes grow even wider than Carlie's did when we were still in the hallway. "What?" he almost whispers. "When?"

"It kind of started back in February," Kieran says, and he visibly cringes even before his mom shrieks—as loudly as she can shriek with her whispery voice—"*February?*"

"I know, I know." Kieran holds out his hand as if he's trying to push back her surprise. "I didn't want to say anything because I wanted to be sure I was remembering more than a few things here and there." He glances at me again quickly before shifting his gaze back to his parents. "But now I'm starting to think everything's going to come back."

"So, what...what started this?" Carlie asks.

Kieran steals a glance at me before addressing his mom, and I almost forget we're technically not together anymore and reach up for his hand, stopping myself just in time. "It was that one Saturday back in February when the weather was really warm, remember? You and Dad were in Sumner doing something, and Kayla was in Evanston. I'd gotten my license and I wanted to take the car out, and I ended up spending the afternoon with Zip."

178

I give Jim and Carlie an embarrassed smile as Kieran continues.

"We drove out to the farm where we were on Prom night last year, and then we went down to the river," he tells them. "I didn't remember anything at the time, but later I had a headache."

"I remember," Jim interjects. "You asked to be excused from dinner so you could go lie down."

Jim and Carlie exchange glances, and she says "That's right. I'd hoped then you might be remembering something because Cooper had headaches when his memory started coming back, but you never said anything."

"Well, now I'm saying something." Kieran smiles. "I wanted to be sure first. I didn't want to get everyone's hopes up in case I was only remembering a few random things."

Carlie leans forward, resting her elbows on her knees. "So, what's come back to you?" she asks as she naturally would. I suck in a breath because, according to Kieran, most of what he's remembered so far has to do with kissing me.

Kieran holds a hand up near his ear. "You had shorter hair once," he tells her. "Right below your ears. I keep getting this memory of you and Dad on a beach somewhere...you're in this light blue bathing suit and Dad's got on navy swim trunks. And Kayla...you're sitting near them and building a sand castle. I can't really tell how old you are, but you're definitely younger than you are now. I mean, you kind of look like a little kid, but you might be older..."

"She's nine," Carlie interjects, before cupping her hands over her mouth and nose for a moment, tears springing to her eyes. "So you would have been ten. That was the last summer we took you kids to the house on Martha's Vineyard."

Jim narrows his eyes as if he's thinking, and once Carlie notices him doing so, she says, "I remember the swimsuit. I hated it—

179

didn't go with my coloring at all but I didn't realize it until after I'd bought the thing and gotten it home."

Kayla nods in sympathy, as she's apparently also had the same shopping regret before.

"So why was that the last summer we went to Martha's Vineyard? Did something happen? Maybe I'm remembering it because something happened," Kieran asks.

The Laniers—Kayla included—exchange glances, and Kayla's the first one to jump in with an explanation.

"I'd started running track," she explains. "The more I got into it, the more time it took up. So we didn't always have time for long vacations."

She doesn't say anything else, her wide-eyed expression seeming to appeal to her parents to continue the story.

"By the next summer, we'd started to be concerned about your dreams," Jim begins. "You told us you were dreaming about Kayla winning medals in races, but you couldn't see what color they were in order for us to know where she would place. Inevitably, Kayla would medal at the next race."

"I made you stop saying anything to me about your dreams when Mom and Dad told me," Kayla says. "For about a minute, I thought it might be cool to find out how my races would go before they actually happened, but then I changed my mind."

"And that's why you never wanted me talking to you about my dreams at all," Kieran says to her, apparently having puzzled through something he's read in either his dream journals or in the mini-autobiography he wrote before he underwent the treatment for his sleeping disorder. Kayla nods in confirmation.

"Two years after our last trip to the Vineyard, when you were twelve, we'd reached a point with your condition that your dad..." Carlie begins, nodding at Jim for reasons which become instantly apparent, "Your dad went to New York to meet with Morgan to find out if he could give us any insight into your condition, and he became convinced Morgan would try to come after you once he was out of prison as a way to get revenge on us for adopting you and moving away."

"He was a bit threatening then," Jim adds, but quickly says, "Although we know now he isn't, of course. Morgan went through a lot in prison in the years after I met with him that helped turn him around."

Kieran nods, his eyes narrowed as if he's slightly confused. The Morgan situation has been—and in some ways, always will be—complicated. While Kieran can read in his journals and notes about his recent relationship with Morgan and the nightmare scenarios he dreamt of before they met, I'm guessing that hearing about how his family struggled with his initial dreams about Morgan must be a strange experience.

"Not too long after Dad's trip back to New York, Mom and Dad sat me down and told me everything—about your real parents, about how they adopted you, and about how they were scared your dreams could mean Morgan would come for you one day," Kayla continues. "They wanted me to be able to watch out for you and help keep you safe. So, if I seem a little weird with you sometimes, that's probably why."

"Sometimes?" Kieran asks, and everyone titters a little at his joke, but he and Kayla exchange warm glances. I know the two of them are only brother and sister by law, but they've been in the same family from a young enough age that their relationship seems as natural and effortless as any of the blood siblings I know—maybe even more so. Given Kieran's current condition, the fact their sibling bond is still just as strong is almost incredible.

"Have you remembered anything else?" Jim asks Kieran. "Maybe something from our years in North Carolina?"

"The beach memory is the only thing I've seen from my childhood," Kieran says, stealing another glance at me. "Pretty much everything else has been from the last year or so."

Carlie gets up and crosses the room, stopping in front of Kieran and reaching out to ruffle his hair. "This is only the beginning, Kieran. You'll see. The memories will all start coming back now," she says as if she's confident, even though she's told all of us over and over there are no guarantees with anything having to do with Kieran's condition or with the treatment. "We'll go to Jillian's next week, and once you're in North Carolina again, I'm sure you'll start remembering more."

Next week is our spring break from school, and Kayla had mentioned to me the Laniers were going to Asheville for the week not only for a visit with Jillian, but also in the hopes of stirring up some of Kieran's memories of living there. Obviously, now that Kieran's started remembering things, Carlie's placing more importance on this trip than ever.

"I hope so," Kieran says, looking up at his mother and then over at me. "I want to remember everything."

I smile at him because I don't know what else to do, and Carlie looks at me as if she's realizing I'm in the room for the first time since we all walked in here.

"Zip, when are you having surgery? Sometime over the break, correct?"

"Tomorrow, actually," I tell her. "I have to recover at home for two weeks, and I couldn't undergo surgery until the swelling in my knee went down. Luckily, the timing's worked out to where I won't miss too much school."

"That's good," Carlie says. "Although now I'm wondering if we shouldn't get you home. You have a pretty big day ahead of you tomorrow."

"I'll be asleep through most of it, though, I guess," I tell her.

"Good point," she says, reaching out to squeeze my shoulder. "Even so, tonight's been quite a night for everybody. Kayla, are you still awake enough to drive Zip home?"

Kayla's been sitting with her feet tucked up under her in the easy chair, but she pulls them out and plants them on the floor, springing to attention. "Nobody's tired but you, Mom. But I'll take Zip home. Don't want her waking up in the middle of her surgery because she didn't get enough sleep."

"Oh, my God," I mumble, covering my face with my hands and wishing I'd never mentioned anything to her about my fear of waking up during surgery.

"Kayla, that's not how anesthesia works. You're well aware of that. Don't make Zip nervous," Carlie scolds, and I add "Yeah, Kayla. Don't make Zip nervous."

Kayla laughs and walks over to pull me up from the chair as Carlie grabs my crutches. "Sorry," she says. "I'm only kidding around. Let's go."

We make our way to the porch, and as Kayla's holding my crutches while I use the railing to hop myself down the stairs, I'm too scared to turn around and look for fear of falling down when I hear the front door shut behind me.

"Kayla, can I talk to Zip for a minute?" Kieran says as he steps down next to me, taking my crutches from her.

"Sure," she says, walking off toward the driveway and leaving us alone. Kieran holds my crutches and puts his other arm around me as we go down to the path one excruciating step at a time.

"I'm really, really sorry about what happened at the party tonight," he says, once we're on the walk. I'm busy arranging myself on my crutches, and so only after a few seconds am I able to lift my eyes to his.

"Kieran, it's okay. I'm serious."

"No, it's not." He runs a hand through his hair and darts his eyes away. "You had every right to say you need more from me. You deserve more, whether it's from me or from someone else."

"Thanks," I say, which seems like the stupidest thing I could say at the moment, but nothing else is coming to mind.

"Look, we're leaving for Asheville on Sunday," he says, returning his eyes to me once again. "You'll be in the hospital at least overnight, right?"

"Yeah."

"I'll call or text or something to make sure everything went okay, but after that, I'll give you some space. We'll be gone until next weekend, so I won't be around anyway, and you won't be at school the week after that. Maybe not seeing each other or talking for a while will be a good thing." He darts his eyes to the ground, where he's kicking at the sidewalk with the toe of his shoe. "And it'll give me some time to think about how to make up for being such an ass tonight."

"You weren't an ass," I insist. "But I don't want to kiss you and wonder if the only reason you're kissing me is because you need to in order to bring your memory back. I want you to *want* to kiss me." I shut my eyes. "And wanting you to want to kiss me is ridiculous because I have no idea how I'm going to be able to tell the difference."

Part of me feels like I'm being way too stubborn. Falling into Kieran's arms would be the easiest thing in the world right now—or, it would be if I didn't have these stupid crutches in my way—but somehow I know I'd hate myself if I gave in.

But how will I be sure when I can trust him—and trust his kiss—again?

My eyes are still shut so I don't see Kieran step to me, but I can feel him plant a kiss on my forehead. When I open my eyes, I find myself staring at his throat, his Adam's apple moving up and down as he swallows.

"Have I ever done that to you before?" he asks, and I watch his neck muscles expand and contract along with the words.

"What?"

"Kissed you on the forehead."

"No," I say, straining to recall a time when he'd kissed me on the forehead rather than the lips, and if he had, it must not have been too significant. "At least I don't remember if you have."

He steps back enough for me to stare into his eyes. "That wasn't me doing something I'd read about in my journals," he murmurs. "That wasn't me trying to do something to bring my memory back. That was me *wanting* to kiss you." He moves back even further so he can put his hands on my shoulders. "But I'm going to give you your space for the next two weeks, like I said. You need to focus on your surgery and on getting better instead of thinking about me right now."

As if I would stop thinking about him ever, but I keep quiet and let him continue.

"And after two weeks, whatever I have to do to prove myself to you, I'll do it."

We've gotten so serious, I can't help but interject my bad sense of humor onto the situation. "This could get interesting," I say, narrowing my eyes.

"Just don't make me jump out of an airplane or wrestle an alligator or fight someone or something," he says, thankfully joining in the joke. "Promise me we'll stick to the romantic stuff. I think we're both going to be better off."

"I promise," I say, smiling, just as Kayla rolls her window down and yells from the driveway "Zip, I think I'm supposed to be taking you home *tonight*."

"Guess I should go," I mumble.

"Sounds like it," Kieran says through a laugh. "Let me help you to the car."

We walk off together to the driveway, where Kayla puts the car in gear almost before Kieran's helped me get settled in the front seat and put my crutches in the back. His hand on the door, he leans in for another forehead kiss, whispering "Good luck tomorrow," before he pulls away, the words tingling against my skin even after we've backed down the drive.

CHAPTER 16

Cassie stands with her hands on her hips in the school lobby, a sheet of blue butcher paper with the words *An Evening to Remember* written in silver glitter block letters taking up most of the wall behind her.

"What do you *mean*, you're not going to Prom?"

I've spent most of the last two weeks at home dodging Cassie's phone and text questions about whether or not Kieran had asked me to Prom the night of Cody's party. But now that I'm back at school and she can harass me in person, the Prom conversation isn't going to be so easy to avoid.

"It's not complicated, Cass," I say through a sigh, glancing to my right at the table of Junior Class officers—including Stephanie Hull—selling Prom tickets. "I'm not going. That's all."

Cassie crosses her arms over her stomach, her pose still defiant.

"Okay, first of all, I thought you and Kieran got back together after Cody's party. And, second of all, it's *Prom* and we're *seniors*. How can you not go, even if the theme is totally lame?"

She casts a glance at the banner on the wall behind her, and I can't help but agree.

"Seriously. It's like they didn't even try."

"Juniors are such a waste of space," Cassie hisses, rolling her eyes at Stephanie and her fellow class officers. "And I thought *In Your Dreams* was a nightmare theme to decorate. *A Night to Remember* doesn't even mean anything."

Or it could, at least to Kieran. Part of me wonders if going to Prom might not knock loose more of Kieran's memories, but I'm also worried it might knock loose some of *my* memories about that night, which I've been trying to file away into a dark corner of my brain for nearly a year. And, anyway, Prom is in a little over two weeks and regardless of whatever's going on between Kieran and me right now—which is almost nothing, considering I only received a few texts from him to check in on how I was doing after my surgery and then he stuck to his plan to give me some space—two weeks isn't much time to find a dress and rent a tux and make plans for the evening. Last year, he asked me over a month before the dance and, considering some people at this school start making Prom plans in late February and early March, even then we were cutting things kind of close.

"Well, anyway," I begin, trying to shake thoughts of last year's Prom out of my head. "Kieran and I aren't back together, and we may never be back together. We're not even close to being ready for something like Prom."

"So what were you two *doing* behind the grain silo for so long?" Cassie demands. "Discussing your college plans?"

"Yeah, actually," I say with a smirk. "Among other things. But what we definitely *weren't* doing was getting back together, and we definitely weren't making Prom plans." I catch sight of the clock above the gym doors and exhale with relief, finding my escape from Cassie's Prom obsession. "Look, my grandfather's probably waiting outside to take me to physical therapy. You can give me all the crap you want about not going to Prom later—I promise."

Cassie rolls her eyes at me and wishes me luck at therapy, and I scoot out the front door of the school and hop down the few steps to the parking lot, where Gramps is parked in one of the guest spaces near the flagpole. On seeing me approach, he gets out of the car and puts my crutches and backpack in the backseat as I arrange myself in the passenger side, sliding the seat back as far as it will go so I can stretch my leg out.

188

"So, how are things, Zip-i-dee-doo-dah?" Gramps asks.

"Fine, just…" I pause, not sure if Gramps wants to hear about my silly high school dramas. But then I remember he's Gramps and he loves me, and he'd probably be willing to listen to me babble on about pretty much anything, silly high school dramas included.

"Cassie was giving me a hard time about not going to Prom, so she's kind of bumming me out. She said I should go whether or not I have a date because it's Prom and we're seniors."

"And you don't want to go because of what happened last year?" Gramps asks, pulling out of the parking lot and onto Main Street.

"Partially, I guess," I begin tentatively, and then I'm talking so quickly my brain almost can't keep up with my mouth. "Plus, I'm dateless. Kieran and I aren't back together, and I don't know if we ever will be, so I don't really feel like going alone even though all my friends will be there. And, anyway, I'm probably still going to be on crutches and I'll look like a huge raging dork in a dress with this gigantic leg brace hanging out."

I don't think I'd realized until now, as I'm spitting out this stream of word vomit at Gramps, how deep my aversion to going to Prom this year actually runs. Sitting on the bleachers or hobbling around on crutches while all my friends enjoy the dance is yet another good reason to stay home with my mom and watch movies.

"Well, I don't think you should go if you don't want to," Gramps says, exiting onto the four lane highway and picking up speed toward Sumner. "You've never been the kind of person who does things because of peer pressure or obligation."

"I know. I think I'm letting Cassie get to me because we're about to graduate and we're running out of time to spend together."

"You'll have almost a whole month after Prom before school gets out, and then you'll have the entire summer before everyone

189

leaves for college. It's not exactly like Prom is your last chance to be with your friends."

"True," I say, crossing my arms over my stomach. I was sure Gramps would get it.

"And Prom holds some pretty intense memories for you," he continues. "I know Cassie isn't aware of the full story of what happened at the river, but even what she did hear about should be enough for her to understand why you wouldn't want to go. I mean, everyone in town remembers how you ended up in the hospital that night."

"And I ruined my dress and lost my shoes. So traumatic," I say, my voice serious but my lips forming a smile. Gramps laughs.

"Cassie probably thinks you need a do-over after what happened last year," Gramps suggests after sobering up. "But what Cassie thinks doesn't matter. You know, over and over in your life, you're going to be confronted with situations that require you to consider other people's feelings before making a decision."

"And?"

"And this is *not* one of those times," he says, shifting his eyes to me just enough so I can see them twinkling. "If you decide to go to Prom, you don't owe it to anyone but yourself. And if you decide to stay home, maybe I'll come over and hang out with you."

"Thanks, Gramps."

About forty minutes later, we pull up in front of Med-West Medical, a white building across the street from Med-West Hospital.

"Physical therapy should be on the first floor, right inside," Gramps tells me, and I remember he had knee replacement surgery when I was a freshman and had therapy appointments here for a few weeks. "Sure you don't want me to go with you?"

The whole reason Gramps is driving me is because he comes to Sumner once a week anyway for coffee with some of his former

190

colleagues at the college, so we arranged my therapy appointments around his usual meet-ups. "I should be fine," I tell him. "Go meet up with your friends and take your time." I nod toward the backseat, where my backpack rests in the passenger floorboard. "I've got more than enough school stuff to catch up on, so I can always hang out here and do homework if you're not back by the time my appointment's done."

Gramps nods and helps me out of the car, holding my backpack out so I can slide my arms through the handles and handing me my crutches so I can hobble inside the building. As he said, the physical therapy offices are right inside, and after I check in at the front desk, I watch an afternoon talk show on the waiting room TV for a few minutes until a tall redhead in a green Med-West polo shirt and white pants pokes her head through the door to the waiting area and says, "Zara McKee?"

I get to my feet and crutch myself over to her. She holds the door wide and allows me to walk through ahead of her.

"My name's Jane," she says, and I glance over my shoulder to see her smiling at me, revealing a small gap between her two front teeth. "I'll be your therapist. We'll go back to the office for a few minutes and talk, and then we'll get you started on some exercises, okay?"

"Sure," I tell her, my voice full of confidence. I had to start doing some therapy exercises at home before my surgery in order to increase mobility in my knee, so I'm certain whatever she'll ask me to do will be a piece of cake.

We walk through the therapy room, which looks sort of like a health club with different stations. Some of the stations are equipped with weight machines like the ones I recognize from school, but other stations are simply everyday objects, like jump ropes and hula hoops. I focus my attention on one station with a five-stair staircase leading to...nowhere. A guy who seems to be about my age in a leg brace similar to mine hobbles up the stairs and slowly turns to head back down, his hands on the rails on either side.

"You'll be doing that eventually," Jane says, noticing me staring at the guy. "We'll work up to it."

An hour and a half later, after Jane and I have talked about my therapy plan and I've cycled through a rotation of exercises, I'm done for this visit and we schedule another session for the day after tomorrow. Physical therapy ends up giving me a weird kind of rush—different than, but not completely unlike, the surge of adrenaline I experience when I'm on the basketball court. Both basketball and my therapy exercises require sweat and effort, kicking my endorphin levels up and getting my heart beating faster. But basketball was almost always unconscious for me. Even when I'd be trying to master a new move, like the no-look pass, once I'd mastered it, the move became as natural as breathing. I had to focus in order to play well, but I almost didn't need to think.

Act, react, act, react—simple.

Physical therapy, on the other hand, is all thinking. If I lift my leg this high or try to squat this low, how bad will the pain be? If I do a certain exercise for a minute or two longer—despite the pain—will my recovery time be shorter?

So at the end of my session, I'm pretty exhausted, both physically and mentally, which leaves me certain I must be hallucinating when I venture out into the waiting area and find Kieran waiting for me instead of Gramps.

"Kieran?" I ask, blinking, but each time I refocus, I discover he still hasn't turned into Gramps.

"Surprise," he sings. "I thought I'd pick you up. I mean, if it's okay with you, of course."

192

He shoots me the grin that will forever be my downfall, and I blink and refocus again.

"Does my grandfather know you're here?" I ask stupidly. I'm clueless as to how Kieran knows I'm here, much less what he's doing here picking me up.

"Yeah. He's outside in the trunk of my car," he replies, totally serious.

"Okay—not funny." But I'm smiling. I can't help it.

"You're right. Not funny at all. But, seriously, I was on campus meeting with one of the advisors in the Art and Design Department for the forty-millionth time, and I ran into your grandfather in the hallway. He said he was meeting some people for coffee before he had to pick you up from therapy, so I volunteered to take you home so he could stay longer. He tried to call you, but you didn't pick up."

I'd heard my phone buzzing in my pocket while I was on the leg flexor machine trying to lift a ludicrously miniscule amount of weight. By the time I'd finished my set, I was so worn out I'd forgotten about my missed call.

"Look," Kieran begins when I don't answer. "If my being here isn't okay, your grandfather told me you should call him and he'd come get you—"

"No, Kieran—it's fine. I mean it." I say, nodding. "Let's go."

We walk out to the parking lot, where Kayla's Jeep is parked in a space a few feet from the Med-West entrance.

"Kayla let you borrow her car?" My disbelief is obvious, and a part of me wonders if he didn't get a set of spare keys somehow and made off with her vehicle while she was still at track practice.

"Only on the condition that if she finds so much as a chip in the paint, she gets to kill me, bring me back from the dead, and kill me again."

"Sounds about right," I say, smiling.

Kieran takes my crutches from me and helps me into the passenger side, and once we're both settled in, he asks, "Do you need to be home right away?"

"No."

"I'm only asking because I passed this ice cream place on the way here. I thought maybe we could hang out for a while."

Ice cream? Good. Hanging out with Kieran? Usually good, but who knows anymore?

I'm willing to take the chance.

"Sure thing. If it's Buster's Ice Cream, I've been there before. It's pretty awesome."

He pulls out of the parking lot and starts heading down Four Mile Road toward Buster's.

"So you were talking to people at Sumner again?" I ask. "Does that mean you've made a decision?"

"No," he says with a little laugh. "I keep hoping if I talk to people enough, the right decision will magically come to me."

"We've been over this, Kieran. I'm pretty sure college decisions require a person to, you know, *decide*, rather than getting some sign from the heavens."

"Me, too. I just can't seem to make the decision to commit to one school. And I realize people at Sumner aren't going to tell me anything different than what they've told me before. I guess I'm still hoping for a sign anyway."

"Well, at least you already have your major picked out," I say, trying to put the best spin on the situation. "So there's one less decision you'll need to make once you finally decide where you're going to go."

He shoots me his usual grin. "True. But now I'm hoping I don't change my mind about my major, too," he says. "I have this fear that I'll finally choose a school and then I'll get there and discover art isn't what I want after all."

"Don't you wish someone had warned us growing up was going to be this hard?" I say through a laugh.

"Knowing my parents, they probably did," he starts. "I just don't remember it anymore."

"Good point."

We pull into the parking lot at Buster's Ice Cream, a little outdoor shop with picnic tables scattered throughout an enclosed area off the parking lot. We find a parking space and after he turns off the car, he begins the several-minute ordeal of helping me out of the passenger side.

"So what's going on with your college decisions?" he asks as I settle onto my crutches.

"Not much. I should hear from Northwestern any day now, I hope. And Sumner's still an option. Last time I spoke to their coach, he said they have no problem redshirting me while I recover."

"Redshirting?" Kieran shoots me a confused look as we walk toward the windows where we'll place our orders. I'd forgotten he has only a basic knowledge of most sports.

"It means I'd sit out a year but still have a full four years of eligibility left once I'm healthy," I explain. "My doctor said my recovery's going to take about a year, so it's not like I'd be able to play by November anyway. I *hope* I'd be able to play by my sophomore year, but then I'll be a year behind on conditioning and drills...I mean, I'll be rusty. I'm trying to accept that there's a good chance I might never get playing time in a game during my college career." I glance down at my leg brace.

Kieran gives me a sad smile as we lean up against the order window and wisely changes the subject to the most important matter at hand. "What do you want?" he asks. "It's on me."

195

"You're sure? We're inching painfully close to a date here."

The last sentence is out of my mouth before I can think about the implications of my words, but Kieran smiles at me.

"I'm sure. What's good here?"

"Pretty much everything, but they make this red velvet cake milkshake that's basically the most spectacular thing ever invented."

Kieran turns to the guy manning the window and says "Two large red velvet cake milkshakes, please."

We watch in silence as the guy fills our order, and then Kieran carries our shakes to a table. I slide my crutches underneath and carefully lower myself to the edge of the bench, allowing my bad leg to hang out in the aisle between the tables. Since it's so close to dinnertime, we're the only people here and so I don't have to worry about tripping anyone as they walk by.

As Kieran sits down across from me, I remember another time when we had milkshakes together, and I decide the possibility of jarring his memory is worth the awkwardness of discussing another incident from our past.

"So, this isn't the first time you've taken me out for a milkshake, you know."

"Oh, really?"

"Yeah. So you remember how we were in Asheville last summer?" I start.

"I remember reading about running off to Asheville," he says, and my heart instantly plummets into my stomach. I hate that most of our relationship has been reduced—for him, at least—to pages in a notebook or words on a computer screen.

"I don't know if you remember reading about the night we went out with our families and then we were able to get some time alone for a while," I begin. "We were walking around downtown and you took me to this coffee place in an old double-decker bus and we had milkshakes."

"Sounds interesting," he says. "But I don't remember that at all. Jillian and the rest of the family dragged me all over Asheville pretty much non-stop while we were visiting, but it didn't do any good. Nothing about living there came back to me and, I mean, the Asheville years are the biggest chunk of my life."

A darkness settles over his face. The Laniers lived in Asheville for about fourteen years. Fourteen years of Kieran's life just…gone. I can't even imagine, and because I don't know what else to do, I keep talking about our brief time in Asheville in the hopes I can bring something…anything…back to him.

"We were getting milkshakes and we met Cooper for the first time," I tell him. "But we didn't know he was Cooper until later. He was hitting on me and you basically told him what he could go do with himself."

I'm embellishing the story a little—Kieran did get pissed off at Cooper, but Cooper had pretty much backed down as soon as he realized I had a boyfriend. Of course, we would find out later he was well aware I had a boyfriend and Kieran was the one he was trying to contact. But, Cooper being Cooper, when he found me sitting alone, he couldn't pass up the chance to act like an ass.

"Well, it's nice to hear I defended your honor," he says after a long sip of his milkshake.

"You did an admirable job," I tell him, tipping my milkshake cup in his direction.

"Speaking of being admirable," he starts, his expression shifting into seriousness. "I want to apologize again for what happened the night of Cody's party."

"Kieran, you've apologized enough already. I'm okay—I swear."

197

"Maybe, but I still feel bad for coming off like I was using you to get my memory back. And, I mean, getting my memory back is probably the most important thing in the world to me right now, but I'm also realizing that getting my memory back isn't going to mean anything if I've pushed away the people who are supposed to be closest to me. Every significant thing that's happened to me in the last year, you've been a part of whether I remember it or not. I don't want to lose you."

He seems almost heartbroken, and so I reassure him with "We've been over this before. You're not going to lose me. I'll always be a part of your life."

Kieran shakes his head. "I'm not talking about us just being friends," he says, looking at me so intensely I dart my eyes away, taking a sip of my milkshake and focusing my gaze on the picnic table. "I want to be with you, Zip. I knew it in some way even when I was with Steph—the whole thing with her didn't feel right once I got into it. But you..." He pauses and I look up. "That afternoon we spent together? When we went to the river and you kissed me? That was the most like...*me*...I've ever felt. I can't even put a finger on what I mean exactly, but I think I'm closer to the person I probably was when I'm with you. And the person I was seems like he was a pretty okay guy from what I've read."

"He was," I mumble. "He still is."

"Well, I'm not sure I'm making much sense, but I want the person I was and the person I am now to be the same person. And I know we made a big deal about your kiss being this sort of magic thing that was going to solve all of our problems, and so I'm sorry if that night at Cody's I came off like I wanted to make out with you just to jar my memory." Now he's the one focusing on the tabletop and avoiding my stare. "To be honest, I really just wanted to make out with you."

I really just wanted to make out with you, too, I want to say. I almost want to scream my thoughts at the top of my lungs, but the words don't come. Why is this so hard?

Maybe it's hard because he broke up with me. Maybe it's hard because he remembers almost nothing about what we've been through together.

"You have no reason to believe any of this," Kieran says as if he can read my mind. "I pushed you away and then acted like the only reason I wanted you back was because of what you could do for me. Like I said the night of the party, I know I need to prove myself to you, and I've been thinking about how I can start doing that."

"Okay," I say. "I'm listening."

Kieran sits back and flexes his hands as if he's just done a strenuous workout.

"Well, according to everything I've read, we never went on many dates."

"True," I say, realizing he's right—other than Prom and a few movie double-dates with Kayla and Brad, we were always more of a "hang out at home and watch movies" kind of couple, mostly because once you've gone to the Downtown Diner, the Burger Barn, and Paulie's Pizza, you've hit all the hot dating spots in Titusville, and on a teenager's allowance, going out in Sumner all the time can get expensive.

"Well, I was thinking—you're going be in physical therapy for awhile, right?"

"For pretty much the rest of my life—yeah," I grumble.

"So, you're going to need somebody to drive you back and forth from Sumner once a week."

"Twice a week, at least for a while," I correct him.

"Okay—twice a week. So, twice a week, I'll drive you to therapy after school, and when you're done, we'll do something here

199

in Sumner for a while until we need to be home. Whatever you want to do, we'll do. If you want to stop here and get ice cream every time, fine."

"You know, there's a mini golf course and batting cages out by the mall," I suggest, warming up to this whole "date" idea. "In a few weeks when I'm off my crutches and hobbling around in this big stupid leg brace, I'd love to take you on at mini golf."

Kieran squints in a way I've noticed he does now when he's trying to call forth a memory that may or may not be there.

"I'm not sure, but I'm guessing I like mini golf," he says. "Batting cages might be another story."

"*Everyone* likes mini golf," I tell him in a teasing tone. "I think that's one of the few simple facts of life." Reaching down, I tap my leg brace, which is sticking out from the table enough he'd be able to see it. "But I think batting cages are out for me for the immediate future. It'd be hard to pull off a decent stance in this monstrosity."

"Okay, then," he begins, shooting me that grin. "Mini golf twice a week once you're off your crutches, if that's what you want." The grin disappears as he turns serious. "I'll do whatever it takes to prove I want you for *you* and not just for what I think you can do for me."

Part of me hates that I've made Kieran feel that he has to prove himself to me, but the bigger part of me doesn't want to feel like I'm being used. I need to know that Kieran—whichever version of Kieran is going to exist from here on out—truly wants to be by my side.

And yet another part of me is excited for the chance to behave like we're a regular couple, going places together that aren't Titusville eateries or my living room. Normalcy isn't exactly something Kieran and I are familiar with, regardless of the state of our relationship.

"You've got a deal, Kieran Lanier," I say, reaching out for the hand that isn't curled around his milkshake cup. "My next therapy appointment is the day after tomorrow."

"I'll find out which one of my family members is willing to part with a car," he replies, lacing his fingers together with mine. He stares at me for a second before getting up, our hands still joined, and crossing over to my side of the picnic table. The table as a whole is pretty small, so there's not a ton of room for two people on a bench, and he has to sit right up against me.

I'm not complaining.

"Can I kiss you?" he asks quietly.

"On the forehead or on the lips?" I ask.

"Well, I know we're not having the best of luck with kissing on the lips at the moment, but we just made a deal on something and I think we should formally seal it, you know?"

"And somehow a forehead kiss doesn't seem formal enough?" I ask, keeping my face expressionless. I shouldn't tease him like this, but I can't help myself.

"Zip, I'm sorry…" he says, letting go of my hand, and I decide I don't want him to leave my side. I'm suspecting he didn't just *happen* to be at Sumner talking to people and he didn't just *accidentally* run into my grandfather, and I'm wondering which family member of mine he spoke with to find out I was going to be in Sumner after school.

If he's trying to prove himself to me, he's off to a pretty good start.

Before he can stand up and return to the other side of the table, I grab his face in my hands and plant a kiss firmly on his lips. He slides his arms around my waist and pulls me to him as best he can considering my leg hanging out in the aisle means I can't completely turn my body toward him. We cling to each other for what seems like a small eternity, kissing to the point I'm afraid we're going to lose our minds right here in front of Buster's Ice Cream. We both seem to sense our lack of control and pull away at the same time, but stay close enough together our foreheads are still touching.

"I think we've sealed the deal," he whispers, rubbing his nose against mine. "We're officially dating."

"Yup. We're officially dating," I whisper back, before allowing my mouth to close over his again.

CHAPTER 17

By my fourth physical therapy session, I'm almost more frustrated than I've been about anything in my entire life. I tried to move up a weight level on the leg press and I couldn't, and Jane reminds me—as she has to remind me after every therapy session— that my recovery is going to be a long process and I can't expect huge improvements after only a few sessions. While I know she's right, knowing the end date to my recovery is so far in the future doesn't make me any less impatient.

My grumpiness over my therapy appointment disappears the moment I walk out into the lobby and find Kieran waiting for me, just as he has been every time I've been to therapy so far. True to his word, he's taken me out somewhere in Sumner before taking me home; in addition to our trip to Buster's, we've been to the movies and to the Titusville baseball game versus Sumner over at Veterans' Park, where Kieran wisely brought lawn chairs for us to sit on off to the side since navigating the bleachers with my crutches and leg brace would have been more than a little difficult. And every time he comes to pick me up, he manages to keep our destination a secret until we arrive, and today is no different.

"So, where we headed?" I ask, walking up to him as he slides his phone, which he'd been playing with as I walked into the lobby, into his front jeans pocket.

"It's a surprise," he says, reaching out to squeeze my shoulder. "You okay? You seemed kind of bummed out just now when you walked out."

"Yeah," I say as we start for the parking lot. "Therapy's harder than I thought it would be, I guess. All my life, pretty much anything involving physical activity has been kind of easy for me, you know?

And this is so, so difficult and stressful. I had no idea therapy would be this grueling, both physically and mentally. Right now, I can't even imagine walking under my own power again."

"But you will," he says. He pauses since we're almost at the car, and he takes a few minutes to help me get settled in before continuing with his encouragements. "I mean, you know after a while you'll be off your crutches, and you know after a while you'll be out of the leg brace. These things take time." He starts the car and backs out of the parking space. "I can imagine it's frustrating, though. You know you're going to improve and you'll be all healed eventually, but you want it to happen today."

"Exactly."

Kieran heads down Four Mile Road past the mall, and I quickly realize we're heading toward downtown Sumner. "So, we're going somewhere on Main Street?" I ask, hoping to fool him into revealing a few clues about our destination, if not the destination itself.

"*Near* Main Street, and I'm not telling you anything else," he insists. "I swear, I'm going to start blindfolding you when we go on these dates."

"Or you could just tell me where we're going every time."

"And what fun would that be?" He grins. "I like surprising you—makes the whole thing seem like even more of an event."

I laugh a little as Kieran heads down Main Street past the coffee shops and antique stores and college bars and takes a right turn onto College Avenue in front of the Sumner College campus. There's nothing else on College Avenue other than a grocery store and some houses, so I ask, "We're going to the college?"

"You're getting warmer," he says, turning right onto campus and driving through the traffic circle in front of the main building and heading out to the large parking lot adjacent to the fine and performing arts center, and I think I can guess where we're headed. I've been here enough times with Gramps I know the Sumner Art Museum is inside the building, but I've also been here enough times to know what time the museum closes.

"Kieran, if we're going to the art museum, I think it closes at five," I point out, nodding at the clock on the dashboard. "We only have ten minutes."

"The museum may close at five for other mere mortals, but it doesn't close at five for us," he says, parking the car. "You're forgetting—I have connections here."

"Of course—your dad," I say, although, as things turn out, his connection isn't the dad I thought it would be. Morgan, in his maintenance crew uniform of a Sumner College polo shirt and jeans, is waiting for us outside the museum's entrance inside the building when we arrive, a mere two minutes before the museum is scheduled to close.

"We're all good?" Kieran asks him.

"All good," Morgan says, nodding a "hello" at me. "The desk clerk just left, but you guys have the place until five-thirty if you want it. As long as I'm here to lock up and make sure you two don't walk off with anything, you're fine."

"No offense," I ask, narrowing my eyes at Morgan, "but how did you get permission to do this?"

"Kieran told me he wanted to set this up, so I asked your grandfather if he could contact someone in the Art and Design Department to make it happen." He nods at the clock over the door to the museum. "I'm off work at five, so I'm not cutting into my work time by being here keeping the place open, but Gramps said the Art and Design people would only give us until five-thirty."

"See?" Kieran says, shoving his hands into the front pockets of his jeans. "We worked *your* connections, too."

"Smart." I nod at both of them. "And I've been here before. Trust me—it's not going to take us a half-hour to look at everything."

Morgan laughs and opens the glass door, allowing Kieran and me to enter the art museum, which really isn't much more than a large room with paintings lining the walls and sculptures evenly spaced throughout the room.

"I know you've been here a million times before," Kieran starts, his voice apologetic, "but I thought it might be kind of cool to experience the place by ourselves after-hours."

The museum is small and under-utilized enough that we probably would have been here by ourselves even if we'd been able to come during regular business hours, but I appreciate the lengths Kieran's gone through to make this happen, so I don't say what I'm thinking. Plus, being here when we're technically not supposed to be does kind of add a special feeling to the visit.

"This *is* pretty cool," I tell him, rubbing elbows with him since I can't hold his hand without letting go of my crutches.

We walk over to a photograph just inside the main door, a photograph that's always here no matter what exhibition is going on. The black and white picture shows the main building here at Sumner, simply known as Sumner Hall, the ground surrounding the castle-like building covered with about two or three inches of snow. The evergreen trees and bushes at the front of the building are dusted with snow as well, and the handwritten date in the corner of the photo tells us we're looking at the building in 1894, about twenty years after the college was founded.

"So, since we've got college on the brain," Kieran begins, taking his eyes from the photograph and glancing sideways at me. "Kayla keeps asking me if you've told me what's up with your college decisions. She says there's no way you haven't heard from Northwestern by now."

"How polite of her not to pester me herself," I point out.

"She's showing some uncharacteristic restraint," he says, and I laugh as he continues, "Although I'm guessing she's been harassing you anyway?"

"Oh, yeah," I confirm. And Kayla's right—I *did* hear from Northwestern. They sent my acceptance letter last week and a financial aid letter a few days later offering me enough scholarship money that I won't need to pay a dime for my education. And while Sumner says they'll still offer me a full basketball scholarship regardless of the state of my knee, it's going to be a while before I can tell whether or not I'll ever play again, and I know with some degree of certainty I'll never again play at the same level. So, Sumner could be offering me money and I'll end up riding the bench for four years.

Mom and I have done almost nothing but talk about my decision for the last few days, and although I'm going to wait until the end of the month to be sure—because I don't have to accept anywhere until May first—I've basically decided to go to Northwestern. Taking a basketball scholarship away from someone who might actually be able to play right away doesn't seem fair, and Northwestern's always been my dream school. Of course, my ultimate, wildest dream would have been to play basketball at Northwestern, but I always knew that was a long shot. As far as academics, though, Northwestern has top-notch programs in everything I'm considering as a major, and with my dad living close by, he can help me find a good place to continue my physical therapy and drive me to appointments if need be. And my dream has always been to go *away* to school. Not even leaving the county for college isn't exactly going away to college, and even though I've kind of made my peace with having grown up in the wasteland that is Titusville, I don't want to spend the next four years within easy driving distance, either.

But I haven't mentioned anything about my college decision to Kayla, no matter how much she bugs me to tell, nor have I said anything to Kieran—until right now.

"I did hear from Northwestern," I admit, walking over to a painting hanging to the right of the old Sumner photograph, a painting composed of nothing more than multi-colored shapes and lines and squiggles that don't seem to add up to anything recognizable. I swear I don't get art at all.

"And?"

"And I don't want to say anything else," I answer, looking at the painting and not at him.

"Okay," he says flatly, and since I can't tell if he's hurt or confused or what, I take a deep breath and start explaining.

"Kieran, look—you're still confused about where you want to go to school, and I don't…" I pause. "Okay, this is going to sound totally arrogant."

I sneak a peek at him and find he's giving me a version of his usual grin that nearly undoes me.

"I know you're trying really hard to prove yourself to me right now," I continue. "I don't want you making your college decision based on what I decide to do. So that's why I haven't said anything to you or Kayla. I even made my grandparents promise not to tell Morgan anything so he wouldn't slip up and tell you."

I half expect him to laugh and tell me to stop being so full of myself, but instead he says, "Yeah. That's fair. I mean, you're making complete sense."

"I am?"

"Uh huh." He shrugs. "You know I've been kind of looking for, like, some kind of a sign or whatever telling me where I'm supposed to go to school. If you told me where you were going to go,

208

I'm so confused right now, I probably *would* make my decision based on yours, even if you told me not to."

I exhale, a weight lifted from me. "I'm glad you understand," I tell him.

"Completely."

"I guess I thought our college decisions were important enough that we shouldn't make our individual choices dependent on what the other one does," I insist, although my heart is saying *Even though I want to*. I want so badly for Kieran to end up in Chicago so we can be close to each other, but I can't let him make a college decision that might not be what he truly wants.

"And what happens if one of us chooses Sumner and one of us chooses Chicago now that we're dating again?" he asks "I mean, I know we haven't been back together for very long, but..."

As Kieran's voice fades out, I think about how to answer his question and realize there's no good answer.

"Then we trust everything's will work out somehow, I guess." I say finally. "Things have been rough for us, but they've always managed to turn out okay somehow. I mean, I know you don't *remember* they have, but one way or another, they have. We just need to believe this whole college thing is going to turn out the same way. Sumner and Chicago aren't *that* far apart, and as long as our families are living in Titusville, we'll always be coming back home to visit, so I guess we could use that as an excuse to see each other—*if* one of us ends up here and the other one ends up in Chicago, that is."

Kieran smiles. "You've done a really good job not giving yourself away," he tells me.

"Well, it's not easy. I hate that I've made up my mind and I can't tell anyone, but I think this is the best decision for right now."

"And like I said, I understand. Kayla won't, but I do." Kieran grins, turning us toward an African-looking sculpture of a young man in the middle of the room. "I think she wants to start brainstorming decorating ideas for your dorm room."

I roll my eyes. "I'm sure she does," I grumble. "And we can take all summer to brainstorm decorating ideas for our room—*if* I go to Northwestern."

He nods and glances around the gallery. "So, what do you want to look at next?" he asks, easing us out of our conversation about college for now.

I move my head back and forth, taking in the various works of art. "I don't know," I mumble. "Thanks for bringing me here, and I'm really glad you set this whole thing up and all, but I'm probably the worst person in the world to take to an art museum. I mean, I appreciate art and I understand being an artist takes a lot of time and talent, but I guess art's not my thing, you know? Books, I get. Art baffles me most of the time."

"Baffles you how?"

I hobble back over to the first painting we'd examined. "Like, take this thing, for example," I start. "I mean, what the hell is this supposed to be? This little card here on the wall says it's called 'Community,' but to me, this painting is just this total mess of lines and dots. How's that supposed to represent 'community'?"

"It's a painting of people," Kieran says as if his response is obvious. I can sense my brow wrinkling, and so he points to the canvas, moving his finger around as he explains. "The lines and shapes and squiggly things are faces and arms and legs. The different colors represent different races, I'm guessing."

Tilting my head, I stare at the painting, and almost as if they've popped out from hiding behind other objects, the abstract shapes of people start to emerge with the help of Kieran pointing them out to me. "Okay, I can kind of see them now," I tell him. "But I could have stood here and stared at this thing for a million years and

210

never figured things out on my own. How were you able to look at this and just instantly say, 'Oh. Okay. People.'?"

Kieran shrugs. "I don't know," he starts. "I mean, someone else may look at this and see the different colored lines and shapes and squiggles and think, 'Oh, it's some kind of a metaphor. The different colors and different shapes are supposed to *represent* diversity,' and they might not find people at all."

"I wouldn't have even gotten far enough to think it was a metaphor," I grumble.

"Maybe it's..." Kieran pauses. "Maybe I'm just able to see things as more than what they appear to be at first glance. I can see the possibilities in things. I can see what *might* be."

"That's kind of a beautiful thought," I say, and I'm not teasing him.

"Thanks," he says, giving me his usual grin. "I totally just came up with it."

I elbow him in the ribs and he laughs a little before continuing "I think being able to sense the possible is why I enjoy art so much, and why I've apparently always enjoyed it, according to what I've read in my journals. You can create something, and you have an idea of what it's supposed to represent, but then you put it out there for other people and they interpret it however they want—and what they get might be something you've never even thought of. Art is all about possibilities. And my life, based on what I've read and based on what I'm going through now, has kind of always been about *im*possibilities and uncertainties and 'No, Kieran, you can't do that.' I think I like that art is all about uncertainty, too, but it's about positive uncertainties."

I lean forward as much as I can to gaze past Kieran and through the glass front door of the museum, where Morgan is pacing back and forth aimlessly in the lobby, waiting for us to finish so he can lock up.

"And sometimes, maybe art's about negative uncertainties that turn out to be positive," I say, still focusing my attention on Morgan. Kieran follows my gaze and narrows his eyes at me.

"I don't get what you mean."

"You've seen all the pictures you used to draw of Morgan when you were dreaming about him, right?" I ask.

"Yeah."

"You used to call him the 'Boogey Man,'" I remind him, assuming he's also read the descriptions of Morgan he wrote down along with the drawings. "You were afraid of him."

"Until my dad—Jim, I mean—convinced me I was drawing future versions of myself so I wouldn't think of him as a threat," he recalls, but he says the words in the flat way I've come to identify as meaning he's remembering what he's read and not what lives inside his mind as a memory.

"And then he turned out to be one of the good guys," I say, still gazing out into the lobby, where Morgan has stopped milling around and is now leaning against the wall next to the door, only his right arm visible to me from this angle.

"Yeah," Kieran starts. "I guess there are good possibilities and bad possibilities. I'm just lucky he turned out to be one of the good ones."

"Well, maybe I need to start focusing more on the positive possibilities rather than what I think already is," I suggest, glancing back at the painting. "There," I say, pointing at a collection of lines and dots and squiggles in the corner. "That looks like kind of a stick figure almost and the dots are eyes…the curved lines are her hair…a little girl, maybe?"

"I think I see her," Kieran says, following my finger with his eyes as I point out the various shapes that make up the little girl.

I can't help but laugh in an almost weird kind of relief. I've felt so stupid ever since we've walked in here and started looking at things that finding the little girl in the painting makes me feel like a total genius. "You know, one of these days I might just get this whole art thing," I joke, because I don't really believe I'll ever "get" art, at least not in the way Kieran does.

"I think you get it," he says, leaning down to me tentatively. I raise my head and wish I could stand on my tiptoes like I used to in order to kiss him, but he seems to sense I'm inviting him in anyway and leans all the way in for a brief kiss.

"You know, you already see the possibilities in things—the good possibilities," he whispers when we part enough so he can speak. "You've always believed I'll get my memory back. You believe no matter how our college decisions end up, everything's going to be okay. And you believe in the possibility of us, or I'm guessing you wouldn't be here right now."

"True," I murmur, and his lips close over mine again. I want so badly to toss these stupid crutches to the floor and throw my arms around him, and I realize what I've missed most these last few months of being apart and in this short time of being together but being hampered by my injury is the ability to press up against him, to feel his arms around me completely and to measure our heartbeats as they race in unison. Even though we're kissing right now, a measure of distance still exists between us.

But don't get me wrong—kissing is awesome. And if kissing's all the closeness I can get right now, I'll live.

I hear footsteps behind us, and Kieran pulls back from me. Turning to glance over my shoulder, I see that Morgan's entered the museum and stopped a few feet from us. "Just wanted to let you know you've only got a few more minutes to enjoy all this wondrous art," he says, his voice flat.

"I've got all the wondrous art I need right here," Kieran says to him, but he's looking down at me. Morgan smiles and then makes a little gagging noise in the back of his throat as he heads back for the lobby.

"So, was that a little overboard?" Kieran asks, his hand caressing my back.

"Comparing me to a wondrous work of art?" I ask. Kieran nods and I say "Yeah—maybe a little. Maybe a lot, actually."

"Well, I can't help it if I think you're the most beautiful thing in here." He grins and I roll my eyes.

"Okay—you need to stop now."

His grin widens until he starts laughing, and then he says, "All right. Sounds like we have limited time, so what should we focus on next?"

"Um," I swivel my head around until my eyes come to rest on a basket with intricately woven designs on a pillar across the room. "Let's go look at that Easter basket thing over there."

"You mean the Native American woven basket?" he corrects me and I shoot him a look, to which he responds "Sorry, but we studied a slide of that exact basket in art class earlier this semester."

We start walking off toward the basket and I sigh. "I'm never going to get this whole art thing," I mumble, and Kieran just laughs and puts his hand on my back to guide me as we make our way to the other end of the museum.

CHAPTER 18

It's Prom night—or, as tonight is going to be known in my life, it's "Have dinner at your grandparents' and hang out and watch bad movies with your mom" night. And I'm cool with that. I've been to one Prom, and given everything that happened, it may have been one Prom too many. And even though I'm now once again dating the guy I went with last year, he doesn't remember much about last year, Prom night or otherwise. So I'm more than happy to pretend what's going on at the high school and at the Stanley Farm tonight has nothing to do with me.

"Ready to go?" Mom says, jingling her keys at me. We would normally walk over to my grandparents' house, of course, but since my injury, much of what we normally do has gone right out the window. I nod as I turn off the playoff basketball game I'm watching and hoist myself up from the couch. It's been a little over a month since my surgery and I'm finally off crutches. Now, I have enough strength to half-walk, half-drag myself around under my own power, my right leg still hampered by my enormous leg brace.

We head outside and settle in for the millisecond drive to my grandparents' house, where we can smell the steaks Morgan's grilling outside the carport even before we're out of the car. Mom heads over to him at the grill while I go inside to the kitchen, where Gram is tossing a green salad with wooden tongs.

"Where's Gramps?" I ask, planting a kiss on her cheek.

"He's out in the studio," she tells me, and a smile that seems a little more wide and crooked than her normal smile crosses her face as she stares out the window over the sink at the art studio in the backyard. "I'll send you out to get him when we're ready to eat. He's immersed in some new project right now, so I don't think he had any problem leaving the cooking to Morgan and me."

"Do you need any help?"

"Well, the potatoes should be almost done," she says, nodding toward the oven. "You can grab a fork and check on them for me."

I rummage in the silverware drawer for a fork and do as she asks, reaching into the roasting pan to spear a potato, blowing on it as I shut the oven. "I think they're done," I tell her after a few nibbles. I grab two potholders from the counter and take the potatoes out as Mom and Morgan enter with a plate piled high with steaks.

"If we're ready to eat, guess I should go get Gramps?" I ask.

Mom looks at Morgan, Morgan looks at Gram, and Gram looks at Mom, all of them having some kind of silent conversation with their eyes I can't manage to translate.

"You guys are acting like a bunch of freaks," I point out. "I didn't exactly ask a difficult question. Gramps *is* eating with us, right?"

Gram nods her head rapidly as if I've pulled her out of a trance.

"Of course Gramps is eating with us, sweetheart. Go on out to the studio," Gram says.

I back out of the kitchen, afraid these pod people I thought were my family might do something weird if I don't keep an eye on them. Only once I reach the art studio do I understand what's going on.

"Gramps?" I say, knocking and entering at the same time, immediately stopping in my tracks. Instead of the usual harsh fluorescent lights over the workbench, the studio is bathed in a soft glow from tiny white Christmas lights strung around the perimeter of the room near the ceiling. A small votive candle on a card table in the corner near the lithography press also adds some light, and then

216

there's Kieran, standing in the middle of the room, his smile so wide he could probably light up the space by himself without any help.

"What…what is this?" I ask.

"Isn't it obvious?" Kieran says, turning at the waist as he sweeps his hand out in front of him. "This is Prom."

I notice the glow from another light—Kieran's phone, plugged into some speakers on the workbench, the music player emitting soft music.

"I think we're missing about a hundred other people," I point out.

"They weren't invited. I thought we could let them keep their big, crowded Prom with bad music and cheap decorations and throw a private one of our own."

"You seem to know a lot about Prom for a guy who doesn't remember going to one before." I smile, but my hands at my sides are twitching with nerves.

"I read a lot," he says, shooting me that grin and stuffing his hands in his pants pockets. I look him up and down—he's wearing dark khaki pants and a light blue button down Oxford shirt with a white t-shirt underneath, while I'm in a gray Titusville Basketball t-shirt and baggy navy mesh shorts along with my latest stylish accessory, my giant black leg brace.

"I'm a little underdressed for the occasion," I admit.

"You look amazing," he says, taking a few steps to close the distance between us. "You look like *you*."

"And that's a good thing?" I ask through a laugh.

"That's a *very* good thing." He eliminates the space between us completely and takes my hands as I hear a throat clear in the doorway behind me. I swivel my head around to find Morgan with a plate of food in each hand and my grandmother right behind him carrying drinks. Kieran and I step aside and they enter, taking the food and

217

drinks to the two place settings atop the white tablecloth. I watch in stunned silence as they do their work, Kieran telling them a polite "thank you" as they make their way out of the studio. As Morgan shuts the door behind him, Kieran leads me by the hand to the table and pulls my folding chair out for me. I sort of sit, sort of fall into the seat, even more ungraceful than usual thanks to my knee. Kieran tries to push the chair in with me in it, but my usual weight combined with my leg brace is a little too much for him to handle.

"Sorry," he mumbles, standing back and allowing me to scoot myself up to the table by grabbing the underside of the chair and hopping both the chair and myself forward until I can reach my food. So dignified.

"I'm the one who should be apologizing," I tell him. "You're trying to be all sweet and chivalrous and my stupid leg is getting in the way."

"So I get credit for trying?" he asks, grinning as he takes his seat on the other side of the table.

"You get credit for *succeeding*." I glance around the room at the lights, the phone playing music on the workbench, the amazing dinner before us. "I can't believe you did all this."

"I had a lot of help," he says, shrugging as he cuts into his steak.

"So was everyone in on this?" I ask. "My mom, too?"

"Yeah. Once I told everyone I wanted to give you a Prom, she and your grandmother came up with the idea of getting you over here for dinner. And your grandfather's been upstairs in the house this whole time, by the way. He and Morgan helped me set everything up out here." He pauses. "Everybody at school has been so hyped up over Prom the last couple of weeks, and I started to feel bad because I hadn't asked you—"

"Kieran, we've been back together for, like, five minutes," I say, spearing a potato with my fork. "I wasn't expecting you to ask me to Prom."

"I know. But still—every other couple in school is at the dance right now."

"I kind of didn't *want* to go, if you want the truth. I mean, last year definitely had its moments, but there was so much other stuff…" I shake my head as my voice trails off. "And once you've seen one Prom, you've seen them all, so whatever."

He laughs as I blow off the idea of Prom with a wave of my hand and continue shoveling in food.

"Well, last year's Prom *did* have its moments," he says, avoiding my eyes and focusing on his plate. "I seem to remember one in the barn at the Stanleys' when we were dancing. I pulled you to me and kissed you, and you rested your head on my shoulder and closed your eyes. A few minutes later, the lights went out."

I nearly choke on a piece of steak as our eyes lock. He sounds so confident, I almost wonder if he isn't recalling last year from memory, but I don't want to get my hopes up.

"So, you remember *reading* about us dancing, right?" I check with him after I swallow.

"No." He points to his temple. "I *remember* remember. Two days ago, after school…I had a headache when I got home, so I took a nap and when I woke up, I could recall the moment as clear as anything. I checked my journals to make sure the details matched up."

At a loss for words, I don't know what else to do but reach across the table for his free hand. He rubs his thumb across my skin before shrugging his shoulders and saying, "Anyway, after everything I've put you through over the last few months, I thought you deserved a Prom—or the good parts of a Prom, anyway. Like

219

good food." He sweeps his free hand in the air over our plates for emphasis. "And slow dancing to music we get to pick out ourselves."

"And kissing?" I ask when he doesn't say so himself.

"Oh, yeah. Definitely kissing. Although I don't think we'll want to risk much more with your family and my dad just a few yards away."

"Good point. And you don't owe me anything, by the way," I'm quick to point out.

"So, I should grab Morgan and your grandfather and we should just tear all of this down?" he asks, rising from his chair and making like he's going to take his plate and walk out.

"I didn't say that," I tell him with a little laugh. "I mean, you went to all this trouble. We might as well stay and enjoy ourselves."

"Thought so," Kieran says, shooting me his grin. He rests his plate on the table and sits back down. "Now, when we left off, I think we were talking about kissing..."

As if she could hear our conversation, my mom knocks on the door and sticks her head inside the studio without waiting for a response. "Everyone decent in here?" she asks.

"Mom, please," I whine as she walks inside carrying a rectangular pan and two dessert plates. Kieran gives her a little laugh as she sets the pan and plates on the edge of the table.

"Sorry," she says. "Just here to deliver Gram's red velvet cake." She turns back to the door, but before she slips out she tells us "You two can go back to groping each other now, or whatever you were doing."

"Mooom," I moan, putting my head in my hands as Kieran has another good laugh.

"I really like your mom."

"Good thing," I mumble, lifting my head. "Because I sort of don't right now. She's embarrassing."

220

We finish our meals and dig into the cake, and as I'm trying to press every last morsel of a giant slice onto the tines of my fork, Kieran says, "Oh, wow. I almost forgot."

He gets up and crosses to the workbench as I put my fork down and twist in my chair to see what he's doing. When he turns back around to face the table, he's holding a plastic container with a red rose corsage.

"It's not a Prom without a corsage," he points out.

I pull myself up from the table with about as much grace as a moose and hobble over to him.

"You really thought of everything, didn't you?" I smile, offering him my hand. He slides the elastic band up to my wrist and caresses my palm before letting go.

"I tried." He reaches back to the workbench, setting down the plastic container and cranking the volume on his phone up a few notches so music fills the room, but not so loud that we can't talk to each other. "So, since this is Prom, should we dance?" he asks.

I cast a sad glance down at my stupid leg brace. "I'll do my best," I promise him. "I probably won't be too graceful, but, then again, I'm not exactly graceful on the dance floor when I'm not wearing a thousand-pound leg brace, either."

"Well, other than the brief memory of us dancing together last year, I have no memories of dancing before, like, ever. So I'm guessing I'm not exactly Mr. Smooth." He reaches out and places his hands on my waist. "I guess at the very least we can put our arms around each other and rock back and forth."

"Sounds pretty good to me."

I wrap my arms around his neck and the two of us sway together, our feet not moving much from their designated places on the floor.

"So, you know, today is May ninth," he says.

"This is true."

"Which means we both would have had to notify our chosen colleges by now."

"Also true."

We both stop moving but stay in each other's arms as we stare, not saying anything for nearly a minute.

"Where are you going?" he asks.

"Where are *you* going?" I fire back.

"I asked you first."

I take a deep breath and close my eyes. "I'm going to Northwestern," I tell him before opening one eye to find him smiling at me.

"I'm going to the Art Institute."

I open my eye and Kieran rests his forehead on mine, both of us exhaling with relief.

"What made you decide to go to Chicago over Sumner?" I ask, although part of me is so elated right now, I barely care about his reasons. We're going to be a forty-five minute train ride away from each other for the next four years instead of a two-hour car trip, which is all that matters.

"Ultimately, I think I liked the idea of being in the city," he says. "There's more stuff to do, and I'll have easier access to internships and job opportunities. Plus, you may have noticed Sumner isn't exactly home to a bustling art scene."

"You mean the Sumner College Art Museum doesn't count?" I say, keeping my voice flat, but the slight teasing edge to my words gives me away.

He smiles. "Not exactly," he notes. "In the end, I couldn't pass up the opportunity to go to art school in a major city. Plus, Kayla will be close by, and I think that makes my parents a little more comfortable about both of us leaving home." He pauses. "So, why Northwestern?"

"Because, in the end, going there is what I've always wanted. I didn't even think about going somewhere else until a few months ago when Coach told me I might be able to attract some attention from schools as far as basketball. But then my leg got messed up and Northwestern sent my acceptance letter, and it seemed like the universe was telling me what I'd always wanted was the right thing for me, you know? I'll be able to see my dad and Liv and Kathy more often, plus, I'll get to room with Kayla and Brad's already there, so I won't be totally alone on campus.

"Sounds like Kayla's going to be pretty happy with both of us," he comments, and I laugh.

"Yeah—because our decisions were really about her all along."

"I'm sure she'd like to believe that."

"I won't tell her if you won't," I say.

"Deal."

We are quiet for a moment, falling back into each other's arms and swaying to the music floating through the tiny speakers attached to Kieran's phone. But about halfway through the song, Kieran stops moving and steps back from me slightly.

"Good thing we'll be close to each other for the next four years," he says, before lowering his voice, "because I'm pretty sure I'm falling in love with you."

The words give me a jolt to the point I almost buckle, but I fight to stay upright.

"And I'm not talking about falling in love with the person in my notebooks, just so you know. As much as I want to remember her, that girl is only words on a page." He takes a hand from my waist and traces the outline of my jaw with his index finger. "I'm talking about falling in love with the girl who kissed me at the river back in February. I'm talking about the girl who *wouldn't* let me keep kissing her at Cody's party. I'm talking about the girl I've been hanging out with for the last few weeks. I'm in love with *her*." He pauses. "And I'm sure I'd love that other girl, too, if I could remember more than just bits and pieces of her." Another pause. "I'm probably not making any sense…I'm not doing this well."

I shake my head and pull back so we can see each other clearly.

"Kieran, I get it. I'm not sure that girl in your notebooks even exists anymore, to tell you the truth. So much has happened since last year, even just since December…" Now I'm the one to pause because I'm confusing myself. "I guess what I'm saying is, people change all the time to some extent. I mean, the *core* of who we are stays the same, but everything around us is constantly moving forward to the point we either adapt or get left behind. So, in some way, the people we are now won't be the people we are next week, next month…"

My voice fades and blends in with the guitar on the song that's currently playing, and Kieran moves his hands to my shoulders to keep us still.

"You know my memory might never come back completely," he says, looking into my eyes with such a laser-like intensity I can almost sense my retinas burning. "I want so badly to remember everything we had together, but that might not happen."

"I know," I say quietly, but he continues before I can say anything else.

"But if there's nothing we can do to bring my memory back for good, then I'm okay if you are. Like you said—everything's constantly moving forward, and we need to change as things change. Nothing about life is permanent." He runs his finger along my jaw once again. "Or, not much is permanent, anyway. *Me*, the core of who

224

I am…well, I'm pretty sure I'm going to love you next week. And next month. And next year and beyond into infinity. *That's* permanent."

"And I'm pretty sure I'll love you, too," I whisper, resting my forehead against his again. "I never stopped. I loved the person you were before, and I love the person you are now. And I can't predict the future, but I'm guessing I'm going to love the person you'll be then, too."

"Apparently I used to be able to predict the future but I kind of sucked at it." Kieran says. "But I'm finding it's easier to let the future take care of itself."

"Well, the future is coming whether we can predict it or not," I point out. "Even when you were seeing things, they were never complete enough for us to change what eventually happened. The future still came, no matter what we did—we couldn't stop it."

"True," he says, adding, "although there's one thing I can definitely predict about our future that I don't want to avoid."

"Which would be…"

"Lots of this." Kieran lowers his mouth to mine for a kiss so slow and lingering, I almost feel as though time has slowed down, rewinding us back to the past and our first kiss, right here in the art studio, one of the few things about our past Kieran can recall. And I realize I don't care about him only recalling a few things about us.

While I absolutely hope Kieran's memory comes back to him completely at some point, I know we'll both be okay if he never remembers another thing. Both our present and our future seem pretty promising, and the past is in the past, even if only one of us remembers it.

We part just enough for me to breathe against his lips "If this is what the future holds, I'm all in," before we lose ourselves in each other all over again.

CHAPTER 19

Senior year, I've learned, is filled with perks, especially once you've made your college choice and you can kind of coast along on autopilot until graduation. One of the best senior perks at Titusville High is that if your grade is an A or a B grade in a class going into the final, you can choose whether or not to take the exam. And since I have straight A's because I finally conquered physics, my life consists of several mornings' worth of free periods during finals week.

Even finals week itself is a senior perk. Because grades need to be averaged before the graduation ceremony, seniors take finals a week earlier than the rest of the school and, while the underclassmen suffer, the seniors get some time off before graduation. For three years, I've sat in classes on the last day of senior finals, watching the seniors make fun of my classmates and me through the narrow windows set into the classroom doors. Now, I'm the one poking fun, waving and mock pouting at Tori Sandowsky as she sits through her last chemistry class of the year. Tori notices me, checks to make sure Mr. Reynolds is facing the blackboard, and gives me a middle finger salute with both hands. I laugh and head upstairs to my last class ever at Titusville High School—seventh-period English.

But there's no learning going on today. Mrs. Rossdale is busy collecting our textbooks and writing hall passes for those who left their textbooks in their lockers—any responsibility for being prepared is completely out the window since we're not actually having class. Those of us who are still in the classroom are talking freely and loudly knowing there are no consequences for doing so. Having an open conversation isn't going to be enough to get detention on the last day of school, and if anyone did pull a detention-worthy act—which I guess would be something like vandalism or fighting—that person would probably end up banned from graduation altogether.

Because we can without any repercussions, Kieran and I sit with our desks scooted up against each other in the back of the room, the two of us huddled so close together our heads are nearly touching, our bodies and desks forming a little island in a sea of noise.

"So, I was thinking," he starts, propping his elbow on my desk, "It's Friday night, school's out...why don't we go on a date?"

"My next therapy appointment isn't until next week," I point out, not that I need to—Kieran's committed my therapy schedule to memory by now.

"Well, I was thinking we could go out anyway. It's not like we need your therapy appointments for an excuse to go to Sumner."

I arch an eyebrow at him. "Three dates in one week?" I say with mock amazement. "You'll need to take out a loan if we keep this up."

"Yeah. I think I'll find a job once we get to Chicago so I can keep you in the style to which you've become accustomed."

I let out a laugh, and I like knowing I can laugh freely in a classroom and not get in trouble.

"So, what did you have in mind?" I ask.

Before Kieran can answer, Micah Lierman, a sophomore who works in the front office during his study hall period, comes in with a note for Mrs. Rossdale.

"Kayla and Zara, you're wanted in the principal's office," Mrs. Rossdale says over the hum of student conversations.

I turn to Kayla, she turns to me, and the entire class erupts in a chorus of "Ooooooh," to which Kayla says, "Oh, shut up" to no one in particular. Kieran shoots me a puzzled look, and I shrug my shoulders at him as if to say, "I have no idea what's up." I join Kayla

227

in the front of the room, and the two of us head out into the hallway together.

"Any idea why we're being summoned to Rosner's office on the last day of school?" Kayla asks as we make our way to the stairs, and after thinking for a second, I'm hit with an idea of what this might be all about.

"Well, since the last final exam periods were this morning, I'm guessing Rosner wants to talk to us about who's going to be valedictorian. No one's said anything to me yet about which one of us it's going to be. Anyone said anything to you?"

Kayla's forehead furrows. "No, but…we can't *both* be valedictorian?" she asks. "I hear some schools have more than one."

"Titusville gave up on the multiple valedictorian thing a few years ago. One class had three kids with the same grade point average and so they decided to let all three of them give commencement speeches. The ceremony lasted about four days." Kayla laughs and I continue, "So now, if people are tied based on grades, the administration looks at standardized test scores. If people are still tied after test scores, then I don't know what happens."

"I'm hoping some kind of sudden-death scenario comes into play," Kayla says, smiling and narrowing her eyes.

"You would."

"I'm thinking pistols at dawn…a cage match, maybe."

"You're forgetting I'm more than a little incapacitated," I remind her, pointing down at my leg brace, which is currently forcing me to take one stair at a time rather than going down at my usual gallop.

"Oh—trust me. I didn't forget."

I groan at her as we finally reach the school lobby. Kayla hangs back and allows me to hobble ahead of her to the office, where she reaches out to open the door for me.

"Mr. Rosner's expecting you," Mrs. Gillette tells us from her post behind the counter, and the two of us walk across the main office area to Rosner's office. His door is open, and we peek our heads in.

"Zara. Kayla. Please, come in." Rosner says once he notices us. He stands and motions to two navy blue vinyl chairs in front of his desk. As we sit down, he says, "I need to discuss the valedictorian situation with you."

"Okay," Kayla answers for both of us.

"Since neither of you had to take final exams, your grade point averages for the year are identical. But after checking your college entrance exam scores, we found Kayla had higher scores on both national tests. The margin was only a few points, the closest since we've been determining valedictorians by this method, but rules are rules." Rosner sits back in his faded leather desk chair and clasps his hands together over the edge of his desk. "Congratulations, Kayla," he says.

"Thanks," she replies, smiling, "but I don't want it."

The expression on Rosner's face matches my emotions right now—totally stunned. Kayla's never given me any indication she didn't want to be Number One. Kayla always wants to be Number One at everything, so I just assumed being valedictorian would be the next potential victory on her list of things she wanted to accomplish.

"What do you mean, you don't want it?" Rosner asks before I can.

Kayla addresses her answer to me. "This isn't my town," Kayla begins. "You've lived here your entire life. Everyone knows you and cares about you and has since you were a little kid. I have, like, four friends here. I hardly give a crap about anyone beyond a few people." She pauses and gives Rosner a quick glance. "No offense or anything."

"None taken," he says, his mouth twitching into an amused smile.

"I think Zip should be the one who gets to address the class and the whole town," she says, before shifting to speak to me once again. "And this isn't some pity thing because of your leg, either, because I can tell that's what you're thinking."

I bite my lip because the thought had crossed my mind.

"We can't go changing things on a whim, Ms. Lanier," Rosner points out, and I almost laugh out loud at the fact that Kayla is now "Ms. Lanier," probably because she's pissing him off. "Superintendant Turner and the school board put these rules in place for a reason. And the rule is that the valedictorian is the person with the highest grade point average and, in case of a tie, the person with the highest test scores."

"But is there a rule stating the valedictorian has to be the one to give the speech at graduation?"

Rosner's brow furrows, causing the wrinkles in his high forehead to deepen.

"To be honest, I don't know, but I can certainly check." He glances back and forth between both of us before finally settling his gaze on me. "Assuming you're both on board with this plan, of course."

"So, even though Kayla's the valedictorian, I'd give the speech at graduation," I say, making sure I'm understanding everything.

Rosner shifts his eyes to Kayla, who nods at him.

"Yes," he tells me. "As long as the school board says it's okay."

I'm not exactly thrilled at the prospect of having to give a speech in front of the entire town, but I'd expected to give one anyway if I'd been named valedictorian, so this isn't exactly a change of plans for me.

"I'll call Superintendant Turner to make sure the valedictorian handing the speech over to someone else is acceptable, and I'll keep you both posted." Rosner stands up from his desk. "You can go back to class now."

Kayla and I leave his office and head out into the main hallway. "So what was that all about?" I ask her as we make our way to the stairs.

"Are you kidding me? I don't want to give a speech in front of the whole town. And *you're* the one who's probably going into broadcasting, anyway. I figured you needed the practice."

"And you're going to be a lawyer," I point out. "So it's not like you won't ever be talking in front of people."

We reach the bottom of the stairs and gaze up at the landing. I sigh and grab hold of the railing to start pulling myself up, but Kayla grabs my free arm.

"By the time we get back upstairs, the period will be over," she tells me, nodding at the second to last step and sitting down. "It's not like we're going to get in trouble if we don't go back. Kieran will bring our stuff down for us."

I lower myself down next to her. "So, you really gave up the speech because you're too scared to talk in front of people?" I ask, not bothering to mask my skepticism.

"No," she says, shaking her head. "Not at all. What I said in Rosner's office was completely true. I'm more than happy to be valedictorian, but you deserve to give that speech. Like I said, this is your town. You've lived here your whole life. I'm passing through, basically. No one wants to hear what I have to say."

"No one wants to hear what I have to say, either," I insist.

"Zip, think about everything you've been through in the last year or so. You have more to say to people than anyone."

231

"And most of it, I can't say," I fire back, giving her a look. "You know that. I can't get up on stage and tell people about the last year and a half of our lives in gory detail."

Kayla rolls her eyes at me. "You don't do it in gory detail," she says. "You dance around it. Do like Brad did last year—tell a story and spin some sort of lesson out of those details. Get creative."

"If there's one thing I'm not, it's creative," I say with a sigh as the bell rings. Kayla helps me to my feet so we aren't crushed by the herd of people rushing down the stairs, and we wait off to the side for a moment before Kieran, as Kayla had predicted, makes his way down to us, a backpack slung over each shoulder while he carries mine with his left hand.

"Sorry you got stuck carrying all of this," I say to him as he hands my backpack to me.

"No big deal. I thought you guys might not make the trip back upstairs." He lets Kayla's backpack fall from his shoulder and she takes it from him. "And it's not like there's anything in these backpacks anyway since it's our last day."

We head for the side exit, none of us lingering to gaze back on the main part of the school. When we come for graduation next week, we'll line up right outside the gym for the procession to the football field, so this particular moment really is the last time we'll be inside the high school as students. And while I'm tempted to glance over my shoulder at the place I've spent the last four years of my life—six, counting my two years in the junior high wing—I resist the urge and keep moving forward with the Laniers toward the outside doors.

"So what did Rosner want to talk to you two about?" Kieran asks.

"Graduation," Kayla tells him. "I'm valedictorian, but we think we've worked it out so Zip is going to give the speech."

Kieran raises an eyebrow at me. "And you're okay with that?" he asks.

"With losing the top spot in the class to your sister? No." I brace myself as Kayla gives me hard joke-punch to the shoulder. "With giving the speech? I'm mostly okay, I guess."

"Zip doesn't think she has anything to say to anyone," Kayla says, tilting her head forward.

"You have plenty to say," Kieran insists as we walk through the double doors and out to the parking lot.

"Maybe," I mumble, a little more confident now than a while ago when Kayla and I were talking inside the school. "I'm just not sure how to say it."

"Then we'll help you," Kieran offers, glancing over at Kayla. "Right, Kay?"

"Sure," Kayla says, punching a button on her keychain to unlock her car. "Like I told you inside, you've got more to say to this town than anyone after what you've been through this past year and a half. And we lived everything right along with you."

"And just think," I say, linking arms with her before she can get in the driver's side, "if you help me write the speech, it'll be almost like you're giving it yourself."

Kayla strokes her chin and narrows her eyes, thinking through my description. "*My* words coming out of *your* mouth, and I don't have to stand up and say anything in front of the entire population of Titusville?" she starts. "I could totally get into that."

"Kayla," Kieran warns, opening the back door so he can help me inside. "This is Zip's speech. You gave it up. We're just helping her out."

"I'm only kidding," Kayla says, settling into the front seat and fastening her seat belt. "Should we head for the Downtown Diner and start putting some ideas together?"

We get confirmation from Rosner the next day that the Titusville School Board has no problem with Kayla handing the graduation speech over to me, and every day for the next week, Kayla, Kieran and I sit together—either at the Diner or at their house—and puzzle over the experiences we've had over the last year, what we've learned from those experiences, and how I can convey those experiences to the entire town without giving away any of our secrets. We work and write and polish right up until Saturday afternoon, when my mom starts sending me frantic text messages to come home from the Laniers' and rest up before the ceremony.

Kieran helps me gather up the small pile of index cards on which we've carefully copied my notes and offers to drive me home.

"Thanks," I tell him as we walk out of the kitchen, where Kayla's on the phone with Brad and is so invested in finding out his estimated time of arrival from Evanston she's completely unaware Kieran's swiping her keys from a hook on the wall in the hallway.

"If you keep that up, you'll be lucky if she ever lets you borrow the Jeep once we get to Chicago," I say quietly as Kieran opens the front door.

"Once we get to Chicago, I'll be taking public transit everywhere so I won't need to rely on her unless I need a ride back to Titusville," he points out, taking the index cards from me and sliding an arm around my waist so he can help me down the porch steps.

"I'll be so happy when I can do stuff on my own again," I grumble once we reach the walk leading to the driveway.

"You don't like doing stuff with me?" he teases.

"I do—very much, in fact—and you get what I mean," I fire back. "I want to be able to *move* completely on my own again, so people don't have to help me all the time. I can't do anything by myself."

As if proving my point, when we get to the Jeep, Kieran slides the front passenger seat back as far as it will go because he practically has to lift me up into the seat. Once he's buckled in on the other side, he pauses before starting the engine.

"You can do plenty of things without any help," he points out. "You can see and hear and talk. You can eat and read and write. You can go to sleep when you want and wake up when you want."

I give him a weak smile as he finishes the last sentence. "So can you—now," I remind him.

"Yeah," he says, sticking the key in the ignition and starting the car. "And lucky for me, I guess, I can't really remember what it was like to need someone looking out for me all the time because I couldn't control what my body was going to do to me when. But I've read my journals enough to know I did my best to live as well as I could...or as well as my family would *let* me, anyway."

"I sense a life lesson coming on here," I say through an amused smirk, and he puts on the brakes in order to lean in and kiss me on the cheek.

"Just focus on the things you're sure you can still do, Zip, and let those thoughts get you through this," he tells me, putting his foot on the gas pedal once again. "You may never play basketball at the same level again, but eventually, you'll be able to walk down porch steps and get in and out of a car by yourself. Your injury isn't completely irreversible. For a long time, apparently, I didn't have the luxury of believing that about my condition. You're lucky."

I close my eyes, embarrassed, as he turns onto the county road. "I know, and I'm sorry for being such a whiner," I say. "I just get frustrated sometimes. And I'm not looking forward to having to limp up on stage tonight in front of the entire town. I should have made your sister do this."

"So are you more nervous about getting up on stage, or are you more nervous about giving the speech?"

"Yes," I answer, laughing. "I'm terrified of both. I'm afraid I'll trip climbing up to the stage and I'm afraid everyone in town's going to laugh at me while I'm giving this speech."

I run my thumb along the edge of the index cards as Kieran assures me "No one's going to laugh at you, even if you trip and fall and even if they think your speech is the dumbest thing they've ever heard—which they *won't* by the way. And even if they do think it's the dumbest thing they've ever heard, the hell with them. You're out of this town at the end of the summer anyway, right?"

I giggle as he pulls into my driveway and stops outside the carport. "But, like I said, no one's going to laugh at you. And I think it's pretty natural to be nervous before a speech. Aren't more people afraid of public speaking than death?"

"Something like that," I say, pretty sure I've read that statistic before myself. "Which doesn't exactly make me more secure about the whole thing."

"Well, if you get nervous, just stare at me," he offers. "I won't be laughing—except when I'm supposed to laugh—and I'll be smiling at you the whole time. And if that doesn't work, imagine everyone in their underwear."

"I think I'll just look at you," I tell him. "Trust me—there are *a lot* of people in this town I don't want to think about in their underwear."

Kieran gets out of the car and comes to the passenger side to help me, which ends with my sliding out of the seat and into his arms.

"Well, if *this* is what happens when I need help, maybe being stuck with a bum leg for a while won't be so bad," I murmur, just before Kieran's lips meet mine, and I think for the millionth time how glad I am everything worked out and we're back together. With

Kieran by my side, I can do anything, even with a giant leg brace slowing me down.

We break the kiss and he moves his lips to my forehead. "You're going to be great tonight," he breathes against my skin. "You have no idea how incredible you are, no matter what you're doing. I love you, okay?"

"I love you, too," I whisper into the hollow of his neck, and we stand together, the open car door shielding us from the house, for several minutes, the moment only broken by my mom sticking her head out the front door of the house.

"Are you planning on leaving my daughter here, or are you moving in?" she calls out.

"Oh, my God. Mom," I mutter to myself, and Kieran lets out a tiny laugh, his lips vibrating against my skin. He steps back from me, far enough to lob an answer at my mom from the other side of the car door.

"Just helping her out of the car, April," he says, holding his hand out to me. I lace my fingers together with his and we start toward the house as I push the door shut behind us.

"I'm only teasing you guys," Mom says, holding the front door open wide to welcome us inside. "I heard you pull up a while ago but then you didn't come inside, so I thought I'd check."

We stand inside the living room, Kieran rocking back and forth on his heels. I'm sure he wants to give me a kiss goodbye, but with my mother right next to us, laying one on me would be more than a little awkward.

And then things get even weirder. Mom reaches out and puts a hand on Kieran's shoulder before pulling him all the way into a hug. I slide around so I can see Kieran's face, and he's sending me a look that clearly reads *What the hell is going on here?*

All I can do is hitch my shoulders in confusion. I love my mom, but I stopped trying to figure her out a long time ago.

"I'm hugging you now because I might not get the chance to tonight," Mom starts, patting him on the back and then sliding her arms around to his shoulders, holding him out from her enough to be eye-to-eye with him. "Things are probably going to get pretty chaotic after the ceremony."

"Um…thanks," Kieran says with an edge of uncertainty to his voice.

"I want you to know, because you probably don't remember, but there was a time I wasn't too keen on you dating my daughter," Mom tells him.

"Oh, my God—did you just use the word *keen*?" I blurt out, and Mom raises her eyebrows at me.

"Zip, I'm trying to have a moment here if you don't mind," she says, her voice snappish. But her eyes are twinkling at me, so I know she's not really upset.

I mumble an "okay" as she continues having her "moment" with Kieran. "So, as I was saying, at first, I wasn't sure about this whole relationship. I was a little worried Zip might put all of her dreams aside to focus on you." She glances sideways at me. "Turns out, I severely underestimated my daughter."

Kieran shifts his eyes to me and gives me a little grin.

"And I severely underestimated you," Mom says to Kieran. "You—both of you—have been through so much more than I could have handled as a teenager. And here you are, mature, well-adjusted, and heading off to college."

"Not sure how mature and well-adjusted we are, but if you think so, I won't argue," Kieran says, still grinning.

Mom reaches out to ruffle his hair and tells him "You deserve all the happiness that's coming to you, Kieran. And I couldn't have picked a better guy for Zip to be with—I wanted you to be aware of that."

"Thanks, April," Kieran replies, and Mom drops her hands from his shoulders. "I promise to take care of her as much as I can while we're in Chicago—not that she needs anyone to take care of her."

"True," she says. "But it makes me feel better sending my baby away from home knowing she'll be around people who care about her."

I grumble as Mom calls me "my baby" but then I smile to tell her I'm not really too mad. As annoying as she is sometimes, I know how lucky I am my mom loves me and worries about me so much.

"Well, I'm going to let you two say your goodbyes and see if I can't find something for us to eat before we have to go to the ceremony. Tell your parents I'll find them tonight at the stadium before everything starts."

"I will," Kieran tells her, and she heads off for the kitchen, where she would still be within earshot and so Kieran and I have to whisper.

"That was weird," he mumbles in my ear.

"It was," I whisper back. "But my mom kind of deals in weirdness, so I guess it wasn't totally bizarre."

"Good point." He moves his mouth from my ear until his lips are only a millimeter from mine. "So, now that we have her complete and total blessing to be together or whatever, do you think it's okay if I kiss you right here in your living room?"

"It would be okay even if we *didn't* get her blessing. And you don't remember, but you've kissed me in my living room before. So I think you should go for it."

His mouth closes over mine almost before I can completely speak my last sentence. And while kissing Kieran will always be one of my favorite things to do, something about my mom's words to him make this kiss even more special, more fulfilling, as if Kieran is fully a part of my life now, and I am fully a part of his.

We've conquered almost unimaginable hurdles and here we are after everything—together. We belong to each other, and my body relaxes against his, the weight of a year and a half of anxiety and fear lifting from me and floating away.

When we part, Kieran steps back and reaches for the door. "I'll see you in a few hours," he says, opening the door and stepping outside. "And don't worry about tonight. You're going to be amazing." He pauses and glances down at my leg brace. "So, um, break a leg? Isn't that what people are supposed to say when someone's about to go on stage?"

A mischievous version of his usual grin tells me he's well aware of the joke he's made, even if my leg isn't exactly broken.

"Oh, shut up," I say as he turns toward the driveway, the smile in my voice giving way to a full-on laugh as he laughs as well.

CHAPTER 20

My stomach lurches as soon as I hear the concert band begin playing, signaling to the gathered crowd that the Titusville High School Graduation is about to begin. Since I'm giving the class speech, I have to sit on the stage with Principal Rosner, Superintendant Turner, the faculty, and the county circuit judge who's been asked to give the inspirational "grown-up" speech this year, which typically inspires nothing more than drowsiness in the Senior Class and the rest of the crowd.

Dr. Turner starts walking forward toward the football field, and I realize my last chance at escape is gone. This—my having to give a speech in front of the entire town of Titusville—is going to happen, barring a natural disaster in the middle of the ceremony. I glance up at the early evening sky, completely free of clouds or other threats, and sigh inwardly, accepting that a thunderstorm or hailstorm isn't likely to sweep in and save me.

My stomach churns again once we've walked onto the field and are making our way to the stage set up between the ten and fifteen yard lines. Now I can see everyone, the bleachers on both sides of the field filled to capacity. Before the stage are seemingly endless rows of folding chairs soon to be occupied by my classmates, all of whom at the moment are shuffling along behind the faculty and out of my view.

Rosner and Turner climb the stairs to the stage ahead of me and I, momentarily forgetting my limitations, follow suit. But as soon as I try to lift my right leg to pull myself up to the second step, I wobble because I haven't regained the range of motion in my knee I used to have. If the staircase had a railing, I could grab it and sort of swing my leg up each step. But there's no railing—these are just temporary platform stairs that will be thrown in a storage room somewhere after the ceremony. Panic freezes me on the bottom step, Mr. Circuit Judge behind me clearing his throat as if to say, "Move it, kid."

Great. This is awesome. I'm not even giving my speech yet and already I'm making an ass out of myself.

Luckily, Dr. Turner is still close enough to me I'm able to reach out and yank the back of his robe, which shocks him to the point that, for a second, I'm afraid he's going to topple over onto me, which would definitely be the cherry on the nightmare sundae I seem to be constructing here. He turns around and raises his eyebrows at me as if to say, "What?"

"My leg, sir," I respond to his silent question. "I'm having a little trouble getting up the stairs."

Immediately, Dr. Turner offers me his arm, which is enough for me to struggle my way up the remaining stairs. By the time I'm in my seat in the front row on the stage, my face is so hot and red from embarrassment I feel as though I'm about to explode.

Of course, if I exploded, I'd be unable to give the speech, so maybe bursting into flames wouldn't be such a bad thing.

After a few minutes, my fellow graduates are all seated before me on the football field. My eyes search wildly before I finally find Kieran and Kayla sitting next to each other in the middle of the section on the left and whispering to each other. I so wish I could be out there with them right now instead of being up here on the stage, the only teenager in a crowd full of adults.

The band finishes and Dr. Turner takes the podium, welcoming everyone to the festivities and droning on about the high school's academic achievements for the year, which are few. He mentions the girls' basketball state championship, which produces a few cheers and whoops from the crowd, which I'm tempted to join in on, but given my prominent place on the stage, I force myself to stay quiet. Finally, he introduces Mr. Circuit Judge, who gives the standard, boring "Congratulations, Graduates. You are our future. We're proud of you. Do big things" sort of speech dignitaries have been giving at high school graduations as long as there have been high school graduations, probably. Dr. Turner retakes the podium to announce the honors society members and detail their college plans, and when my turn is up, I stand as Turner says, "Zara McKee, who will be attending Northwestern University," and I realize I'm shaking, because my speech is up next.

"And now, I'd like to introduce our final speaker for the evening," Turner begins. "This young woman truly represents the best of Titusville High School..."

Oh, God. I swallow hard, bile burning a trail down my throat.

"Chief among her many extracurricular activities, she was co-captain of this year's state champion girls' basketball team..."

More whoops and shouts from the crowd.

"...and is graduating as this year's salutatorian. Ladies and gentlemen, Zara McKee."

The crowd bursts into polite applause, and since the weather event I'd hoped for still looks like it's not going to happen, I step to the podium and rest my pile of index cards in front of me, certain a breeze will blow up from somewhere and scatter them and I'll be forced to improv this whole thing. I swallow down some more bile and clear my throat a few times—which sounds *really* loud through a microphone—and look out onto the crowd, my gaze immediately falling on Kieran and Kayla, both of whom are sticking their tongues out at me along with giving me the "thumbs-up" sign.

Okay. I can do this.

"Fellow graduates, Dr. Turner, Principal Rosner, members of the faculty and school board, esteemed guests, family, and friends..."

I'm suddenly reminded of the "Friends, Romans, Countrymen" speech from *Julius Ceasar*, and I'm half-tempted to throw in some comment about how I've come to bury Ceasar and not to praise him. But ninety percent of the people sitting here wouldn't get the joke, and the ten percent who would probably wouldn't think I was being very funny under the circumstances. So…moving on.

"Good evening, and welcome to the end—the end of our high school careers, the end—almost—of our time in Titusville, and, soon, as I'm sure you're all hoping for, the end of this ceremony. Unfortunately, you have to listen to me talk for a few minutes before the diplomas are handed out."

Polite laughter bubbles up from the crowd. I'm off to a good start.

"But I promise I'll be brief." I clear my throat and continue. "Tonight is also a beginning, which is why graduation ceremonies are also referred to as 'commencement exercises.' Soon, we'll be going off to college or to work and leaving behind things that have been familiar to all of us for so long."

I look directly at Kieran, and his smile prompts me to keep going.

"I've spent my entire life in Titusville, and I've known most of you here in the crowd since before I knew anything at all," I continue. "That's true for just about everyone here, since this is such a small town. Over the years, we've all seen each other at our best and at our worst, and we've shared so many hopes, dreams, and fears. Four years ago, I walked into the high school wing for the first time with big dreams, dreams I wasn't always sure I would be able to achieve. For example, I wanted to bring this school its first state championship…"

The crowd whoops and hollers again.

"And I wanted to graduate as valedictorian and go to Northwestern," I continue. "And some of those dreams came true, and some of them didn't. And still other dreams came true, but not in the way I thought they would. For example, as most of you know, I didn't get to play in the state finals…"

Most of you…yeah, right—everyone in town and within a three-county radius is well aware I didn't get to play in the state finals.

"And I'd always pictured myself playing in the final game. But being unable to play helped me realize being part of the team is just as important as playing in the game. Everyone on the team contributed to our win whether they had started every game or only had the chance to play in practice."

I search the bleachers on the far side of the field for some of my sophomore and junior teammates, the girls who never get to play, but I can't make out anyone individually in the sea of people.

"No one can reach a dream without the help of others. Fortunately, we have all been well prepared by our families and by the faculty sitting behind us for whatever comes our way, and because of them, whatever we dream is within our grasp."

Part of what I'm saying isn't exactly true. Several kids sitting in front of me right now have family members who bailed on them a long time ago—even my own dad isn't exactly up for Father of the Year. And many of the faculty members behind me flat out suck at their jobs, and we're graduating from high school in spite of them and not because of them. But Kayla advised me to keep this part of my speech because, as she said, "Half the battle in public speaking is getting the crowd on your side." I don't know how she knows that, but…

"But I've also learned over the last year that it's okay if your dreams *don't* come true, or if they come true in a way you didn't

245

exactly anticipate. Because sometimes, what happens instead of what we wanted is beyond any dream we ever imagined. I've met some people over the last year who've helped me learn this valuable lesson."

I gaze out at Kieran, who's giving me his usual grin, and I keep my attention focused on him for the rest of the speech since most of it is about him.

"None of us here can predict the future, and none of us can predict whether or not our dreams are going to come true. But our years here in Titusville have given us the raw materials with which to build our dreams…"

Again, this part's all Kayla's doing. She's going to make an amazing lawyer someday.

"And they've given us the confidence to forge new paths for ourselves when life tells us we may need to alter those dreams. So don't be afraid to dream big, but don't be afraid when life sends you in a direction you didn't anticipate—because that direction may take you somewhere that's beyond your wildest dreams. Thank you."

I'm pretty sure I've delivered the worst high school commencement speech in the history of high school commencement speeches, but if so, the crowd is apparently willing to give me a pass. As I go to my seat, I hear the applause at my back and when I turn to sit down, I discover I'm the recipient of a standing ovation, so I guess I did something right.

With my speech out of the way, we can now move on to the best part of the ceremony—the diplomas. I watch as each of my classmates takes the stage to receive a diploma and a handshake from Principal Rosner as Dr. Turner announces their names. While I clap for everyone, of course, I'm a little more enthusiastic when Dr. Turner calls "Kayla Danielle Lanier," and Kayla takes the stage, flashing me another "thumbs-up" before she shakes Rosner's hand. Then Dr.

Turner says, "Kieran James Lanier," and Kieran climbs the stairs, winking at me as he accepts his diploma. My eyes follow him off-stage, where Kayla is waiting for him at the bottom of the steps, and the two of them walk arm in arm back to their row of seats.

I sit through a few more names before I hear "Zara Elizabeth McKee," and I struggle out of my seat and hobble over to Mr. Rosner, giving his hand a firm shake as I accept my diploma.

"Nice speech," Rosner says to me, patting me on the shoulder before I can walk away.

"Thank you," I mumble in return, my face reddening as I hear a loud "Yeaaah!" coming from somewhere in the stands, and I'm pretty sure the outburst is courtesy of my mother.

Wisely sensing the crowd's growing boredom, Dr. Turner keeps his end-of-the-ceremony remarks brief before introducing the Senior Class to the crowd as the newest graduates of Titusville High School. A roar goes up from the seats on the field, and although the class is supposed to stand and wait for the stage party to file off the field before following them, every year the scene descends into total chaos once the concert band starts playing the school song. Families flood the field to find their graduates, and while I do walk off with the stage party as I'm supposed to—once again with an assist from Dr. Turner—as soon as I'm on the field, I merge into the crowd rather than moving toward the gates with the faculty and administrators. Pretty much the entire town is wandering around the football field right now, and I worry I'm going to end up standing out here all night and waiting until everyone else goes home before I'm going to be able to find my family. Luckily, my mom texts me that everyone's waiting for me at the other end of the field near the end zone, and so I make my way downfield, waylaid every few feet by one of my classmates stopping me for a hug.

Kayla gets to me first, breaking away from the group of our combined families and rushing over to gather me in her arms.

"We did it," she screams at me.

"We did," I yell back at a slightly lower volume.

"And your speech was awesome," she says. "You actually left all my stuff in."

She's so happy I can't help but laugh. "Of course, I did," I tell her. "One of these days when you run for president, you can be your own speechwriter."

Anything else she wants to say about my speech is cut off by Kieran coming up behind me, wrapping his arms around my waist and spinning me around until my mortarboard almost falls off my head.

"The adults want pictures. Lots and lots of pictures," he tells me when he places me back on the ground.

"Wonderful," I grumble, and Kieran pulls me into a hug as he laughs.

"I'm so proud of you, by the way," he says into my ear. "And completely impressed. You didn't look nervous at all. You were amazing up there."

"I didn't come off like a total idiot?" I ask. "Be honest."

"Not at all. I was hanging on every word. You're a natural."

"Well, I don't know if I'm a natural," I begin, positive that Kieran's playing things up because of how he feels about me. "But I guess if I want to be a sports broadcaster, I need to get comfortable with talking in front of people, huh?"

"Might be a good idea," he says, stepping back but still keeping his arm around my shoulders. As we turn around, Mom comes up to claim a hug, stopping to retrieve my lost mortarboard from the ground.

"The sooner we get pictures, the sooner we can go eat," she points out, handing the mortarboard to me and gathering me into her arms.

"Well, when you put it like that, let's get on with it," I say, wishing we could just skip the whole photo shoot and go back to Gram and Gramps' house, where both my family and the Laniers are going to gather for a barbeque. After Mom steps back, Kieran puts an arm around me and steers me toward our combined families standing near us in the end zone, whispering, "Get ready to smile," in my ear.

After what seems like a never-ending photo session courtesy of Jim and Carlie, my dad, my mom, and my grandparents all wanting to preserve the moment for posterity, everyone heads back to my grandparents' house for the party. Morgan fires up the grill while the rest of us busy ourselves setting up card tables and folding chairs in the backyard, covering the tables with plastic tablecloths. Once the tables are ready, Dad and Gramps drag a giant cooler with cans of soda out from the carport and while everyone else grabs drinks, Kayla, Gram, and I start making trips back and forth from the kitchen, bringing side dishes and condiments to a table near the grill.

I'm carrying a giant bowl of potato salad from the kitchen to the backyard when I stop outside the back door for a second and take in everything happening around me. Mom and Morgan are talking at the grill, Mom rubbing Morgan's back as he cooks. Gram and Kayla arrange food, paper plates, and plastic utensils on the food table, while Dad, Kathy, Jim, Carlie, and Gramps take their sodas and head for the art studio, likely so Gramps can show them some new project he's working on. Kieran, meanwhile, is chasing Liv around, the two of them weaving their way between the card tables, giggling and red-faced from the activity.

This is my family—all of us together in one place, all of us safe and happy. I want to freeze this moment in time and hold onto it forever.

Kieran sees me and catches up to Liv, scooping her up in his arms and carrying her over to the back door.

"You look pretty content right now," he says to me as Liv burrows her face in Kieran's neck.

"I should. I was just thinking about what a lucky girl I am."

Kieran leans in for a kiss, and as our lips meet, Liv says, "Ewww. Gross."

We're both laughing a little as we pull away from each other, and Kieran puts Liv on the ground.

"I'm going to borrow your sister for a minute," he tells her. "Why don't you go find your parents? I think they're in the art studio."

"Okay," Liv mumbles, making kissing noises at us before she goes skipping off.

"So, how old are girls usually when they stop thinking kissing is gross?" Kieran asks. "I obviously don't remember when that happened for Kayla."

"For Kayla, I'm guessing around ten or eleven years old, like most girls," I say. "For me? I was around sixteen. Something about a certain guy..."

Kieran takes the potato salad from me as my voice fades and walks the bowl over to his sister. "Come inside for a minute?" he asks once he's returned to my side. "I don't think we're going to get many chances to be alone tonight, and I want to be alone with you right now."

"I don't think my grandparents will appreciate us making out in their house."

"I don't want to make out with you," he says, and then immediately backtracks. "Well, I *want* to make out with you, but not right at this particular moment. There's something else."

He grabs my hand and pulls me inside the kitchen, gently pressing me up against the refrigerator for a long kiss.

"I thought you said you didn't want to make out with me right now," I breathe when we part.

"The kiss was just a prelude." He reaches into his pocket and pulls out some folded-up tissue paper. "This is the real reason I wanted to get you alone."

He slips the tissue paper into my hand and I unfold it, revealing a silver mortarboard charm.

"We agreed we weren't going to get each other gifts, remember?" I scold him, but I'm smiling to indicate I'm not really mad.

"Couldn't help it. I wanted to surprise you."

"Mission accomplished."

I rub my thumb along the edges of the charm as Kieran reaches for my wrist, unfastening the bracelet. "According to everything I've read, I haven't given you one of these in a while. I thought it was about time, and today *is* a special occasion, after all. It's all about new beginnings," he says as I slide the new charm onto the band. He refastens the bracelet around my wrist and gives me another kiss.

"Thank you," I say when we part. "It's beautiful."

"And I plan on a lot of special occasions in our future, by the way," he informs me, slipping his arms around my waist. "I may need to buy you a few more bracelets."

I laugh as my mom comes into the kitchen. "There you guys are," she says. "We're ready to eat."

"We'll be out in a minute," I assure her, and she ducks back outside. I lean into Kieran and put my head on his shoulder, not quite ready to head to the backyard and join the crowd of our combined families. For just a few more moments, I want to stand here in the quiet, listening to Kieran's heart beating along with mine.

"We can't stay in here forever, you know," Kieran murmurs into my hair. "Someone else will probably be in here in a minute or so to drag us outside."

"I know," I say. "But I want to spend that minute alone with you. So let them come."

He hooks his finger under my chin, and I raise my head to look at him as he says "I love you, Zip. Always."

"I love you, too. Always."

Epilogue—Five Years Later

I'm dizzy from Kieran spinning me around on the dance floor, and the champagne probably isn't helping, either. But when he pulls me in close so we can sway together as the current song fades out, I rest my head on his shoulder and the dizziness is replaced by a sense of contentment and calm.

"Ladies and gentlemen," the DJ booms into the microphone at his booth. "The happy couple would like to thank all of you for coming tonight. Please get home safely, and congratulations once again to Brad and Kayla. Goodnight, everyone."

"Home," for pretty much everyone in the wedding party as well as the guests, is the hotel whose lawn overlooking the beach served as Kayla and Brad's wedding venue, which is a good thing since almost everyone here is exhausted, tipsy, or some combination of both.

I lift the skirt of my floor-length lavender bridesmaids' dress so I won't trip as I wind my way to the other side of the reception tent, Kieran in tow. I don't want to miss saying goodbye to Kayla and Brad now since they'll be catching a flight to Boston early in the morning before heading off on the Hallorans' private jet for a two-week European honeymoon—a gift from Cooper and his father. I'm guessing no one in the wedding party, Kieran and I included, will be awake in time to see them off.

Kayla, resplendent in a strapless wedding dress with a full skirt, breaks away from a group composed of Brad and some of his cousins as soon as she notices us coming over.

"Hey, Maid of Honor," she says, throwing her arms around me.

"Hey, beautiful bride." I squeeze her and let her go. "Seems like I've barely seen you since dinner.

"Yeah," she breathes, her cheeks flushed from a likely combination of champagne and dancing and excitement and love. "No one ever tells you how much *work* weddings are. I'm going to wake up tomorrow and the memory of this thing will be nothing but a big blur."

"That's because you're drunk," Kieran teases, and she joke-punches him in the shoulder.

"We wanted to say goodbye before we missed our chance," I tell her. "You're going to have a lot of people fighting for your attention as they start to turn in for the night."

"Yeah, my cousins just went inside, but I think they're going to continue the party at the hotel bar instead of going to bed if anyone's interested," Brad says as he comes up, having heard the last of what I'd said. He puts an arm around Kayla's waist, and for the hundredth time today, I'm struck by what a gorgeous couple they are. Given that it's the middle of June on Martha's Vineyard, Brad and his groomsmen—including Kieran—opted for lightweight beige slacks and light gray jackets instead of tuxes. Brad's casual look allowed Kayla to stand out even more, which is a good thing for any bride but *especially* for Kayla, who isn't going to tolerate being outshone by anyone, including Brad.

In addition to being gorgeous, the two of them are every bit as accomplished as they'd always planned to be. Brad just finished his second year at Georgetown Medical School, and Kayla just completed her first year at Georgetown Law and will be working in some senator's office this summer once they're home from their honeymoon. Kieran and I have been laying odds on how long it will take her to build an army and stage a coup to overthrow the government—he took Christmas, while I, exercising my full belief in Kayla's capacity for evil, opted for the end of the summer.

Kieran slides an arm around my waist and glances at his newly minted brother-in-law. "I don't think I'm up for hanging out in the hotel bar," he tells Brad before turning to me, "but I was thinking about a walk on the beach before bed if you're up for it."

"I could definitely be up for that," I say, leaning in to kiss him on the cheek. "But we'd better say goodnight to everyone first or we'll never hear the end of it for sneaking off."

We exchange hugs with Kayla and Brad before sending them off to thank more of their guests for coming, while Kieran and I look around to find out who's left among our friends and family. Staring across the dance floor, I spy Cooper sitting at a table with Cassie, the two of them red-faced and laughing victims of too much champagne. Cooper notices me and waves but doesn't signal to me to come over to the table to join them, and I nudge Kieran and nod in their direction.

"Okay. That's not good," he comments after watching them laugh and drape themselves all over each other for a few seconds.

"And, yet, somehow, it makes total sense," I respond, thinking back years ago to the night Cooper's memory started returning at the Titusville Homecoming Dance, not long after he had been slow-dancing with Cassie. "Assuming they end up being more than a one-night thing, at least Coop will treat her better than Cody ever did."

"Cody Hull," Kieran says, shaking his head. "That guy hasn't crossed my mind in *years*."

"He's recently engaged and living somewhere in Chicago, in case you were wondering," says a voice behind me. "His mom comes into the store every now and then." We turn to find Mom and Morgan holding hands and watching Cassie and Cooper over our shoulders.

"I wasn't wondering, but I guess it's good to know we might run into him sometime," I tell Mom before turning to Morgan. "By the way, have I told you how handsome you're looking this evening?"

Kieran snickers at me because my constant comments on Morgan's appearance tonight have become a running joke. Morgan's wearing a suit for the occasion, and Morgan never wears a suit—for any occasion. Since Dewayne Masters died unexpectedly last year and left the Downtown Diner to him, whenever I'm back in Titusville, I rarely see Morgan in anything other than a t-shirt, jeans, and a grease-stained apron unless we're having dinner with my mom and grandparents.

"I think my appearance has come up more than a few times— thanks," Morgan grumbles. "And I don't know how I look, but I *feel* like an idiot."

"Well, Zip's right—you look wonderful," Mom says, planting a kiss on Morgan's cheek. Although they've gotten more publicly affectionate over the years, Mom and Morgan have never attempted to define their relationship as anything more than "hanging out," and those of us who love them are content not to push. They still live separately—Mom in the little house I grew up in and Morgan in the apartment above the Diner—but they travelled to the wedding together and are sharing a room at the hotel. Regardless of how they choose to define their relationship, if they're happy, I'm happy, and in the end their happiness is all that really matters.

"Are Gram and Gramps still here?" I ask my mom, realizing I hadn't seen them in a while.

"They went upstairs about an hour ago," Mom says, shaking her head. "You know, they can't quite party like they used to. Speaking of which, we came over to tell you we're going up to our room. I hear there's an after-party going on in the hotel bar, but we can't quite party like we used to, either."

I laugh at the thought of my mom partying at all. "We're skipping the after-party, too," I tell her. "We thought we might take a walk on the beach before bed."

"Well, be careful," she says, gathering me into her arms. As I step back from her, Morgan pulls Kieran to him for a hug, and I can't help but smile. The two of them will never have a traditional father and son relationship, but they've built enough of a bond over the last few years that they're definitely more than friends—I think Kieran calls Morgan for advice or just to talk at least as much as he calls Carlie and Jim.

Once we're done exchanging hugs in our little circle, I ask my mom if she's seen Carlie and Jim so we can say goodnight to them. She points to the entrance to the hotel, where the Laniers are thanking guests as they head inside, assisted by Jillian, who's attending the wedding alone, she and her occasional girlfriend Marta finally having given up for good a couple of years ago. Since Mom and Morgan are heading inside anyway, we walk as a group toward them and wait our turn to talk to the Laniers behind a group of people I don't recognize whom I assume must be part of Brad's extended family.

"You missed Brad and Kayla," Carlie tells us after dropping kisses on each of our cheeks. "They've already gone upstairs."

"We said our goodbyes a while ago, Mom," Kieran informs her.

Carlie nods, shutting her eyes. "I'm so tired I can hardly stand up," she explains. "No one ever tells you how much *work* weddings are."

Kieran and I exchange knowing glances, both of us probably thinking the same thing—*like mother, like daughter*.

"Well, you pulled it off beautifully," Mom tells Carlie, taking her hands. "No one would ever think today was anything but effortless."

Jim steps forward and puts a hand on my shoulder, but he addresses my mother rather than me. "Just wait, April," he begins, his eyes twinkling. "You'll find out one of these days how much effort goes into one of these things. Although, I think your daughter is a little less high-maintenance than ours."

Carlie laughs her breathy laugh, and out of the corner of my eye, I notice Kieran's face flushing just as red as mine feels at the moment.

"Oh, come on," Jilly says to the two of us through a laugh. "No need to blush. We all know it's only a matter of time before we're standing here—or somewhere—celebrating *your* nuptials. Frankly, I was a little surprised you two didn't get around to this first."

She gives Kieran a pointed glare, as if it's his fault we didn't get married before Kayla and Brad. Kieran and I have been living together for a while now and we've talked about getting married plenty of times—but getting married well into the future, when our lives and careers are a little more settled.

"Sorry we're not working on your timeline, Jilly," Kieran says, and Jilly reaches out to ruffle his hair as if he's a little boy.

"I'm teasing," she assures him. "Whenever and wherever you two finally decide to tie the knot, you can expect me to be there with bells on."

"I'm pulling for Vegas, personally," Mom deadpans, and I elbow her in the ribs as Morgan laughs at both of us.

Still more people I don't recognize—I can't believe I don't know so many of the people at this wedding—are lingering behind us to get their chance to speak with the Laniers, so we all exchange goodbye hugs and wave Mom and Morgan off to the hotel, while Kieran and I wind our way back through the maze of now mostly empty tables. I note to myself that Cooper and Cassie have disappeared somewhere, and I'm kind of hoping we don't run into them on the beach because if we do, who knows what they'll be doing.

"Still up for that walk, I assume?" Kieran asks once we've reached the edge of the tent.

"Absolutely. I want to be alone with you right now. I've had enough crowds and excitement for one day."

"I'm with you."

I slip off my high heels and walk barefoot through the grass, hand in hand with Kieran. After a few yards, we reach a weather-beaten wooden staircase leading to the beach, and at the bottom of the steps, Kieran strips off his shoes and socks, leaving them where the sand meets the grass. I set my shoes beside his and we head off for the water, not caring if our shoes will be there when we get back.

Between the clear, star-speckled sky, the moon, and the lights from the hotel and the reception tent, we're able to walk to the shoreline without fear of losing our way. A slight breeze kisses our cheeks, a brief but welcome respite from the salty humid air that always seems to hang over the island in the summer. But despite the humidity that makes my hair even more of a nightmare than usual, I never get sick of this place. With the ocean and the beaches and the gingerbread houses and the lighthouses, the island almost seems like something out of a dream sometimes, it exists in such sharp contrast to our daily life in Chicago.

Carlie and Jim have invited me to Martha's Vineyard several times, the first being for an extended weekend a few weeks before Kayla, Kieran, and I started college. I was pretty excited to visit the gingerbread house Kieran had led us all to believe he'd run away to when he had really run off to North Carolina. And Kieran was eager to visit the house, too, because he had no memory of it—no memory of visiting his grandparents here as a child and no memory of writing the fake journal entries depicting the wicker furniture on the front

259

porch slick with summer humidity. Other than a few brief flashes of going to the beach with Kayla and his parents, the Vineyard was every bit as new to him as it was to me that summer.

Kieran's memories have never come back completely, and we've both accepted that maybe they never will. Much like he used have flashes of the future, now he gets flashes of his past, incomplete memories that don't make much sense to him in isolation. Every once in a while, he'll get a far away look in his eyes and I'll ask, "Do you remember something?"

And sometimes the answer is yes, and sometimes the answer is no. And sometimes, the answer is maybe...and he'll describe a scene, and it will be up to me to fill in the remaining details.

This is how we live, and how we've lived for the past five years. I fill in the blanks when I can, and we move on when I can't, and we've made new memories regardless. For example, right before we left for college, Kieran and I had a second first time, which was even better than our *first* first time but more bittersweet because now our night at the Hallorans' lives in my memory alone. I've told Kieran about that night, and I've even written down the details as if I'm writing a short story about two people who aren't us. And on the rare occasions we talk about our *first* first time, I remind myself he's only remembering the *story*, and not the actual event itself.

But this is how we live, and how we've lived for the past five years.

We hung out as often as we could while we were in school, our busy schedules preventing us from being together every day until we rented a tiny apartment on the North Side right before senior year so we could live not quite halfway between our respective campuses. And we still live in that apartment, but our commutes are a little different. I write copy and get some occasional on-air time as a sports reporter for a local cable channel in the suburbs. It's not quite my dream job, but for a first job out of college, I'm pretty happy—although I've learned more about high school tennis and lacrosse than I ever thought I would in my lifetime. I'm not much of an athlete myself anymore, so at least I still get to be around sports on a regular basis. I played intramural basketball for a while in college until I tore my ACL again sophomore year—I still play when I can, but I can't go as hard, and I've accepted my knee will never be the same.

Kieran, on the other hand, commutes south every day, but now he travels even further south than he did while we were in college so he can teach art classes at a middle school. The pay isn't great, and the art, music, and sports programs are always in danger of succumbing to budget cuts, but he's so happy because he's doing exactly what he's always wanted to do, whether he remembers or not, which is helping people through art.

Thanks to his stories, I've learned almost as much about his students this past year as he has. And the tales he tells of the things that come out in their work and in his conversations with them are heartbreaking—kids who don't know their fathers, kids who have never seen either parent and are being raised by their grandparents, kids whose older brothers are running with gangs, kids who have serious emotional or mental issues simmering under some pretend surface happiness. Whenever he tells me these stories, he almost always concludes with some version of the same sentiment—

"I know I had it rough, and I know I had it rough for a long time, but the things I went through don't seem so bad compared to what many of these kids go through every day. At least I had a family behind me, and I had you and your family. Some of these kids hardly have anyone."

And I always remind him "They have you."

Those kids and I are pretty lucky.

We've reached the shoreline, the water lapping up over our bare feet and dampening the hem of my dress and the cuffs of his pants, but neither of us steps back. Another breeze kicks up, and even though the night is still warm, I shiver as the humidity dries on my skin.

"Cold?" Kieran asks.

"A little bit."

"Here." He takes off his suit jacket and hands it to me, but not before I catch him pulling something from an inner pocket, something small enough he can hide within the palm of his hand. I slide the jacket around my shoulders, my attention on the fist he's making to conceal the object from me.

"The jacket actually kind of goes with your dress," he points out, but I shake my head.

"Nice try. What are you trying to hide?"

"Tissues?" he offers, smiling.

"I don't think so," I say, laughing and reaching for his hand. He doesn't fight me, allowing me to pry his fingers from the object, which I discover is a purple velvet ring box.

Of course—Kieran was Brad's Best Man, so he was responsible for Kayla's wedding band.

Which doesn't explain why Kieran felt the need to take the ring box from his jacket and try to hide it in his palm. And there's no good explanation as to why the ring box would be on him in the first place since he handed Brad the ring straight from his pocket during the ceremony.

"So, this is Kayla's ring box, right?" I say with a dopey smile on my face because I think I'm starting to sense how this scene is going to play out.

"No," he says, with a loopier-than-usual version of his grin overtaking his lips. "It's *your* ring box. Open it."

I do as Kieran suggests, opening the box to find a tiny diamond ring nestled in the velvet.

"Oh, my God," I whisper. "Kieran?"

"I figured since everyone was already in a wedding mood, now would be the perfect time to do this," he explains. "Although I was kind of a mess before the wedding, walking around with *two* rings on me. I kept hoping I didn't screw up and hand Brad the wrong one."

I laugh a little, and he continues.

"And I had no idea Jilly was going to give us crap about getting married, by the way. That was entirely unplanned."

I don't say anything, but I examine the ring resting in the velvet folds, the moonlight glinting off its surface.

"Anyway, I don't think I'm doing this exactly right," he says, taking my hand and pulling us back a safe distance from the shoreline so he can drop to one knee. "Zara Elizabeth McKee, also known as 'Zip,' also known as 'The Greatest Thing That's Ever Happened to Me,' will you do me the incredible honor of becoming my wife, whether we decide to get married in Vegas or on Martha's Vineyard or on the moon or at the bottom of a sewer somewhere?"

"Yes, Kieran James Lanier, I will," I tell him through a smile so big it actually kind of hurts my face a little. "But I'm personally pulling for us not to get married in a sewer."

He stands up and takes the velvet box from me before sliding the ring onto my finger. "I don't endorse the sewer idea, either," he assures me. "Just making the point that I'd marry you anytime, anywhere."

We kiss, the sound of the water lapping against the shoreline making for the perfect romantic proposal background, while I try to block out the faint conversations and general clanking around of the hotel staff clearing off the tables under the reception tent, which seems a little less romantic.

"I don't think we should tell anyone for a few days, though," I tell him when we part. We, along with our families, had planned to stay on the Vineyard for a few more days to vacation. "This is Kayla and Brad's time, so I definitely don't think we should tell anyone tonight."

"I agree," he says, resting his forehead on mine. "If there's one thing my sister hates, it's having her big moment ruined by someone else."

"True. And think about it—if we wait a few days, right when everyone's coming down off their wedding-high and starting to get depressed, we can swoop in with the big news."

"Sounds like a plan," Kieran says, stepping back so he can hold the ring box out to me. "So, we should put the ring away for now?"

I shake my head. "Not on your life," I tell him through a laugh. "You couldn't pry this thing off my finger right now if you tried. I think we can make it back to our room without anyone seeing us." I step to him again, my lips nearly on his. "Tonight, I want to stare at this ring and know that I'm your fiancée. Tomorrow morning, I'll take it off and our engagement will be our little secret for a few days."

He nods in agreement and kisses me. "So, what do you say we go back to our room and practice being married?" he asks, giving me the grin that will forever be one of my favorite things. "I hear marriage isn't something you should jump into without truly understanding what you're in for."

"I think by now, you know *exactly* what you're in for."

"I do," he tells me as we turn and start to head back to the hotel. "And I can't wait to be in for it for the rest of my life. I love you."

I stop and put a hand to his cheek, giving him one last kiss before we start walking again. "I love you, too, Kieran," I whisper, and we walk hand in hand up the beach, the moon at our backs.

THE END

ACKNOWLEDGMENTS

When I started writing the *In Your Dreams* series, I knew—in general terms—how I wanted the series to end. What I didn't know was how many wonderful people would want to join Zip and Kieran on their journey (honestly, I thought maybe four people in my family would read my books and no one else). Now that the series has come to an end, I want to thank the friends, family, and fans who have embraced Zip and Kieran's story and sent me emails screaming "Write the next book already! I need to know what happens to those kids!" If I could reach through the Internet and across the miles to give each of you a great big hug, I would.

I'd also like to thank the many people who gave me early feedback on *Beyond Your Dreams* and the previous *In Your Dreams* books. My ideas often sound better in my head than they read on paper—actually, my ideas *always* sound better in my head than they read on paper—and your comments have helped me greatly as far as getting my work to a point that it's actually understandable by other human beings.

As always, I'd like to single out Stacey McNamara for believing in my work. Part of the reason I started writing the *In Your Dreams* series was that I wanted people with young daughters to be able to give those daughters a book featuring a strong heroine. Now that Stacey's daughter is old enough to read my books, the fact that she's doing so is beyond humbling. Thanks so much, Stacey and Sarah—I hope to give you both reading material for years to come.

I also need to thank my ferocious attack tabby, Cleocatra, who always sits by my side or in my lap as I write...until she needs to eat, use the litter box, or chase invisible things across the floor in my office. Thank you for being the best cat in the universe.

Last but never least, I want to thank my amazing husband, Heath Martin, who has always been my biggest fan. He's supported me through countless writes and re-writes, insisted that I'm a good writer whenever I didn't believe it myself (which is pretty much daily), and calmed me down when I'm about to throw my computer across the room because I can't get the electronic formatting right and I'm convinced that [insert name of *In Your Dreams* book here—I've had formatting issues with all four] will never see the light of day. Thank you for loving me, for encouraging me, and for not moving into a hotel when I'm having a crazy writer moment.

ABOUT THE AUTHOR

Amy Martin wrote and illustrated her first book at the age of ten and gave it to her fourth grade teacher, who hopefully didn't share it with anyone else. She currently lives in Lexington, Kentucky, with her husband and a ferocious attack tabby. You can find out more about her books and sign up for her mailing list at http://www.theamymartin.com.